SON OF A STITCH

A Knitorious Murder Mystery

REAGAN DAVIS

COPYRIGHT

FOREWORD

Dear Reader,

Despite several layers of editing and proofreading, occasionally a typo or grammar mistake is so stubborn that it manages to thwart my editing efforts and camouflage itself amongst the words in the book.

If you encounter one of these obstinate typos or errors in this book, please let me know by contacting me at Hello@ReaganDavis.com.

Hopefully, together we can exterminate the annoying pests.

Thank you!

Reagan Davis

CONTENTS

CHAPTER 1

Six across. Jolt from Joe, eight letters. Easy! C-A-F-F-E-I-N-E. My drug of choice.

"Murder!"

I clutch the crossword puzzle to my chest and turn around. "You startled me!" I scold. "Murder?"

"Four down."

I hold up the puzzle where we can both see it.

"A collection of crows is called a murder," Eric says, pointing to four down. "I didn't mean to scare you."

"I know. You can't help that you're freakishly light on your feet for such a big guy."

"It's my superpower," he winks and kisses my forehead. "Maple pecan latte with extra whipped cream and a drizzle of chocolate." Eric hands me a to-go cup from the local coffee shop, Latte Da. "Hope I got it right."

I put down the crossword puzzle. "Thank you," I say, giddy with anticipation and caffeine withdrawal. I take the cup from him and take a sip. "It's perfect."

Eric Sloane is my boyfriend and tenant. He lives in the apartment above my yarn store, Knitorious. We met last year when the Harmony Lake police department borrowed him from a nearby police force to investigate our town's first murder. He solved the murder, then accepted a job offer from Harmony Lake PD and relocated here. We've been dating since the end of January.

Eric and his cup of dark roast double-double position themselves behind the counter. He never stands on the business side of the counter.

"Are you alone again today?" he asks.

I nod. "Connie is still taking care of Archie and his new hip, and Marla is helping at Artsy Tartsy."

Connie is my mother-friend. She's the original owner of Knitorious. I worked for her part-time until she semi-retired last year and passed the store onto me. She moved out of the upstairs apartment and into a condo with her boyfriend, Archie. Now, we've come full circle. I own the store, and she works here part-time. Archie had his hip replaced last week, and Connie took time away from the store to care for him.

My other part-time employee, Marla, is helping at Artsy Tartsy, the local bakery that my best friend April and her wife, Tamara, own.

"How's April's dad? Any news?" Eric asks, bending

down to rub my corgi, Sophie, who's pawing at his knees in a desperate attempt to get him to notice her.

"They're hopeful the surgery he had yesterday was the last one. She expects the doctor to discharge him tomorrow."

April's dad fell off a ladder while tending to his eaves troughs. He broke a leg, shoulder, and his collarbone. April rushed out of town to help her mum look after him. Since Tamara can't bake and work the front counter at the same time, Marla and I decided she would work at Artsy Tartsy this week instead of Knitorious. We're a small community, but we're tight-knit and look out for each other.

"You have no sidekicks this week," he teases.

"I have you and Sophie," I remind him.

"I have a meeting with my boss late this afternoon, but until then, I'm all yours. Put me to work!"

His boss is the chief of police, Charmaine Solomon.

"What do you mean?" I ask, confused. "You're working from the store today?" Not that I mind, but even in small doses, Eric's six-plus-foot muscular hotness messes with my concentration. To say he's a distraction is an understatement. I don't know how I'd be able to focus with him here all day.

"No," he clarifies, "I'm working *at* the store today and tomorrow. You're alone all week, and I have a ton of personal time I have to use. It makes sense." He shrugs and smiles. The honey-coloured flecks in his brown eyes momentarily sidetrack me, and my insides flutter.

Focus, Megan.

"You don't knit," I point out, coming to my senses. "Knitorious is a yarn store. We cater to knitters and crocheters. It's really sweet that you want to help…"

"I don't have to know how to knit to help," he interrupts. "Megan, you've helped me with my job, and you're not a cop."

I can't argue with that, so I pick up a random skein of yarn from the nearest shelf and drop it on the counter. "I'd like to purchase this, please."

"Of course, ma'am." Eric smiles, picks up the skein of yarn and proceeds to process the transaction. I'm shocked. I pay for the yarn with the app on my phone. He places the skein in a bag with my receipt and hands it to me across the counter with a smile. "Have a nice day."

"I'm impressed! I didn't realize you pay attention when you pop in and out of the store."

"I'm not just a pretty face, you know." He winks.

Oh, I know.

I drop the bag of yarn on the counter. "I'd like to return this, please."

Processing the refund takes more focus than the purchase, but he does it. The money reappears in my account and I return the skein of yarn to its shelf.

"You're hired," I say, "but there probably won't be much to do. October is one of the slowest months of the year. You might be so bored, you'll beg to go back to the station."

Harmony Lake is nestled snugly between the lake to the south and the Harmony Hills mountain range to the north. Nature left no room for expansion but provided the town with the perfect foundation for a tourism-based economy.

Between the two ski resorts in the Harmony Hills mountains, and all the rental cottages in and around town, Harmony Lake is full of skiing and snowboarding tourists in the winter. In the summer, city-escapees flock here for the lake and the small-town living experience.

During the busiest weeks, there are more visitors than locals in Harmony Lake. This is not one of those weeks. The summer tourists have returned home to their normal lives of school and work, and the winter tourists won't descend on us until December. Right now, the town is blissfully quiet and doesn't belong to anyone except us locals.

"I doubt it," he replies. "There's nowhere else I'd rather be."

Eric is prone to say romantic things that sometimes verge on sappy. It comes naturally to him, unlike me, who needs several days' notice to think up a reply that could be considered even vaguely romantic. If, however, a comment requires a quick reply that's either awkward or sarcastic, I'm your woman.

Taking her position as greeter seriously, Sophie

springs into action immediately upon hearing the jingle of the bell. She trots to the door and meets my almost-ex-husband before he has both feet inside the store.

"There's nothing else to do, Meg. She's practically dead," Adam announces, closing the door behind him.

"Well, it was a longshot. Thanks for trying. I guess it's time to put her out of her misery."

Adam places the terminally ill laptop on the counter and squats down to greet Sophie properly. Shamelessly, she rolls onto her back and exposes her fluffy belly for him to rub. "Do you want me to pick up a new one? I don't mind."

New technology is Adam's happy place. He has yet to meet a new gadget or device he doesn't love.

"I'll take care of it," I respond. "Knitorious is my store, my responsibility. Thank you, though. But can you give me a list of features and specs I need? You know, techy stuff like RAM, and Gigs, and whatever."

I return the laptop to its place under the counter and plug it in. For what good it'll do.

Technology might be Adam's happy place, but it isn't mine. I can think of a dozen things I'd rather do than research and comparison shop for a new laptop. Normally, I'd be thrilled to let him choose a replacement. But our divorce will be finalized this month, and we need to establish a few boundaries. This laptop is a good start. It's high time I step outside my technological comfort zone.

Because we live in the same small town, our lives

are more enmeshed than most divorced couples. We share a nineteen-year-old daughter, Hannah, and have brunch together every Sunday. I do the bookkeeping for his law practice, and he provides tech support for my personal life and the store.

During our almost-twenty-year marriage, Adam was a workaholic. He was a partner at a large law firm in the city, and his sixty-hour weeks meant we hardly saw each other. That was then. After we separated, Adam left the firm and started a small practice right here in Harmony Lake. We've seen each other more in the last twelve months than we did during the last five years of our marriage. His constant presence in our tiny hometown and my life makes our situation complicated. We've had to learn to spend time together as friends while working out the details of the divorce and keeping our family intact; something we both want for our daughter.

Adam and I have known each other our entire adult lives. I can't imagine not being in each other's lives in some capacity. We met at university when I was eighteen. By the time I was twenty, we were married, and I became unexpectedly pregnant with Hannah a few months later.

"I'll text you some computer specs later today, Meg." Adam moves toward the door and puts one hand on the doorknob.

"Thanks." I smile and busy myself with gathering online orders that need to go to the post office.

He glances around the empty store. Why is he lingering? He looks at me awkwardly with his hand still on the doorknob. I pretend I don't notice that he's working up the nerve to say something. I won't take the bait.

"Do you guys have plans tonight?" Adam finally asks.

Eric and I look at each other and shrug.

"I don't think so, why?" I ask.

Adam takes a deep breath and exhales slowly. "I'm thinking of inviting Jess to Thanksgiving dinner, and I'd like you to get to know each other first, before she meets Hannah. I was hoping the four of us could have dinner tonight."

Jessica Kline is the hygienist from our dentist's office. She and Adam have been dating for about five months. Adam is secretive about their relationship. He even denied they were seeing each other at first until he couldn't deny it anymore. A few months ago—completely by accident—I saw them together, and that's when Jess went from his secret girlfriend to his not-so-secret girlfriend. Only Eric and I know about them. If he wants her to meet Hannah, they must be getting serious.

"Jess isn't spending Thanksgiving with her kids?" I ask.

Jess was married to our dentist, Dr. Arnie Kline. They have three teenagers. They've been divorced for almost ten years, a fact I didn't know until she and

Adam started dating. I already like Jess. She's been cleaning my teeth every six months since we moved to Harmony Lake almost eighteen years ago. But we've never gotten to know each other beyond discussing the weather, how quickly our kids grow up, and how effective my flossing habits are.

"They're going to BC with their dad to visit his side of the family," Adam explains.

BC is British Colombia, the western-most province in Canada.

"We'd love to," Eric intervenes, putting Adam out of his misery.

Relief washes over Adam's face.

In an unexpected and strange turn of events, Eric and Adam are friends. Eric was new to town and didn't know anyone, and Adam was a local resident without any local friends because he was always at his office in the city. They bonded over a mutual love of golf, and now they're friends. Is it weird that they have a relationship with each other that doesn't include me? Yes, but it's far from the weirdest situation in this cozy, quirky town.

"I was thinking we could meet at the pub after you close the store. Sound good?" Adam asks.

"Great. We're looking forward to it," Eric replies.

Should be an interesting dinner.

"What do you think, Sophie?" I ask after Adam leaves. "Are you ready to meet Adam's girlfriend at Thanksgiving dinner?"

Sophie thumps her little corgi tail in response and twitches her eyebrows at me.

ERIC IS GOOD FOR BUSINESS, I'll give him that. We're busier than usual for October, and customers stay in the store longer than they usually do, lingering in whichever section Eric currently occupies. Knitters who never ask my opinion on anything yarn related have a sudden, urgent need for Eric's opinion on which shade of blue matches their eyes or which yarn would be "most huggable" as a sweater. At least two knitters have offered him private knitting lessons, and one asked him about the size of his gun. He's had a few opportunities to show off his cash register skills ringing up sales.

"You said it wouldn't be busy," he says, holding the door for a customer as she leaves.

"I suspect word got around about the handsome new associate at Knitorious," I respond.

The speed at which the Harmony Lake gossip network spreads news rivals high-speed internet.

"I wouldn't call you handsome, beautiful for sure, but not handsome." Another romantically, corny comment from Eric while he checks his phone. "I need to leave to meet Charmaine. Will you able to cope on your own?"

I know he's teasing. "I think I'll be OK. If I can't

handle the rush, I'll text you. I'll meet you at the pub later."

"It's a date." He pulls me into a hug. "A double date with your ex. Is that awkward for you?"

"Yes," I admit, "but I'm trying to go with the flow."

"Better you than me," Eric says. "I wouldn't have dinner with my ex-wife ever again. Not for any reason."

"After our walk, I'll take you upstairs and you can wait in Eric's apartment until we get back from dinner. I promise to tell you all about Jess." I explain how the evening will unfold to Sophie as I attach her leash at the back door.

I go over my mental checklist before we leave. Turn the OPEN sign to CLOSE. Check. Lock the front door. Check. Turn off the store lights. Check. Feed Sophie dinner. Check.

Sophie and I step into the parking lot, and when I lock the back door, the thud of a car door closing catches my ear.

"Hi, Megan!"

"Jess?" Why is she here? "Hi!"

"I'm glad I ran into you. Adam suggested I park here. I hope it's OK. I can move the car…"

I wave away her comment, cutting her off mid-sentence. "Of course. There's no chance of finding a spot at the pub on a Friday night. You can park here whenever you want."

"Thanks. Could we walk to the pub together?"

"Sure! If you don't mind a quick walk with Sophie first?"

"Not at all. I was hoping to get you alone. There's something I want to talk to you about."

What could Adam's not-so-secret girlfriend want to talk to me about?

CHAPTER 2

We walk and talk, stopping at every tree, bench, and rock bordering our path so Sophie can sniff and mark her territory.

The conversation starts with the obligatory weather chat. We catch each other up with how our kids are doing, while pretending there isn't an air of tension hanging between us because of whatever she wants to talk to me about.

"Megan, I just want to say thank you for being so open to meeting me and being supportive of Adam and me." Jess says, finally addressing the elephant in the room.

"Of course!" I reply. "You're both great people, I hope it works out for you. And I'm not just saying that because I dread finding a new dentist if it doesn't." I'm kidding about the last part. Sort of.

Jess giggles and flippantly flicks her wrist. "I've got

your back. If it doesn't work out with Adam and me, he has to find a new dentist, and I get to keep you and Hannah. I've already told him, so don't worry."

In addition to being friendly and easy to talk to, Jess has a wicked sense of humour, and she's gorgeous.

Her long, straight, strawberry blonde hair looks almost rose gold in the light of the setting sun. She has perfect teeth—she's a walking billboard for her dental practice—and her sea-foam green eyes are captivating. Like me, she has fair skin, except hers is dotted with clusters of reddish freckles. I'm the Veronica to Jess's Betty. My hair is brown and curly, my eyes are hazel, and I have a curvy hourglass figure, whereas Jess is lean and muscular. I don't know if she works out, but she looks like she does.

The only physical feature we have in common is our lack of height. To be honest, our physical dissimilarity is a relief. The only other relationship Adam embarked on since our separation was with someone who resembled me. It was unnerving and ended in murder.

"But seriously," Jess adds, "I know how awkward it is to meet your ex's new partner. I was so nervous the first time I met Arnie's new wife. She didn't do anything to make me uncomfortable, but it was still stressful. I hope you don't feel like that. I have no expectations. You and I don't have to be friends, but I'd love it if we were. If not, I hope we can at least get along for the sake of our families."

Wow. Such a brave and vulnerable statement. How am I supposed to not love her?

I stop walking and look at her, summoning the most serious facial expression I can muster. "I already like you more than Adam."

We both burst out laughing.

With the awkwardness out of the way, Jess and I spend the rest of our walk getting to know each other better. We're both from Toronto. Though she's eight years older than me—I'd never have guessed she's forty-eight—we have similar taste in music. We were at the same concert twice, Beastie Boys and The Rolling Stones. We both read mysteries, watch true crime documentaries, and have perfectionist tendencies. She finds the same satisfaction from dislodging a huge nugget of tartar from a tooth that I find in fixing a knitting mistake that other knitters say isn't fixable. We don't look alike, but we have a lot in common.

"ARE YOU READY FOR THIS?" I ask Jess as I'm about to open the large wooden door to The Irish Embassy. "This is as public as it gets. Five minutes after we join Adam and Eric, the entire town will know about your relationship. You're about to become the most talked-about person in Harmony Lake."

Jess nods, then giggles. "I'm ready. Adam warned me about the rumour mill in this town. Hopefully, something else big will happen, and our relationship won't be the trending topic for very long."

"If nothing else gossip-worthy happens by dessert, I'll text Connie and ask her to start a rumour to take the heat off." I wink.

It's a joke, but I'm sure Connie would gladly accept the challenge.

We giggle as I open the door and gesture for Jess to go ahead of me.

The Irish Embassy—known simply as the embassy or the pub to locals—is one of the largest buildings in Harmony Lake and one of the few businesses on the south side of Water Street. The main floor has a double-sided bar in the centre with bar stools lining both sides. The bar is surrounded by various types of seating, booths along the walls, tables and chairs in the centre, and a couple of cozy sitting areas with sofas and club chairs around the fireplaces. Out back, there's a patio overlooking the lake.

During tourist season, it would be standing room only on a Friday night, but this isn't tourist season. Most of the booths and tables are occupied, but it's not crowded.

Scanning the room, Eric catches my eye and waves to me from one of the semi-circular booths.

"Over here." I nudge Jess.

"What took you so long?" Adam asks. "The store closed almost an hour ago. We were getting worried. You didn't answer my texts."

"We took Sophie for a walk, dropped her off, then walked over," Jess explains. "We took our time." She slides into the booth next to Adam while digging through her purse. "Shoot! I left my phone in my car."

Adam offers to retrieve her phone, but Jess declines. I offer her my phone so she can text her kids and let them know they can reach her at my number. She accepts and sends a quick text from my phone, which I leave on the table where we can both see it.

After an order of Irish nachos, plus two orders of steak and mushroom pie, and two of fish and chips, we're all full to bursting. Jess and I polish off a bottle of wine and order another, lamenting that we both have to work tomorrow and should have planned to have dinner on a Saturday night instead.

I can leave my car at the store and stagger home from the pub, but Jess lives and works in Harmony Hills, a half hour drive from here. So, we decide Adam will be her designated driver, and she'll pick up her car from Knitorious tomorrow.

The laughter and wine flow freely until someone touches my shoulder.

"Hey, Jamila! How are you?"

Jamila Jagger owns Bits and Bytes, Harmony Lake's electronics store. She's a tech wizard, and I trust her to guide me toward the perfect laptop for my store. I debated going to Electric Avenue, one of the big-box electronics stores in Harmony Hills, but I try to support local whenever possible. We small business owners need to stick together.

"Hi, Megan," Jamila smiles. "I just popped over to tell you I'm not ignoring you. I know you left me a message today. I didn't have time to call you back, but I'll call you tomorrow."

"No worries, Jamila! I'm glad Bits and Bytes is busy!" If I'm more enthusiastic than this conversation merits, I blame the wine.

"Hi, I'm Jamila," Jamila introduces herself to Jess and extends her hand for Jess to shake.

Ah! The real reason Jamila stopped by our booth—to check out Adam's girlfriend up close.

"Hi, Jamila." Jess shakes Jamila's hand. "I'm Jess." She flashes Jamila a wide, toothy smile and lets out a small hiccup. "If you'll 'scuse me, I hafta visit the ladies' room now." She slides out of the booth, takes a moment to confirm her footing, then walks a bit unsteadily toward the ladies' room.

I gesture for Jamila to take Jess's vacated seat. She slides into the booth next to Adam and leans over the table toward me.

"I need a laptop," I tell her. "I have specs." I pick up my phone, open my text thread with Adam, and forward the text with the computer specs to Jamila.

"Leave it with me," Jamila says. "I'll look at your text and my inventory and call you sometime tomorrow."

"Thank you," I reply. "Who are you here with? Do

you want to join us?" Apparently, slightly drunk Megan is extra welcoming.

"I'm waiting for the Solomons. I was just at their house for dinner. We decided to meet here for a drink. They'll be here any second. I should get back to our table before someone takes it." Jamila smiles.

Charmaine Solomon is the chief of police. Her husband, Dr. Emory Solomon, is a local psychotherapist who specializes in family therapy. His office and Adam's office are in the same building.

"You have good taste in girlfriends." I wink at Adam and take a sip of wine.

"And you were worried they wouldn't like each other." Eric grips Adam's shoulder in that friendly way men do.

After finding her way back from the ladies' room, Jess slides into the booth.

"You were worried we wouldn't like each other?" she asks, rubbing what I hope is Adam's knee under the table.

"I had two worst-case scenarios," Adam explains. "You either wouldn't get along at all, or you'd get along too well and gang up on me."

"We promise we'll only gang up on you sometimes," Jess assures him.

"Welcome to your worst-case scenario," I add.

As we near the end of our second bottle of wine, Jess remembers her phone is in the car and announces her intention to walk to Knitorious to get it. Adam suggests he should go with her because he's steadier on his feet. Eric, also sober, agrees with Adam, but Jess rejects his offer of assistance and instead decides she and I can retrieve her phone together. The semi-intoxicated leading the intoxicated. What could go wrong?

Stepping out of the stuffy, loud pub into the crisp October night is a breath of fresh air. Literally. I inhale deeply and revel in the coolness. I glance up the alley beside the pub. Two people are standing close together in the midst of what appears to be an animated discussion. I can't hear what they're saying, but their spirited gesticulations make me think that whatever they're discussing, they don't agree on it. As my eyes adjust to the darkness, I realize the two people who are arguing are women. Then I realize one of them is Jamila. I recognize her high pony-tail bobbing when she speaks. The other woman is Charmaine Solomon. What would they be arguing about? Didn't Jamila say they had dinner together tonight? I didn't realize they knew each other well enough to have dinner parties and argue in dark laneways.

"Let's go!" Jess shouts. She locks her arm in mine, and zigzagging, we amble up Water Street toward Knitorious.

She entertains me with dental-hygiene stories. Like the patient who would only brush the teeth they wanted to keep, the patient who has names for each of their teeth, and the patient who insists on being called "Your Highness" since getting their dental crown.

By the time we're close to the store, we're laughing so hard I'm afraid I might pee.

"Nice parking job, jerk!" Jess shouts, nudging me.

When I look up, there's a white Tesla parked in front of my store with its passenger-side tires on the sidewalk.

"Oh my," I say, suddenly feeling more sober. "It looks like they hit the lamp post."

Approaching slowly and assuming the vehicle is empty, we take in the scene. The car isn't wrapped around the pole, so I don't think the driver was going very fast when they hit it.

"Do you think they were drunk?" Jess asks.

"I don't know," I reply, inching closer to the car.

The car is silent, but it's electric, so that doesn't mean it's not running. The headlights and rear running lights are on, so it could be running. Could the driver be inside?

"People who drive luxury cars are so entitled!" Jess yells with a slur. "Like, how entitled are you if you think you can park like that jus' cuz you have an essspensive car?"

Her comment makes me laugh.

"Whasso funny?" she asks, starting to giggle without knowing why.

"Your boyfriend drives a JAGUAR!" I blurt out between fits of laughter.

Laughing so hard she bends forward, I reach out to

steady Jess, and we approach the Tesla. Someone is in the driver's seat.

I knock on the window. "Hello?" I knock again. "Are you OK?"

The realization that someone could be hurt focusses Jess on the task at hand. Squinting, and with her nose pressed against the window, she says, "His eyes are open. I think he's all right." She raps on the window with her car key. "We'll get you help, sir."

The driver's head is turned mostly toward the passenger side of the car, so we can't see his entire face. We jog around the back of the car to the passenger window. With her hands cupping the sides of her face, Jess looks inside. "It's Dr. Armistead." She knocks with her fist. "Dr. Armistead? Look at me!" She turns to me. "Why won't he look at me?"

I squint and put my face up to the window next to hers. "Because he's dead."

CHAPTER 3

I REACH for my phone in my back pocket and panic when I realize it's not there. "Darn it! I left my phone on the table at the pub!"

"Mine's in the car!" Jess and I race toward the parking lot behind the store as she repeatedly presses the remote on her key chain. The car is blinking and chirping when we turn the corner. "Do you really think he's dead?" she asks, grabbing her phone from the passenger seat.

"Yes," I reply, nodding.

"9-1-1?" she asks, trying to unlock her phone with her fingerprint. Her hand is shaky, and the phone won't unlock. I place my hand over hers to stop the device from moving while she concentrates on steadying her thumb over the sensor until it unlocks. "Here." She thrusts the unlocked phone at me. "I can't," she says, shaking her head.

Jess sits on the pavement beside her car. I think she's about to throw up, but I can't worry about that now.

A text from Adam appears on her screen.

Adam: What's taking so long? You and Meg find a body or what?

Adam likes to poke fun at my knack for finding dead bodies. This will teach him to make light of dark situations.

Me responding on Jess's phone: Yes.

I swipe out of her text messages and dial 9-1-1. I'm about to hit *talk* when the phone rings. Unknown number. But I recognize it. Eric.

"Hello?"

"Where are you?" A thudding sound in the background. He's running.

"Parking lot. I have to call 9-1-1." I'm about to end the call, but he speaks again.

"Adam's calling them. Stay on the line with me. I'm almost there."

"A car. On Water Street. In front of Knitorious."

"Are you hurt? Is Jess hurt?"

I can hear him in stereo now. He's within earshot.

"No. The man in the car is hurt." I end the call.

"Megan!" Eric runs around the corner.

"Sorry, I hung up." I'm crouched beside Jess now, rubbing her back and listening to her whisper, "Don't puke" to herself repeatedly under her breath.

"Stay here! Adam's right behind me!" he shouts, then disappears around the corner.

I assume he's running toward the Tesla, toward Dr. Armistead.

"Let it out," I advise Jess, twisting her long hair and gathering it in my fist. "You'll feel better. You can freshen up upstairs."

Jess nods in agreement, lurches forward, and proceeds to heave while I hold her hair back.

As she wipes her mouth with a tissue from her purse, I gently steer Jess toward Knitorious.

"Your phone is in your bag!" Adam is beside us now, thrusting my forest-green tote bag toward me.

Instead of taking the bag from him, I reach in and grope around for my keys. I unlock the door and hold it ajar with my foot while I drop my keys inside my bag and take it from Adam. All the while keeping my arm supportively around Jess. "Can you text Eric and tell him we're upstairs?"

"Of course," Adam replies, holding the door open while I usher Jess inside.

Still supporting her with my arm, and with Adam behind us prepared to catch her if she falls, Jess and I wobble slowly up the stairs.

I situate Jess on the sofa and use the hair elastic on my wrist to pre-emptively secure her hair in a messy bun in case she needs to throw up again.

"Thank you," she mumbles.

"Don't thank me until you see it," I reply. "It might be the messiest messy bun I've ever made."

She chuckles under her breath and reaches up to

touch the monstrous pile of hair on her head. "I think my hair is the least of our problems right now."

Adam hands me a glass of water, then hands one to Jess and sits next to her on the sofa, rubbing her back.

Pointing, I show Jess where the washroom is and tell her she'll find washcloths and towels in the linen closet behind the washroom door. "There's toothpaste and mouthwash in the drawer on the right," I explain.

Nodding, she starts to get up. Adam helps her to her feet, and she walks gingerly toward the washroom.

"It's not just the alcohol, she's in shock," I explain quietly to Adam after Jess clicks the washroom door.

I sink into the chair next to the sofa, and Sophie jumps onto my lap, excited to see me and oblivious to the chaos happening downstairs.

"She's not the only one," he responds. "Are you OK?"

I nod. "Definitely much more sober now."

"What happened?" he asks. "Did you guys see the car hit the pole?"

I explain what happened, leaving out Jess's remarks about luxury car drivers being entitled, and my comment about her boyfriend—Adam—falling into that category.

"Dr. Armistead?" he asks. "The same Dr. Armistead we went to for marriage counselling a few years ago?"

I nod. "I didn't recognize him at first. Jess recognized him. Then I remembered their offices are in the same medical building in Harmony Hills. She probably runs into him all the time, so of course she recognizes him."

From inside my bag, my phone dings almost constantly. Word has gotten around about the incident outside my store. Red and blue flashing lights reflect off the walls inside Eric's apartment. The accident scene is directly below his living room window.

I retrieve my phone and unlock the screen without scrolling through the dozens of unread messages that pop up.

I type a text to the Modern Family group chat.

Me: A car hit a pole outside Knitorious. We're all fine. Will update you soon.

The Modern Family group chat is a text thread Eric started a few months ago when I was in a car accident, and he was inundated with texts about my wellbeing. Originally, it included me, Eric, Adam, April, and Connie. It quickly grew to include Connie's boyfriend Archie, Archie's son Ryan, and Ryan's girlfriend Lin. April also added her wife, Tamara.

Now that the people who matter most know what's going on and that everyone is safe—everyone except Dr. Armistead—I lock the screen and toss my phone onto the coffee table.

"How are you feeling?" Adam asks Jess upon her return from the washroom.

"I've been better," she replies, resuming her seat on the sofa next to Adam and taking small, cautious sips from her glass of water.

"Did you know Dr. Armistead well?" I ask.

She shrugs. "Kind of. We've worked in the same medical building forever. He's a patient at the dental practice, and years ago, Arnie and I went to him for marriage counselling. He was a nice man. I think he's between wives right now. He has a son, about Hannah's age or a year or two older."

Between wives. What an odd way to describe someone's marital status. It gives the impression that Dr. Armistead has had several wives. I'm about to probe Jess for more details about his relationship situation when she continues speaking.

"Poor Dr. Armistead." Jess shakes her head. "If it weren't for bad luck, he'd have no luck at all this week."

"What else happened to him this week?" I ask.

"His office was robbed on Monday. The whole place was turned over. In the middle of the day."

"Wow," I respond. "That's awful." I'm about to ask what was taken, but Adam beats me to it with his question.

"I wonder why he was in Harmony Lake tonight?" he asks. "I've never seen him around town before."

"I have no idea." Jess shakes her head.

The thud of footsteps makes us stop talking and turn our heads toward the apartment door. The thudding grows louder until the door opens.

"How's everyone doing?" Eric asks, holding the door for one of his uniformed colleagues. "We need to speak to each of you briefly"—he looks back and forth from me to Jess—"then we'll get more detailed statements in the morning when you're not under the influence."

Jess and I nod.

"We'll each take one and split up?" Eric's colleague asks. "One up, one down?"

Eric nods.

"I'll go downstairs, I should take Sophie outside anyway," I offer, less out of concern for Sophie and more out of concern for Jess navigating the stairs again.

I INHALE DEEPLY and savour the crisp night air when Sophie, Eric, and I step into the parking lot. After a long, silent hug, we walk north into the residential streets behind the store, instead of crossing Water Street and walking through the waterfront park, like we normally would. To the best of my alcohol-clouded recollection, I tell Eric everything that happened from the moment Jess and I left the pub until he called me on Jess's cell phone.

"Do you think he had a medical episode?" I ask.

"Possibly. It's too early to tell," Eric replies. "But we have to treat it like a crime scene until foul play is ruled out."

"Maybe he fell asleep at the wheel, or maybe he was

using the self-driving feature Teslas have, and it steered him into the pole," I suggest.

"At this point, it could be anything." Eric shrugs. "When I saw him earlier, he seemed fine. I didn't notice any signs of medical distress."

We stop walking while Sophie investigates a fire hydrant. I look up at Eric. "You saw him earlier today? Where?"

"Who's questioning who?" he teases. "He showed up at Charmaine's house as I was leaving. He was one of the Solomon's dinner guests tonight."

"You were at the Solomon's house? Is that where you met with Charmaine? Not at the station?"

"She asked if we could meet at her house because she had to get ready for a dinner party tonight. She prepared duchess potatoes while we talked. I wasn't there very long. When I was leaving, Dr. Armistead was arriving. We said hello and goodbye at the door on my way out."

"Duchesse potatoes, mmm, yummy," I observe.

"They looked good. She piped them and put them in the fridge, so she could put them in the oven when the chateaubriand was almost done."

"Chateaubriand with duchess potatoes. Now, I'm hungry. I bet she made chateaubriand sauce too. With mushrooms."

"Apparently Emory makes that. It's one of his specialties. Along with the sautéed brussels sprouts. But we're getting off track." Eric steers our conversation back to the issue at hand.

"Sorry, I'm looking for a distraction from the dead body in front of my store," I explain.

"I know," he says, taking my hand. "Are you sure you're all right? Finding a dead body is traumatic, even if it's not your first time."

I nod. "I think I'm fine. I'll know for sure when the rest of the alcohol wears off. Jess was quite shaken, though. She might need some extra support. Did you tell Chief Solomon that one of her dinner guests is dead?"

"Yeah. By text," Eric replies. "Not ideal, but I wanted to tell her personally instead of sending a patrol car. And I couldn't leave the scene since I'm the only detective in town."

"That's awkward, having to question your boss," I point out. "But aren't you a witness too? Since you saw the victim a few hours before he died?"

"Yup, among other reasons," he agrees.

I assume he's referring to the fact that the scene of Dr. Armistead's death is outside his front door.

We arrive back at the store and I pause before opening the door. "Are we done? I'd like to go home."

"We do have to talk. I need to ask you some more questions, and I need to tell you some stuff, but it's best to wait until you're completely sober."

"I'll walk home, for obvious reasons, and leave my

car here. I just need to go upstairs and get my phone and bag. I guess you won't be working at the store tomorrow after all. Your new fan club will be disappointed."

"A patrol car will drive you home. I have to get back to work. I'll talk to you in the morning." Eric kisses me goodnight.

"I don't mind walking. The fresh air is good for me."

"You're still under the influence, and there's a small chance this wasn't an accident. Please humour me and let a patrol car drive you home?"

"Fine," I agree.

"Text me when you get there. Lock the doors and turn on the alarm. I love you," he reminds me as he turns the corner.

Watching Eric disappear toward what I hope is an accident scene, the knot in my stomach swells and tries to convince me Dr. Armistead's death isn't an accident at all, but murder. I try to ignore the knot, and my instincts, but it's hard because they haven't been wrong yet.

CHAPTER 4

Saturday, October 3rd

"I go away for a few days and you replace me, Megawatt? The rumour mill is buzzing with stories about the dead body you and your new bestie found outside Knitorious."

April likes to come up with punny nicknames for me. Apparently, this morning I'm Megawatt. She's done it since we met seventeen years ago at a mummy-and-me playgroup with our girls.

"It would be impossible to replace you," I reassure her, even though I know she's teasing. "But Jess is cool, you'll like her." I stop walking while Sophie sniffs a tree. We're only a few driveways away from home. At this rate, we'll never get to work. "How's your dad feeling?"

"Grumpy," April replies. "My mum says it means he's getting better. She says he's happiest when he's crotchety and complaining. He hates it when we fuss over him. Honestly, I love him to death, but he doesn't make it easy."

"To be fair, if I had three broken bones, I'd be grumpy too," I tell her, adjusting my AirPods. "Don't worry about anything in Harmony Lake, just focus on your parents. Marla is filling in for you at Artsy Tartsy, and Zach is helping out between school and hockey. Connie and Ryan take turns chauffeuring him to and from hockey when T has to work."

Zach is April and Tamara's son. He's a sixteen-year-old hockey player with a massive appetite. They also have a daughter, Rachel, who's the same age as my Hannah. Rachel and Hannah are best friends and attend university together in Toronto.

"I know. T says everyone is supportive and amazing. She makes it sound like everything is running so smoothly without me that I never have to come back."

T is short for Tamara.

"She just doesn't want you to worry. We all want you back, we just don't want you to worry about what's happening here while you're helping your parents. We miss you!"

"I miss you too. I'll be home by next weekend. There's no way I'm missing Thanksgiving dinner if Jess is making her debut. I'll bring my parents with me if I have to." We laugh. "So, you and Adam knew this Dr. Armistead guy?" April asks.

"Weird, right? He was the marriage counselor we

went to a few years ago in Harmony Hills. He was a nice man. What are the odds he'd show up dead outside my store?"

"Why did you and Adam go all the way to Harmony Hills for marriage counselling? Why not stay local and see Dr. Solomon?" April asks. It's a fair question.

"You know what it's like here," I remind her. "Everyone knows everyone else's business. We didn't want to broadcast our marital issues, and we didn't want Hannah to find out. If anyone saw us coming or going from Dr. Solomon's office, it would have spread through Harmony Lake faster than a viral infection."

"It's true," April agrees.

April and I chat until I arrive at the store. We end our call, and I walk to the front of the store to make sure the Tesla and Dr. Armistead are gone. They are, but crime scene tape cordons off most of the sidewalk in front of Knitorious, and a police officer and his patrol car direct traffic around the now-crooked lamppost.

Water Street is to Harmony Lake what Main Street is to other small towns. It's our main drag. Most of Harmony Lake's stores and businesses are on the north side of Water Street. The south side has a narrow park in front of the waterfront—the park where I walk Sophie before the store opens. Water Street is charming and picturesque. It's old with limited on-street parking and no new architecture at all. But I think this adds to its charm.

On the way to the back door, I notice that in addition to Jess's car and my car, Eric's car is still here, as well as a couple of cars I don't recognize. Strange. When Eric has a case, he's usually out the door early, interviewing people and gathering evidence. Hopefully, the fact that he's home means the coroner has already determined the cause of death and ruled out foul play. But if that were the case, he would've mentioned it when we texted earlier this morning. Something's not right. Something else is going on.

I detach Sophie's leash and freshen her bowl of water. After checking the clock on the cash register, I realize there's more than enough time to walk to Latte Da and get a maple pecan latte before it's time to open the store. Phone in hand, I stash my bag under the counter and head toward the back door. I'll text Eric on my way and ask him if he wants anything.

"I was just thinking about you," I say when he comes down the stairs and intercepts me at the back door.

"Good thoughts I hope." He smiles and kisses my forehead.

Eric is almost a foot taller than me. I get a lot of forehead kisses.

"I'm going to Latte Da. Do you want a coffee?" I ask.

"I'd love one," a familiar, deep voice booms from the top of the stairs. "Dark roast, two milks, please, Megan."

"Hi, Darby. What are you doing here?" Darby and I hug and exchange a cheek kiss.

Darby Morris is a friend of Eric's and a detective with the Harmony Hills police department. He doesn't belong here; this isn't his jurisdiction. Now I *know* something is going on.

"Darby is here to work the Armistead case," Eric explains. "There are too many conflicts of interest. The HLPD can't investigate it."

HLPD is the Harmony Lake Police Department.

"Does this mean Dr. Armistead was murdered?" I ask.

Eric shakes his head and shrugs. "There's no evidence to suggest it was murder, but until the coroner officially says otherwise, it's a suspicious death. That's why Darby is here."

I take a step back and realize Eric is wearing the same clothes he wore last night. He hasn't shaved, and his eyes are bloodshot and heavy.

"Have you been up all night?" I ask.

He nods.

"Who wants to tell me what's going on?" I demand. "I don't like secrets."

"Why don't I go to Latte Da and leave you two to talk," Darby announces. "Text me your orders."

Before either of us can respond, Darby leaves, closing the back door behind him.

Eric and I take a seat at the wooden harvest table at the back of the store. I wait while he texts our coffee order to Darby, then gives Sophie some love before she explodes from trying to get his attention.

"If you and I are witnesses, shouldn't we be separated until Darby questions us individually?" I ask, drawing on my unfortunate previous crime scene experience.

"He already questioned me, and he has your preliminary statement from last night. It's fine." Eric takes my hands. "Remember last night when I told you I saw Dr. Armistead at Charmaine's house yesterday evening?"

I nod. "He was arriving for dinner as you were leaving after your meeting with Charmaine."

"That wasn't the first time Dr. Armistead and I met. My ex and I went to him for marriage counselling right before we split up."

"You too?" I ask. "It's like he's the only marriage counselor in the world."

"Why do you say that?" Eric looks confused.

"You went to him for marriage counselling, Adam and I went to him for marriage counselling, and last night Jess said she and her ex-husband went to Dr. Armistead for marriage counselling too."

"Huh, that is a coincidence," Eric agrees. "And of all three couples, none of them stayed together."

"You're right," I acknowledge, shocked by the realization of Dr. Armistead's unfortunate track record. "I hope the three of us aren't indicative of his overall success rate. Is that the only reason Harmony Hills PD was called in?"

Eric shakes his head. "No. Charmaine is a witness. She was one of the last people to see Armistead alive. He was at her house for dinner. I can't question her impartially because she's my boss. In fact, she's everyone's boss, so there would be a conflict of interest if any cop with the HLPD investigates the case. Last night, we secured the scene, notified the coroner, and took preliminary statements. When Darby got here, I handed off the case to him, and he questioned me. By the time we finished, it was so late, or early depending on your perspective, that I decided to stay up and talk to you."

"Are you OK with Darby taking over?" I'm sure Eric isn't happy about being shut out of a case in his own jurisdiction.

"I'm not thrilled," he admits, "but if it has to be anyone, I'm glad it's Darby. Armistead probably died of natural causes, but if his death does turn into a murder investigation, the case is in good hands."

"What will you do now?" I ask. "Will you work on other cases?" Harmony Lake is so small, there probably are no other cases.

"I'm sticking to my original plan," Eric replies. "I'll use the time I have owing to help at the store until Connie and Marla come back. I'll fill in as your sidekick." He grins.

"Before you do anything, you should get some sleep," I suggest.

"And a shower," he adds, smiling weakly.

I don't hear the back door, and Sophie doesn't make

a sound, so I'm shocked to find Darby suddenly beside us. It's hard to imagine Darby sneaking anywhere without being noticed. It's not just his voice that's big; he's a big man all around. He's as tall as Eric and thicker. It's amazing how stealth-like these huge men are when they walk in and out of Knitorious.

"One maple pecan latte with extra whipped cream and a drizzle of chocolate sauce." He pulls a cup from the tray and places it in front of me. "And one dark roast double-double." He pulls a second cup and sets it in front of Eric. "And one whipped cream for Sophie." Darby pulls a third cup from the tray and puts in in front of me.

"It's nice of you to think of Sophie," I say, cracking the lid on the whipped cream.

"I didn't," Darby admits. "When I placed your very specific order, the cashier asked me if it was for you. When I said it was, she insisted on giving me whipped cream for Sophie."

"Small town service." I smile and put the cup on the floor for Sophie.

"Do you think we have time to talk before you open the store?" Darby asks me.

I check the time on my phone. "I think so. I can open a few minutes late if necessary. I expect the store will have more nosy neighbours than knitters and crocheters today, anyway."

By now, everyone in town knows Jess and I discovered Dr. Armistead and his car outside the store last night. Lots of "well-wishers" and "concerned neighbours" will show up with questions. Some will pretend they're shopping for yarn and knitting supplies, and some will just mill around the store talking to other customers and listening for gossip.

"I'll leave you to it," Eric says, standing up and pushing his chair in. "I'll grab a quick shower then come downstairs. If you and Darby aren't finished, you can use my apartment, and I'll watch the store."

"Or you can get some sleep. Darby and I will figure something out if we aren't finished when it's time to open the store."

Eric nods. "You and I aren't finished talking," he says, looking at me. "There's another conflict of interest I need to tell you about with this case."

"There probably isn't a case," Darby reminds him. "Poor Dr. A probably had a heart attack, or a stroke, or something."

Eric's footsteps disappear up the stairs in the back room, and Darby takes a seat across from me at the harvest table.

"Tell me, Megan, why do all murders seem to lead back to you?" he asks lightheartedly and winks while he opens his leather folio.

"I wish I knew," I reply, watching Darby uncap a fountain pen.

While we sip our coffees, I tell Darby everything that happened last night, starting from the moment Jess declared her intention to walk from the pub to Knitorious to retrieve her phone, until I went outside with Eric and Sophie to give Eric my statement.

Recalling the events with a sober mind, I also tell him I noticed Jamila Jagger and Charmaine Solomon having a lively discussion in the dark alley beside the pub—a detail I'd forgotten last night when I spoke to Eric.

"Are you one hundred percent certain it was them? I mean, it was dark, and you'd been drinking."

"One hundred percent sure it was Jamila, and at least ninety percent sure about Charmaine," I reply.

"Are Ms. Jagger and Chief Solomon close?" Darby asks.

I shrug. "You should probably ask them that. Harmony Lake is a small town. Everybody knows everybody to some extent, but until last night, I didn't realize they were friendly enough to have dinner parties and private conversations in dark allies."

"They have dinner parties?" Darby asks while making notes in his folio.

"I assume so," I reply. "When Jamila visited our booth, she said she'd just had dinner at the Solomon's house."

"She did? You're certain?"

"I'm certain." I nod.

Why doesn't Darby know Jamila was at the Solomon's house for dinner last night? Wouldn't Charmaine or Dr. Solomon have told him? Or Eric?

"I'm surprised Eric didn't mention it in his statement," I say. "I'm sure I remember my conversation with Jamila correctly."

"He mentioned that Ms. Jagger joined your table briefly, but said he couldn't hear your conversation. He assumed you were talking about a laptop."

That makes sense. The pub was busy and noisy and Jamila doesn't have the loudest voice. She had to lean toward me so I could hear her.

"He's right," I confirm. "Jamila came to talk to me because I left a message for her earlier yesterday about a laptop. The store laptop finally died, and I'm hoping she has one at her store to replace it."

"And which whimsically named store does Ms. Jagger own?"

I tell him Jamila owns Bits'n'Bytes, then I disclose to him the previous, professional relationship Adam and I had with Dr. Armistead.

"About three to four years ago," I reply when Darby asks me when we last saw Dr. Armistead for marriage counselling.

I also mention to Darby that, according to Jess, Dr. Armistead's office was broken into on Monday.

"I'm aware," he says, acknowledging the break in.

We stop talking when we hear the back door open, then close.

"Good morning, my dear," Connie sings. "Oh, you have company. How nice. You carry on, and I'll open up."

"Connie Coulson, this is Darby Morris. Darby is a

friend of Eric's and a detective with the Harmony Hills Police Department."

"A pleasure to finally meet you, Mr. Morris." Connie and Darby shake hands, and as I walk toward the front door to unlock it and switch the sign from CLOSED to OPEN, I hear Connie thank Darby for his "hard work on Megan's unfortunate car accident a few months ago." Connie refers to my "unfortunate car accident" as though it were a minor fender bender when it was actually a planned, almost-successful attempt to murder me. Connie still tears up if I mention it. I think calling it an accident makes it sound less scary and easier for her to deal with.

I unlock the door, and the first few customers—or nosy neighbours—of the day file into the store. Connie excuses herself from Darby and rushes to the front to take the lead on crowd control.

"Do you need me for anything else?" I ask, returning to Darby.

"Not right now, but I might need to speak to you again soon," he replies.

"Darby, sometimes the locals are…hesitant to talk to outsiders," I explain as quietly and tactfully as possible. "It takes a while for residents to warm up to new people. It's not personal. Eric had the same problem at first. I'm sure if you ask him, he'll tell you about it. If you need help, I'm happy to do whatever I can. Eric found that having a community liaison helped witnesses feel more comfortable disclosing things."

Harmony Lake residents spend months each year inundated with tourists who are looking to exchange their city lives for an authentic small-town living experience. We've learned to give tourists what they want while still protecting the core of our community and preserving it for just us. We accomplish this by being cautious of outsiders and not opening up to them more than absolutely necessary.

"I understand what you're saying, Megan. And I appreciate your offer. But I'm hoping the coroner will phone any minute and tell me Dr. A died of natural causes. Then, I can close the file and go back to Harmony Hills where I belong." He laughs.

Darby's not the only one hoping the coroner will conclude Dr. Armistead's death wasn't the result of foul play.

CHAPTER 5

TOGETHER, Connie and I manage the flow of questions about what happened last night. I answer honestly and briefly.

Yes, a man drove his Tesla into the light post outside the store.

No, I didn't get a good look at him.

No, the police don't think it was murder.

No, he wasn't local.

Yes, I was with Adam's new girlfriend.

No, our divorce isn't final yet.

Her name is Jess.

No, she's not local, either.

Yes, we were slightly drunk—this might be an understatement.

Yes, I like her.

The truth must be less exciting than the rumours

because, within an hour, the masses stop gathering at Knitorious.

The first few visitors likely spread the word that there's nothing exciting to see or hear. Also, the crooked lamppost means driving on Water Street is a nightmare today with a police officer directing traffic in both directions on the one lane that's still open.

With the store now empty, Connie and I make ourselves comfortable on one of the sofas in the cozy sitting area and pick up our knitting.

"This is the first time I've picked up my needles since Thursday," I remark, starting a new row of the cardigan I'm working on.

"Well, you've had a lot going on, my dear," Connie responds.

"Why are you here?" I ask. "Aren't you supposed to be doting over Archie and his new hip?"

She dips her chin and looks at me over the top of her stylish reading glasses. "Ryan is on Archie-duty this morning." She smiles and tucks a few strands of her sleek silver bob behind her ear. "I wanted to make sure you're OK and help you manage the nosy neighbours. I figured with Eric having to work because of this chaos, and Marla helping at Artsy Tartsy, you'd be outnumbered. I didn't think you should be alone."

"That's very sweet, thank you. But Eric is upstairs, and the local busybodies have already lost interest, so if you want to get back to Archie, I completely understand."

47

"It's nice for Archie and me to have a break from each other," Connie explains. "And it's nice for Ryan to have some quality time with his father. I'm quite happy to stay here and spend some time with you. Now tell me, why isn't Eric at work, and why is Darby walking around town asking lots of questions, hmmm?"

I tell Connie about the various conflicts of interest with Harmony Lake PD working this case. I also tell her the dead man's name and how Adam and I, Jess and her ex-husband, and Eric and his ex-wife, all knew him professionally. Then I tell her that Darby didn't know Jamila was also a guest at the Solomon's dinner party last night.

"Well, Charmaine will *not* like having her name dragged into any of this!" Connie declares. "Her term as chief of police is almost over, and according to the rumour mill, the mayor doesn't intend to renew Charmaine's mandate."

"Really?" I ask, laying my knitting on my lap and giving Connie my full attention. "I haven't heard about this."

Connie nods. "You have to remember, my dear, Harmony Lake went from no murders in the town's history to more than our share of murders since Charmaine's appointment as chief of police. If the mayor renews Charmaine's mandate, she'll lose the next election for sure."

"I guess," I respond. "But is it fair to blame Charmaine Solomon for the murders? In her defence, the town has no unsolved cases, and she created the Major Crimes Unit and hired Eric to head it up."

"Exactly," Connie concurs. "Rumour has it Eric is at the top of the list to replace Charmaine as the new chief of police."

"If that's true, Eric would have mentioned it, and he hasn't said a word to me about it."

Before he went upstairs, Eric said we weren't finished talking. Could this be what he meant?

Except for the occasional interruption when I get up to help a customer, Connie and I pass the rest of the morning knitting and chatting about anything and everything until she gets a text from Ryan.

"Ryan has to leave Archie. He has to fix a furnace," Connie says, looking at her phone screen. "I have to go." She looks at me. "Will you be all right here on your own, my dear?"

"Absolutely," I assure her. "Thank you for being here today, but I'll be fine. How about you? Can I bring dinner to the condo tonight for you and Archie? Or can I cook something? You deserve a break from looking after everyone."

"That's a lovely offer, my dear." Connie opens her arms and we meet halfway for a hug. "But I won't be home at dinnertime. If Ryan's furnace emergency is over, I'm driving Zachary to his hockey game in Harmony Hills tonight."

"What if Ryan's furnace emergency isn't over?" I ask, about to suggest that I can take Zach to his game.

"Why don't I take him?" Eric offers, entering the store from the back room. "I love watching Zach's team play, they're great. I can pick up Archie, and he can come with us."

"Thank you, Eric!" Connie walks toward Eric with her arms open for a hug. "It'll do Archie a world of good to spend time with someone other than me or Ryan."

"I'm happy to do it," Eric says. "Text me the details."

Connie gives Eric a few highlights of what he's getting himself into with Archie and his walker, then, excited about having an evening to herself, she composes a text message inviting her fellow book club members to an impromptu meeting this evening at her place.

"The mayor is a member of the book club," she whispers when I walk her to the back door. "I'll see what I can uncover." She winks.

Much like a certain long-running, procedural-crime TV show, Harmony Lake is influenced by two separate yet equally important groups: The Book Club that meets twice monthly under the guise of reading best-selling fiction, and The Charity Knitting Guild that assembles on Wednesday afternoons at Knitorious. Dun dun.

Both groups have eyes and ears all over town, and through networks of carefully placed members and allies, they make it their business to know the ins and outs of anything that might affect the town as a whole.

Connie and Marla—who both happen to work for me—are crossover members who belong to both clubs.

The two groups are neither competitive nor harbour any animosity toward one another. They operate independently and have separate yet complementary agendas.

Occasionally, when a serious situation threatens the delicate equilibrium within Harmony Lake, the two groups will join forces and almost invisibly take action to restore the town's natural balance.

While I'm not privy to the organizational structure or inner workings of either group, they seem to have a matriarchal hierarchy. The older, wiser women of the town are in charge and train the next generation to take the reins and continue the tradition when necessary.

Harmony Lake might have a democratically elected town council and mayor, but everyone knows it's the women of The Book Club and The Charity Knitting Guild who wield the real power.

"Thank you for doing that," I say to Eric.

"It's not a big deal. I get to watch a hockey game and spend some time with Archie. I'm sure it'll be fun."

Clearly, we have different ideas of fun.

"You look better," I observe. "Were you able to get some sleep?"

"A couple of hours," Eric replies. "Enough to take the edge off."

"Can I ask you something?" I ask.

"Of course." He furrows his brow, and a look of concern takes over his face.

"Connie said there's a rumour that Charmaine's mandate as chief of police won't be renewed by the mayor, and you could be in contention to replace her. Is it true?"

"I only found out last night," he admits. "It's the reason Charmaine wanted to meet with me. She believes the mayor won't renew her contract. She wants to know how I'd feel if she put my name forward as a potential candidate for her job."

"Wow," I say. "Good for her for recognizing your hard work."

If the mayor is unhappy with Charmaine's performance as chief, why would she listen to Charmaine's recommendation for a replacement? Why would the mayor value Charmaine's opinion? And why would Charmaine care who replaces her?

"I was going to tell you after dinner last night, but Armistead died, and everything's been crazy since then."

"I understand," I tell him. "Do you want to be chief of police?"

"Chief of paperwork?" He chuckles. "Not really. I became a cop to catch bad guys and help people, not manage budgets and get stuck in the middle of local politics."

"Is Charmaine angry about not being renewed?" I ask.

Eric shrugs. "She didn't sound angry. She sounded…resigned to it. But I don't know how long she's had to process it. Maybe she's known for a while."

"What will she do next?" I ask. "I can't imagine there are a lot of police-chief positions around. Each police force only has one, so she'd probably have to relocate if she found another job."

"She hinted that she and Emory might move away from Harmony Lake. She said they don't have any family connections here. They've been fixing up the house lately. I think they might be getting it ready to sell."

"If they leave town, what would happen to Dr. Solomon's patients? Maybe last night's dinner was to talk to Dr. Armistead about taking over Dr. Solomon's patients," I wonder out loud.

"Why would Jamila be there?" Eric asks.

I shrug. "Tech support? If patient files and such are digital nowadays, maybe she'd facilitate the transfer or help them merge everything? I don't know." I shake my head. "I'm just thinking out loud." I smile. "What did you tell Charmaine when she asked if she could put your name forward?"

"I told her I need to think about it. I wanted to talk to you," he replies. "I can't talk to her about it now. I can't talk to her about anything until the coroner determines Armistead's cause of death and the case is closed."

"When you can talk to her, what will you say?"

"I don't know. I'll tell her I'm honoured to be considered. I guess it would be all right to put my name forward and see what happens. I don't have to accept, and the mayor might have other candidates in mind, anyway. What do you think?"

"I think it's your career, and you should do what makes you happy. You have my support whatever you do."

"There's something else…" Eric says, his voice trailing off before he finishes his sentence.

He takes a deep breath and exhales slowly. The last time he acted this nervous was when he asked me on our first date.

"Heavy shoulders, long arms," I remind him. "I'll lock the door and put up the BACK IN TEN MINUTES sign." I get the feeling this is important.

"Heavy shoulders, long arms" is a mantra I learned in a yoga class years ago. I take deep breaths and repeat it when I'm stressed or overwhelmed. It helps relieve the tension in my neck and shoulders.

I join him at the harvest table at the back of the store where we're out of sight of anyone who might look through the window.

He takes my hand. "I hate thinking about this, never mind talking about it."

"I'm listening," I say.

"Being a former patient isn't the only connection I have to Armistead." He pauses and takes another breath. "When my ex-wife and I were his patients, Armistead's sixteen-year-old son was arrested and charged with driving under the influence. He was a new driver. He'd only been licensed for a few weeks, and he was drinking underage. It was a serious situation. Armistead called me and asked if I could help him out with the charges."

"Does 'help him out' mean make the charges go away?" I clarify.

"That's how I interpreted it," Eric replies. "He suggested if I helped him out, our counselling sessions would be free."

"Bribery," I observe. "Did you do it?"

"No!" he insists, then pauses. "You know I'd never do that." Another pause. "But I did a background check on him. To see if Armistead had a criminal record or had tried anything like this before. I didn't know if I should just tell him I couldn't help him and pretend it never happened, or if I should report it to someone. I looked him up to see what kind of person I was dealing with."

"And?" I urge.

"I found out he'd been married four times and one of his wives had a restraining order against him. Apparently, he would call her dozens of times every day in an attempt to reconcile with her."

"Are you telling me Dr. Armistead was giving relationship advice even though he had *four* failed marriages, was harassing one of his exes, and tried to bribe the police?" I'm incredulous.

The movie line, *"I guide others to a treasure I cannot possess"* comes to mind.

Eric nods. "That's exactly what I'm saying."

"So, what happened? What did you do with this information?"

"I told my ex-wife Armistead offered us free counselling in exchange for helping his son's situation, and she went berserk. First, she insisted I misunderstood what he meant, then she accused me of lying about it even happening. She said he would never do that, and accused me of making it up to sabotage our counselling sessions. To try to convince her I was telling the truth, I told her about the background check. About his four marriages and the restraining order."

"Did she believe you?"

"I don't know." He shrugs. "She was so angry at me for checking up on him that whether it was true was irrelevant. Anyway, I refused to see him again, so she went to our next appointment alone and told him what I did and what I found out."

"Why did she throw you under the bus like that?" I ask.

"She said it was another example of me being a cop first and a husband last. And she decided it was proof I wanted a divorce and was purposely sabotaging any attempts to fix our marriage."

"I'm so sorry this happened to you." I squeeze his hand.

"Armistead reported me."

"To your superiors?"

Eric nods. "I was given an official reprimand. It's in my file."

"Reprimand for what?"

"For the background check. He wasn't part of any cases I was working on. We aren't supposed to look up random people. Cops do it all the time, but we're not supposed to do it."

"Did you tell whoever reprimanded you about Dr. Armistead trying to bribe you?"

"Yes. Armistead denied it, of course. The attempted bribery was his word against mine, but there was proof of his accusation against me, a digital trail of the search."

"What happened with you and your ex after Dr. Armistead reported you?"

"I moved out within a week."

"Can I ask you a really personal question?" I ask. "It's totally fine if you don't want to answer. I understand completely."

This is the most Eric has ever talked about his marriage. Before today, he's only ever mentioned his ex-wife's name is Karen, she's a chiropractor, and she still lives in the city. She knew he was a cop when they met, but his job caused stress in their marriage, and she wanted him to leave the force and work for her father's heating and air conditioning company. Eric refused. He wanted to be a cop since he was a little boy.

"Of course. Ask me anything," he says.

"If this situation with Dr. Armistead didn't happen, do you think you and Karen would've worked it out?"

"No," he confirms, shaking his head. "She was right about one thing, I wanted a divorce. I think her goal for therapy was to get the therapist to help her convince me to change careers, and my goal was to get the therapist to help her see our marriage wasn't worth saving."

"Thank you for trusting me enough to tell me this. I know you don't like to talk about when you were married."

"I want you to hear it from me. It's unlikely, but if Armistead's death turns out to be murder, this situation could come up, and I don't want you to think I kept it from you. No secrets."

"No secrets," I repeat after him. "But you're entitled to privacy. Privacy and secrets aren't the same."

Honestly, I don't want to know the details of Eric's past relationships.

Sometimes the past is better left there.

CHAPTER 6

THE JINGLE when I open the door at Bits'n'Bytes sounds similar to the bell over the door at Knitorious. But that's where the similarities end. Bits'n'Bytes is futuristic and sleek. Everything is white, smooth, and shiny. A completely different atmosphere than my cozy yarn store.

"I'll be right with you, Megan!" Jamila's smiling face pokes around a doorway at the back of the store.

"No worries, Jamila, take your time," I call out.

I catch sight of myself on a security monitor just below the ceiling and try to tame a few unruly curls. Other than the local jewellery store and the bank, Bits'n'Bytes is the only other business I'm aware of in Harmony Lake with a security system.

When I wander from the wall of laptops to the wall of tablets, I glance toward the back room and glimpse the back of Jamila's head. She moves toward the back door, and the rest of her body comes into view. Her back is to me. She unlocks the door and moves aside. Someone else comes into view and joins Jamila at the back door. It's Charmaine Solomon again. I've never seen Charmaine and Jamila in the same place at the same time, and now I've seen them together twice in two days. Both times, they're huddled together conspiratorially. Both women speak and nod repeatedly until Charmaine finally leaves, and Jamila closes the door and locks it.

I book it to the front window, hoping to see Charmaine's car drive out of the parking lot behind the store, so I can confirm it's her.

"Sorry to make you wait, Megan."

I turn away from the window and look at Jamila. "No problem. Your text said to stop by whenever, but I practically ran here because the laptop at the store is completely dead."

"Right!" Jamila holds up her index finger. "Give me one more minute to get it. It's in the back."

When Jamila disappears again, I run back to the window, hoping I didn't miss Charmaine's car.

Bingo!

There she is, waiting to turn left out of the driveway that connects the parking lot behind the store to Water Street. I knew it was her.

"Let's take a look!" Jamila places the laptop on one of the shiny, white, round tables in the showroom. She sits in a shiny, white chair, and I sit across from her.

Jamila gives me a tour of the laptop and lists its various tech specs and such. I nod and smile but don't actually understand what most of it means. She assures me it's fast, has enough memory, and plenty of storage for everything I need. She says it's compatible with the programs I use to run Knitorious.

"It sounds perfect. I'll take it," I say confidently, not feeling at all confident.

"Great! Do you mind leaving your phone here for a couple of hours?"

"My phone? Why?"

Jamila explains that because the laptop at the store is dead, but my cell phone, home computer, and store computer sync the same information, she can use my cell phone to set up the new laptop.

"You'll set it up for me?" This makes me happier than it reasonably should. I dread setting it up myself.

"It's part of the service," she explains. "To stay competitive, I have to offer something the big-box stores don't." She shrugs. "I offer free set up."

Jamila taps on the keyboard and occasionally spins the laptop toward me for a fingerprint or to set up a password.

"How are you feeling today, Jamila?" I spin the laptop toward her after setting up my fingerprint. "I mean, since learning that Dr. Armistead died last night."

"Dr. Armistead?" she asks without looking up from the screen.

"Yes, Dr. Armistead. Didn't you have dinner with him last night at the Solomon's?"

"Oh, you mean, Mac?"

Dr. Armistead's first name is Malcolm, or as I'm now learning from Jamila, Mac for short.

"I found him," I tell her.

She stops tapping on the keyboard and looks at me. "I'm sorry to hear that. It must've been awful."

"It wasn't pleasant," I agree. "Probably as unpleasant as finding out someone you just shared a meal with suddenly died."

She nods somberly. "He was a nice man. He was fine when I left the Solomon's. It's hard to believe that less than an hour after I said goodbye to him, he died."

"Did you know him well?"

"I was his tech support. Not very often, because he was pretty technically astute, but I did some tech stuff for him over the years."

"How did he find you? I was told he lived and worked in Harmony Hills."

"He did," Jamila confirms. "Emory referred him to me. I provide tech support for Emory's therapy practice too."

"Well, I'm sorry you've lost a friend, or client, or both."

"Thanks." Jamila's gaze returns to the laptop screen, and she continues typing.

"How are the Solomons doing today? They must be in shock after what happened to their friend."

"I haven't spoken to either of them since last night at the pub," Jamila replies. "Eric texted Charmaine, and she stepped outside to call him back. When she came back, she told Emory she had a work emergency, and they had to leave. I found out about Mac early this morning from a police officer."

Lie. I just saw Jamila and Charmaine together in the back room.

"I haven't spoken to them either," I admit. "And I'm not sure when I'll be able to give them my condolences. Charmaine is Eric's boss, and he says he can't talk to her right now—something about conflicts of interest. I don't want to put either of them in an awkward position, so I haven't reached out to the Solomons. If you speak to them, would you tell them I'm sorry for their loss?"

"Sure." Jamila nods. "Did the police question you?"

I nod. "Detective Morris questioned me this morning."

"Me too," she says, "but he said he doesn't think Mac was murdered. Why is he questioning people if it wasn't murder?"

It takes me a moment to remember that Mac is Dr. Armistead. I'm not used to hearing him called by his first name.

"Detective Morris says every death is treated as suspicious until the coroner confirms it isn't."

Jamila lets out a sigh of relief.

I know how she feels, I've been there. It's unnerving

to think that something as horrible as murder could happen in your hometown. A place where you feel safe and trust the people around you. It unsettles your mind, body, and soul. It makes you second guess everything.

THE JINGLE of the bell startles the ladies who are sitting on the sofas, knitting.

"Hi, Megan," the two ladies say in unison as I enter the store.

"Hi, Megan." Eric waves from his seat, next to one of the women.

"Hello, everyone," I say, crouching down to greet Sophie and fighting back a laugh at Eric's obvious awkwardness.

"He was all alone," Mrs. Roblin says, patting Eric's knee.

"Helpless," Mrs. Vogel adds. "What if someone came in with an urgent knitting problem?"

"He wouldn't know what to do!" Mrs. Roblin continues. "Lucky for him, we came along. We decided we should keep him company and help with any knitting emergencies that might come up."

"It's the neighbourly thing to do," Mrs. Vogel justifies.

Never in my life have I encountered what I would consider a life-or-death knitting emergency.

"Thank you, ladies! I appreciate it. I'm a bit stuck this week with Connie looking after Archie and Marla helping at Artsy Tartsy."

Mrs. Roblin and Mrs. Vogel ask about Archie's hip replacement surgery, then they ask how April's father is doing. Soon they're telling Eric and me about friends and family who have had hip replacements and ladder-related accidents.

"Thank you for coming to my rescue this afternoon, ladies." Eric gives each of them a wide smile and stands up. "Now that the boss is back, I think I'll go upstairs for lunch." He gives them a wink.

Amidst cries of how he shouldn't have to make his own lunch, and if Mrs. Vogel had known, she would have brought him a sandwich, and if Mrs. Roblin had known she would have brought him a casserole, Eric escapes to the sanctuary of his apartment.

Within minutes of his departure, Mrs. Roblin and Mrs. Vogel pack up their knitting bags and leave the store.

"Are they gone?" Eric asks cautiously, his eyes darting from one yarn section to another upon re-entering the store.

"Yes, they left right after you. If you want me to call them and let them know you're back, I'm more than happy to. I'll even run another errand if you want them to hang around for a while," I tease.

"No, thank you! They're lovely ladies, but too much of a good thing is not good."

Eric goes to the backroom/kitchenette and reappears with two plates.

"Lunch," he announces, putting the plates on the harvest table. "Chicken Caesar salad wraps."

"Thank you," I say, joining him at the table. "I'm starving."

I explain how I left my phone with Jamila so she can set up the new laptop. "She said she'll call me on the landline when it's ready."

"Tell me about the new laptop," he replies.

To the best of my ability, I tell him the handful of specs I can remember and describe its appearance. I'm far more comfortable describing its appearance than the specs.

"You really don't know a lot about computers, do you?" He laughs.

"No, I don't. I'm what's called 'an end user'." I take a sip of water. "Charmaine Solomon was there."

"At Bits'n'Bytes?" Eric asks.

With my mouth full of food, I nod.

"Did you speak to her?" he asks.

I swallow before I reply. "No. She doesn't know I saw her. She was in the back room with Jamila. I happened to look up when Charmaine was leaving through the back door. I watched her car turn onto Water Street to make sure it was her." Eric looks down and to the left. He does this when he concentrates. "What?" I ask.

"I wonder if either of them disclosed this visit to Darby?"

I shrug. "I don't know about Darby, but Jamila didn't disclose the visit to me. I asked her outright if she's spoken to the Solomons since Dr. Armistead died, and she said, 'no'."

"Why would she lie?" he wonders out loud.

"It's possible Charmaine was checking on Jamila. Jamila's probably never had dinner with someone who died right after the last course. Also, Charmaine might've wanted to see Jamila with her own eyes to reassure herself that it wasn't food poisoning that killed Dr. Armistead. If one of my dinner guests died, it would cross my mind."

"Possibly," Eric agrees, nodding. "It still doesn't explain why Jamila would lie about it."

I shrug. "Maybe she thought I was being nosy. Connie and I had our share of nosy neighbours this morning. Maybe when they left here, they went to Bits'n'Bytes, and now Jamila is cautious about telling anyone anything. But I remembered something else this morning when Darby questioned me. Something I forgot to mention to you last night."

I tell him about Jamila and Charmaine's conversation in the alley beside the pub.

"Even when you're drunk, you have above average observation skills."

Slightly drunk. Tipsy.

CHAPTER 7

THE BELL above the door turns my attention from the yoke of the sweater I'm knitting. "Jess!" I declare, putting my knitting on the coffee table in front of me. "How are you?" We hug.

"Still in shock, I think, but I'm OK. How about you?" she asks.

"I'm OK."

"Megan, this is my friend Karen Porter. She works at the medical centre too. She drove me here to pick up my car."

"Hi, Karen, it's nice to meet you." I extend my hand.

"You too." Karen shakes my hand weakly.

Karen has been crying. Her face is splotchy, and her large brown eyes are red and swollen. Her dark hair is pulled back into a low ponytail, and a few escaped wisps stick out around her face. She has that raw, tired look that only comes from crying yourself to exhaustion.

"Have a seat," I say.

"There's another reason Karen drove me here today," Jess explains. "She was friends with Dr. Armistead. She was really shaken when she found out what happened. She has some questions about how we found him. I've answered them to the best of my ability, but between the shock and the chardonnay, I'm not sure I'm recalling everything correctly."

"I don't think we're supposed to talk about this together," I say. "Have you given a statement?"

"Earlier today." Jess nods. "I told the detective what happened and answered a lot of questions for him."

I'm hesitant to have this conversation without asking Darby first. My phone is still with Jamila, so I can't text him, and Eric is walking Sophie, so he's not here to ask.

"I was married to a cop," Karen pipes in. "I'm sure it would be fine, as long as we're all honest about what we talk about if the police ask."

I chew the inside of my cheek, still hesitant. Karen is obviously chomping at the bit to talk about it. She seems more distraught than I'd expect from a co-worker. Exactly how well did she know Dr. Armistead?

"Were you and Dr. Armistead close, Karen?"

Her eyes fill with moisture, and she swallows hard. She opens her mouth to speak, but no sound comes out, and she nods sharply instead.

I hand her a box of tissue, and Jess rubs her upper back.

"You loved him," I say softly. Her grief is palpable. "I'm sorry for your loss."

Karen nods again and dabs at the tears streaming down her cheeks. "Did he look…" She pauses while she finds the right word. "Peaceful?"

"It was dark, and I only saw him through the car window for a moment. He didn't look injured or in pain. It didn't look like he suffered."

I have no idea whether he suffered or not, but I know it's what Karen needs to hear, and it's probably what Dr. Armistead would want her to hear.

"Karen, I had no idea you and Dr. Armistead were together," Jess says. "Why didn't you tell me?"

We sit quietly and wait while Karen composes herself enough to speak.

"We didn't tell anyone," Karen explains, looking at Jess. "It was a secret."

"Why?" Jess asks.

"I was his patient," Karen admits. "His profession has a five-year rule. He has to wait five years before dating a former patient. We didn't wait five years."

"How long did you wait?" I ask.

"We've been dating for about a year, and I was his patient between three and four years ago."

"Oh my," Jess says, looking at me. Then she looks at Karen. "You told the police about your relationship, right?"

Karen shakes her head. "I haven't talked to the police. They don't know I exist."

"You have to tell them," Jess advises.

Good advice, Jess.

"Uh-uh." Karen shakes her head. "No way. I don't want to damage Mac's reputation. People will judge him. They'll say he took advantage of me, and he didn't. It wasn't like that. We only had a couple of sessions years ago. We lost touch until I left my practice in the city and joined the practice in Harmony Hills. We met again and had a connection. Why should we wait two more years? We're adults." Her voice becomes louder, and her tone more defensive as she speaks.

"I get it," I say, hoping to calm Karen's emotional state. "The police think he died of natural causes. If they're right, there won't be an investigation into Dr. A —Mac's death, and you won't have to say anything. The case will be closed."

"But if they're wrong," Jess adds, "and his death is investigated, you, me, or Megan will have to tell the police about your relationship."

Karen's silent tears become sobs. I get her a glass of water and place it on the table in front of her.

"Karen, do any of your friends or family know about you and Mac?" I ask.

She shakes her head and sips the water.

"If you tell them, they can support you. Right now, everyone assumes you've lost a co-worker, not your life partner. If your people know the truth about your relationship, they'll understand, and you won't have the extra burden of keeping this secret and hiding your grief."

"Megan's right," Jess agrees. "It's something to think about."

Jess continues to comfort Karen until Karen asks me where she can freshen up.

"Back of the store," I direct. "Turn left in the kitchenette. There's a small hallway. The washroom is on the right."

Karen goes to the washroom, taking the tissue box with her.

Once we're alone, Jess looks at me wide-eyed. "I had no idea she was in a relationship with Dr. Armistead, I swear," she whispers. "I just assumed she's one of those super-sensitive people. I can't believe I didn't see it."

"In hindsight, were there any clues?" I whisper.

Jess opens her mouth to answer, but we're interrupted by the jingle of the door and the sudden appearance of Sophie.

"Hi, Sophie." Jess rubs the corgi's head. "Hi, Eric."

"Hey, Jess. How are you?"

Eric and Jess exchange pleasantries, then Eric looks at me. "Jamila stopped me outside Bits'n'Bytes. The laptop is ready."

"Listen," I hiss. "Jess's friend is here. She's in the washroom. She told us she's Dr. Armistead's secret girlfriend."

Eric's mouth forms a very small **o**. "I'll leave you to talk, and I'll pick up your laptop and phone."

I nod. Eric puts Sophie's leash on the counter and leaves through the front door.

I give Jess a brief explanation about the conflict of interest with the HLPD and Dr. Armistead's investigation.

Jess takes a deep breath. "Before Eric and Sophie came in, you asked me about hindsight. Now that I think about it, Karen and Dr. Armistead had lunch together almost every day but always in his office. They never went out unless it was part of a group. And when his office was robbed on Monday, she helped him sort through the mess. It took them hours. She said they were there all night. I should've seen it."

"You saw what they wanted you to see," I tell her.

"What are you talking about?" Karen asks upon her return from the washroom.

"Jess was just telling me that Dr. Armistead's office was broken into on Monday. She said they made a huge mess."

Karen sighs and nods. "They did. They emptied every drawer, filing cabinets were flipped over, paper was scattered everywhere. It took hours to sort through."

"Did they take anything?" I ask.

Karen shakes her head. "Not even his laptop."

"The office door and his filing cabinets weren't locked?" Jess asks.

"They were," Karen confirms. "The robbers picked the locks."

"Whatever they were looking for, they must've wanted it badly," I observe.

"The police said they were probably looking for drugs."

"In a therapist's office?" It sounds like Jess doesn't buy it. "Dr. Armistead doesn't write prescriptions. He wouldn't have drug samples in his office. If they wanted drugs, there's a pharmacy in the lobby and a dozen other medical offices in the building that have drugs in them."

"But Mac's office was the only one that was empty," Karen explains. "The police think the robbers lurked around waiting for an opportunity, and when they saw Mac leave his office and lock the door, they knew it was empty. The police think the robbers were angry when they realized there were no drugs, and they trashed the office."

Jess looks at me and shrugs. I get the feeling she's still not convinced.

"Karen," Jess says gently, "is your secret relationship the reason you and Dr. Armistead ate lunch in his office every day and never went out? Were you afraid people would realize you were more than friends?"

"It was difficult for Mac to enjoy eating out with his allergy."

"Allergy?" I probe.

"He had a severe caffeine allergy. Very rare but

deadly. He kept an EpiPen with him at all times. He also kept one in his car. You'd be amazed how many foods contain caffeine. Foods you'd never expect. He was conditioned to bring his own food, or he would eat at a handful of specific restaurants where he was comfortable."

While Jess and Karen talk about food allergies, I think back to the conversation Eric and I had last night about his meeting with Charmaine. She was preparing duchess potatoes and chateaubriand with sauce and brussels sprouts. I wonder what they had for dessert. Could any of those dishes have inadvertently contained caffeine? Poor Charmaine! I can't Imagine worrying that I may have accidentally poisoned someone.

Did Dr. Armistead have any visible symptoms of allergic reaction when Jess and I found him? I only saw his face. I'm sure I would have noticed hives or severe swelling. But it was dark. The streetlight wasn't working because of the accident. Think Megan, think! Stupid chardonnay, clouding my recollection.

I'm vaguely aware when the bell over the door jingles, but I'm so focused on my thoughts that it doesn't distract me.

"WHY ARE YOU HERE?" Karen's shout brings me back to the here and now.

"Karen?" Eric sounds shocked.

He closes the door behind him but doesn't come any closer.

As my brain begins to connect the mental dots, I gasp and bring my hand to my mouth.

Is this the same Karen who was married to Eric? She said she was married to a cop. She works in a medical centre. Chiropractors sometimes work in medical centres. She moved from the city about a year ago. Oh my gosh, it's her. I know it's her. The pit in my stomach and the expressions on Eric and Karen's faces confirm it's her.

"Why is my ex-wife here?" Eric asks quietly, looking at me.

He sounds calm, but I can see the panic and confusion in his eyes.

At a loss for words, I shake my head and shrug.

"Why am *I* here? Why are *you* here? What are you doing in a knitting store?" Karen demands. "Don't tell me you're the one working Mac's case?!"

"I don't know what you're talking about, Karen," Eric replies calmly. "Who's Mac?"

I'm on my feet now, standing halfway between the sofa where Karen is sitting and the front door where Eric is standing.

"Leave!" Karen demands. She looks at Jess. "Make him leave." Her voice is shaky now, and her chin is quivering.

"I live here, Karen," Eric states matter-of-factly.

"Fine! I'll leave!" Karen starts to get up, but Jess stops her by placing a hand on her shoulder.

"This is my fault," Jess interjects. "I brought Karen here. I didn't realize you two...know each other."

"None of us did," I add, walking to the front door.

I reach behind Eric to lock the door and turn the sign from OPEN to CLOSED. I don't think the BACK IN TEN MINUTES sign will be sufficient for this situation.

"Thank you," I say quietly to Eric as I attempt to pry the laptop box and my cell phone from his hand. I can't loosen the death grip he has on them. He appears calm and composed, but it's an illusion. Up close, every muscle in his body is tense. He's stiff as a board. His jaw muscles clench and unclench constantly. I take his stiff, free hand and lead him to the back room. I close the door behind us.

"Let go," I grunt, tugging at the box.

He loosens his grip on the laptop box and my phone. I put them on the counter in the kitchenette, then point to the stairs that lead to his apartment. "Sit down," I suggest gently.

Eric sits on one of the steps, takes a deep breath, runs both hands through his hair, and drops his chin to his chest. He's staring at the floor between his feet. He's in shock. Possibly speechless.

I kneel on the floor in front of him so I'm low enough to see his face. "Eric, I'm sorry. I had no idea Karen is your ex-wife. I would never ambush you like this. Jess didn't know either."

"Why is she here?" He looks at me.

I tell him that Karen drove Jess to Harmony Lake so

Jess could pick up her car. And that Karen wanted to talk to me because I was with Jess when we found Dr. Armistead.

"She works in the same building as Jess and Dr. Armistead, but I didn't know she's a chiropractor. Her last name isn't Sloane, it's Porter. I've never seen a picture of your ex-wife, and you said she lives and works in the city. I honestly didn't make the connection. I wish I had. I would've made sure you weren't blindsided."

He looks at me. "It's OK. It's no one's fault."

"I know she was mean and shouty, but that's not all because of you. She's grieving. She's an emotional mess right now."

"Grieving who?" he asks, confused.

"Dr. Armistead."

Comprehension flashes across his face. "Is she the same woman who was in the washroom earlier? The one who is Armistead's secret girlfriend? Mac and Armistead are the same person?"

I nod. "Yes."

He inhales deeply and lets it out slowly. "Not my monkey, not my circus. None of this is my problem," he says, putting his hands on his knees and standing up. He reaches with both hands. I take his hands, and he pulls me to my feet.

I climb the first two stairs, so we're close to eye level. "Are you sure you're all right?"

I genuinely can't tell. He seems fine, but he's good at

hiding how he feels and what he's thinking. It's a cop thing—conceal, don't feel.

"I'm fine. I was in shock, but I'm OK now."

I wrap my arms around him and rest my head on his shoulder. Some of the tension leaves his body, and I feel him relax. "I'm so sorry this happened."

"It's not your fault. It's no one's fault." He kisses me. "I should leave. Connie says it takes up to half an hour for Archie and his walker to get from the condo to the car." He smiles.

"You don't have to go," I tell him. "You've had a rough day. I'll take Zach to his game or find someone else. You can chill at home."

"I want to go," Eric insists. "I'm going upstairs to get a jacket, then I'll leave through the back door. It sounds like Karen has quieted down, and I don't want to get her started again."

"OK."

I trust Jess has filled in the gaps for Karen and explained that Eric lives here, works in Harmony Lake, and that he and I are together.

I grab my phone from the counter in the kitchenette. Before I open the door to the store, I take a deep breath and brace myself for whatever awkward conversation I'm about to have with my boyfriend's ex-wife.

CHAPTER 8

Sᴜɴᴅᴀʏ, October 4ᵗʰ

Adam: Be there in 10 minutes.

Me: Just leaving to walk Sophie. Let yourself in.

Adam replies with a thumbs-up emoji.

Adam, Hannah, and I have brunch together every Sunday. We alternate between his place and mine, but Adam always cooks. Hannah joins us from school via Facetime. Brunch is at my place this week.

"Good morning, gorgeous! I miss you!" I shove my phone in my pocket as I talk with April while leaving the house with Sophie in tow.

"Good morning, Megalodon! Did the coroner decide the marriage counselor died of natural causes?" April asks.

"Not yet," I reply. "But he's only been dead for a day, and I'm not sure the coroner works on weekends. Do you know?"

"I have no idea, but it doesn't sound like a nine-to-five job. People die at night and on weekends too," April speculates.

Fair enough.

"I'll let you know as soon as I hear anything. But I think I might know how he died," I tell her.

"Spill," she demands.

I tell April about Jess and Karen's visit to Knitorious yesterday. "What a horrible allergy. Life would be so boring without coffee and chocolate," I observe.

"Can we back up to the part where everyone realizes Karen is Eric's ex-wife?" April knows which details are important.

I explain how none of us realized who Karen was until it was too late, then tell April about Karen and Eric's reactions when they saw each other.

"How is Eric now?" April asks.

I stop and wait while Sophie greets an elderly couple sitting on a bench. "He seems fine. He was his normal self after Zach's hockey game last night, and our texts this morning were the same as usual. He wasn't OK when it happened. He was in shock. He shut down and went into cop mode."

"What does Karen look like?"

"Hang on." I pull my phone from my pocket and open the browser. A quick web search of Karen's name, the medical centre where she works, and Harmony Hills leads to her chiropractic practice's website. I find her head shot, and text it to April. "I just texted you her pic."

"She's pretty," April comments.

"Very," I agree. "And she was really nice until she saw Eric. Then she returned to being nice after he left. I think they're an example of a couple who are nice people individually but don't work together."

"Did she say how she felt about Dr. Armistead keeping their relationship a secret?"

"She defended him. She told Jess and I that she wouldn't disclose it to the police because she didn't want anyone to think badly of him or to view her as a victim."

"She is a victim, Megastar. He was her therapist. He knows her most personal stuff. It creates a power imbalance. He was in a position of influence over her. There's a five-year rule for dating former patients for a reason." April makes several good points.

"I know," I agree. "Karen said they started dating three years after their last therapy appointment. And she's a healthcare professional too. She knew about the five-year rule when they started dating. I don't know enough about the situation to have an opinion on how inappropriate it was, but it was inappropriate enough for them to keep it a secret, and secrets make me uncomfortable."

We change the subject several times, catching up on anything and everything in our lives.

April updates me on her dad's recovery and how

he's settling in at home since the hospital discharged him yesterday. "He's obsessed with those flipping eaves troughs," she vents. "He has three broken bones and his biggest concern about the whole situation is that the stupid eaves troughs still aren't fixed."

"That's frustrating," I sympathize.

"I'm calling a company first thing tomorrow morning to come and fix them, so he can find something new to complain about."

We talk until Sophie and I make our way back to the front door.

"It smells amazing!" Warm comfort and cinnamon surrounds me when I walk into the house.

"Thanks!" Adam emerges from the kitchen, rapidly stirring something in a mixing bowl. He's wearing my ruffled apron with the cherry pattern which is much too small for his large frame "It's Apple Fritter Breakfast Casserole. I prepared it in advance and put it in the oven when I got here." He stops stirring and tips the bowl toward me. "This is the glaze."

"It's yummy. I love it."

"You haven't tried it yet."

"It smells like dessert. I love dessert," I reason, following him toward the kitchen.

"It'll be ready in ten minutes."

I nod and pick up my tablet to Facetime Hannah. "Are you going to talk to Hannah about inviting Jess to Thanksgiving dinner?"

"Yeah, if you're still good with it," Adam replies, setting the table.

"Of course, I am. I'm sure Hannah will be too."

I unlock the tablet and open the messaging app. Because my devices are "automagically" connected by the wonderful yet mysterious force known as *the cloud*, the last text I sent pops up on the screen.

"Who's that?" Adam asks. Still stirring briskly, he lifts his chin toward Karen's photo on the screen.

I tell him how Karen, Jess, Eric, and I unwittingly ended up in the same room yesterday.

"Jess told me," Adam says. He puts the mixing bowl on the counter and wipes his hand on the apron. Then he picks up my tablet and examines Karen's photo. "I've never met Karen, but I've heard about her. She's one of Jess's work friends." He looks at me, then hands my tablet to me. "But I recognize her."

"From the medical centre where Jess works?" I venture a logical guess.

Adam shakes his head, and I notice the grey around his temples is more pronounced than it used to be. It really stands out against his dark hair and enhances the laugh lines around his blue eyes. "No. From my office. Well, the building where my office is located."

"Oh? Is she there often?"

Adam's office is in a large, renovated Victorian house. He's one of four professional tenants. There's also a financial planner, an insurance broker, and a therapist—Emory Solomon.

"I've seen her a few times waiting for Emory."

Karen Porter is Emory's patient? But Emory and Dr. Armistead were friends. At least, I assume they were friends since the Solomons invited Dr. Armistead to their house for dinner on Friday. Wouldn't it be a conflict of interest for Emory to treat his friend's girlfriend? Did Karen know Emory and Dr. Armistead were friends? Does Emory know Karen was dating his friend, Dr. Armistead?

"That arrangement would be too cozy for my liking," I comment.

"Me too," Adam agrees. "Even if they all know, it crosses a line."

"And I thought we had boundary issues," I mutter.

"What?"

I know he heard me.

"What?" I answer his question with a question.

We Facetime with Hannah while Adam serves breakfast. We catch up with our daughter and hear about her life in the big city. Next weekend is Thanksgiving, and Hannah will be here in person for brunch. We haven't seen her in six weeks, and I can't wait to hug her.

"I told you she'd be fine with Jess coming to Thanksgiving. Have you invited her yet?"

He doles out another serving of casserole to me, then himself. "No. I wanted to make sure Hannah was comfortable first. I'll ask her today."

"Since I'm hosting this year, do you want me to

invite Jess? You know, so she knows we all want her here."

"I'll invite her, and I'll tell her you and Hannah are on board. Thank you, though." Adam smiles.

I sense he wants to say more, but he's hesitant.

"Well, if Jess offers to bring something, say no. The rest of us are bringing enough food to feed a small town. Or she can bring those little loot bags she hands out after she cleans our teeth, and everyone can take care of their dental hygiene after dinner," I joke.

We laugh and Adam makes another joke about all of us speaking to her with our mouths open, to make her more comfortable.

"I'm happy you and Jess hit it off," he says. "And thank you for looking out for her when you guys found Dr. Armistead."

"Of course," I reply. "You always had good taste in partners."

"You guys have been texting pretty regularly," Adam says. "And she stopped by the store with Karen yesterday, when she could've just picked up her car and left."

"We get along well. She's great. Would it make you uncomfortable if Jess and I are friends?" I ask Adam the question he never asked me before he befriended Eric.

He sits back in his chair. "I didn't think so, but it's... awkward knowing you and Jess have your own relationship that doesn't include me. I don't know how to describe it. Do you know what I mean?"

"I have no idea." My voice practically drips with sarcasm.

"I get it now, Meg. I didn't get it before, but now I do. It didn't occur to me that my friendship with Eric might be uncomfortable for you. I should've talked to you about it a long time ago. I'm sorry I didn't."

"Eric and I talked about it," I tell him. "It's all good."

"While we're on the subject"—Adam leans forward and puts his elbows on the table—"Eric is my friend, but you're my family. You're Hannah's mother, and we've known each other forever. I will always have your back. Whatever happens between you and Eric, or me and Eric, or whatever. I'm on your side. Every time."

"I know." I put my hand on top of his. "Ditto."

Navigating our new post-marriage friendship is like walking a tightrope. It's all about balance and planning the next step carefully. Some days we're wobblier than others, but for the most part, we haven't fallen off yet, even though we might be tempted to give each other a little shove sometimes.

"How's the new laptop?" Adam asks, changing the subject.

"It's purple!" I reply, telling him my favourite feature.

"How does it function?"

"I brought it home to show it to you." I leave the table and return a moment later, clutching the laptop to my chest. I shove the dirty dishes to the far end of the table and place the laptop in front of him. "Ta-da!"

"Very nice," Adam says, running a finger along the edge of the device and admiring my first-ever, solo technological purchase. "May I?" he asks, opening the laptop a smidge.

"Of course," I reply. "You should get acquainted with it since you provide all the tech support."

"Same password?" he asks.

I nod.

Adam types in the password and icons fill the screen.

"Have you used it? Everything running OK?"

"It seems fine. But I just got it yesterday afternoon, so I haven't really used it. Just played with it."

"Jamila didn't install the anti-virus software?" Adam asks, furrowing his thick eyebrows.

I shrug. "I have no idea. She said it would sync with my other devices."

Adam installs a cyber security software on all our devices. It scans everything we open and keeps out viruses, and spyware, and such. It works silently in the background of the computer, so I'm unaware of it most of the time. When it comes to my relationship with technology, out of sight is out of mind.

"I'll install it," he says without looking up.

He taps a few keys, we wait a few moments, then he declares the laptop safe from virtual intruders and closes it.

On the table between us, my tablet dings. I unlock the screen with my fingerprint.

Eric: Armistead died of anaphylactic shock.

"That's a relief," I say to Adam as I type a response to Eric.

"Not for Dr. Armistead," Adam responds.

Me: Case closed?

It'll be nice not to have Dr. Armistead's unfortunate death hanging over us.

Eric: Case upgraded from suspicious death to homicide.

"What?" Adam and I say in unison.

CHAPTER 9

ADAM LEAVES, and I text the Modern Family group chat to update everyone on Dr. Armistead's status. Then I load the dishwasher and wipe the counters and table while I wait for Eric to get here. He said he'd be here in ten minutes. This feels like the longest ten minutes ever.

Finally, Sophie yelps and runs to the door. It's impossible to sneak into this house with Sophie on constant surveillance.

"Hey, Soph!" Eric crouches down and rubs her corgi head. "Hey," he says again, giving me a hug and a kiss.

We sit in the family room. Sophie jumps onto the sofa and parks herself between us.

"Murder?"

"Murder," Eric confirms.

"What if he ate something caffeinated by accident at the Solomon's dinner party? Surely if it was unintentional, it isn't murder. Caffeine is hidden in so many foods…"

"Whoa." Eric raises his hand in a stop motion. "Why are you convinced it was a caffeine allergy?"

I forgot Eric doesn't have access to all the information about the case. I'm so used to him being the investigating detective that I forgot he wasn't.

"I think I should talk to Darby," I say after I tell him about Karen's revelation that Dr. Armistead was deathly allergic to caffeine.

"I think you're right," Eric agrees.

Darby sits on the living room sofa, and Sophie sits at attention by his feet. Darby leans forward and opens his leather folio to an empty page then uncaps his fountain pen.

"I take it you've heard about Dr. Armistead's cause of death?"

"Allergic reaction." I nod. "Caffeine?" I ask.

Darby looks at me and tilts his head. "Why would you ask that, Megan?" He grins.

"Because Ka—his girlfriend mentioned that Dr. Armistead had a severe caffeine allergy."

I'm uncomfortable mentioning Karen's name in front of Eric. I'm scared he'll freeze again, or hearing her name will upset him.

"You met Dr. Armistead's girlfriend? I wish I was a

fly on that wall," Darby chuckles as his crinkled eyes dart back and forth between me and Eric.

Obviously, he knows Dr. Armistead had a girlfriend and that his girlfriend happened to be Eric's ex-wife.

"You know about Dr. Armistead's girlfriend?" I answer his question with a question. "She said you don't know about her."

"I went through his phone," Darby explains.

"Ah," I respond.

It's difficult to keep secrets in the age of technology.

"How did you meet Karen?" he asks.

I tell him about Jess and Karen's visit to Knitorious, without mentioning the bit about Karen and Eric's unfortunate reactions to seeing each other.

"But earlier in the day," I add, "before their visit, I went to Bits'n'Bytes to talk to Jamila about my new laptop, and Charmaine Solomon was there."

"Are you sure it was Charmaine Solomon?" Darby asks. He makes a note I'm unable to decipher because I'm too far away, and leaning forward and squinting would be too obvious. Also, from my vantage point, his writing is upside down.

"Certain," I affirm with confidence. "I even watched her car leave the parking lot to be extra sure. It's not so much that she was there, it's that Jamila lied about it. She told me she hadn't spoken to either of the Solomons since the night before. I've thought about it a lot, and I think Charmaine's visit to Bits'n'Bytes was a surprise to Jamila. I don't think it was prearranged."

"Why do you say that?" Darby asks.

"Because Jamila's text said I should come to her store anytime. If she knew Charmaine was coming and wanted to have a private conversation with her, she would have told me to come at a specific time or after a specific time."

Darby asks me what time I went to Bits'n'Bytes yesterday, and I tell him. Eric is able to confirm the time because he watched Knitorious while I was gone.

I ask Darby if it would be considered murder if someone inadvertently fed caffeine to Dr. Armistead without realizing it. "It could happen, right? I'm sure lots of foods and drinks contain caffeine, but people who don't have a caffeine allergy or sensitivity wouldn't realize it."

Darby caps his pen and closes his folio, then looks at me. "Dr. Armistead had at least one gram of caffeine in his system. That's the equivalent of more than five cups of coffee. He ingested it very quickly or all at once. More quickly than he could drink five cups of coffee.

"Oh," I respond. "How is that possible? What food has that much caffeine?"

"It probably wasn't a specific food. It was likely added to something he ate or drank. Caffeine is readily available in pill, liquid, and powder form."

Now, I understand why the coroner concluded that Dr. Armistead was murdered.

"How long does it take for caffeine to kill someone with an allergy?" I ask. "Maybe he ingested it earlier in the day, and it didn't take effect until after dinner," I suggest, grasping for reasons to exclude the suspects who live and work in Harmony Lake.

"The coroner says it was ingested within an hour of his death," Darby explains.

"Ka—his girlfriend said Dr. Armistead carried an EpiPen with him at all times and kept one in his car. Did he try to use it before he died?"

An EpiPen is an auto-injectable device that delivers epinephrine, a life-saving medication for life-threatening allergic reactions. An allergic person uses it if they are exposed to whatever they're allergic to and experiences anaphylaxis, a severe allergic reaction that often results in death.

"I believe when he hit the lamp post, he was pulling over to use his EpiPen but ran out of time."

I adjust uncomfortably in my chair and try to banish the mental image of Dr. Armistead trying to stop his car and reach his EpiPen before it was too late. He must have been full of fear and panic.

"Karen is Emory Solomon's patient." I can't tiptoe around her name forever. I glance quickly toward Eric and notice no reaction from him when I say her name.

"Really?" Darby straightens his spine and sits up at attention. "Did you hear this from a reputable source or the small-town rumour mill?"

Darby is a cop, and cops like tangible evidence, so I don't bother to explain to him that Harmony Lake's rumour mill has a shockingly high accuracy rate.

"A reliable source," I assure him. "Someone in a position to see it for themselves."

I'm sure Adam wouldn't mind if I named him as my source, but I'd rather warn him first.

"Innnnteresting," Darby remarks, re-opening his folio and once again uncapping his pen to jot down a note.

"Now that you know Dr. Armistead was murdered, do you think the burglary at his office on Monday could be related to his death?" I ask.

"There's no evidence linking the two incidents," Darby replies matter-of-factly.

From the corner of my eye, I notice Eric shift uneasily in his chair. I look at him and smile. He smiles back. He wants to tell me something, I can sense it. Sophie senses something, too, and jumps onto his lap. She settles there, and he rubs her.

"Anything you'd like to add, Eric?" Darby asks.

Clearly, he also noticed Eric's sudden unease.

Eric shakes his head. "Nope. I'm good."

"You're very quiet," Darby observes.

"I'm listening," Eric responds. "Listening and learning."

He definitely has something to say. I'm sure he'll tell me when Darby leaves.

"Getting back to the break-in at Dr. Armistead's office," I interject, redirecting the conversation back to the topic at hand. "You mean there's no evidence linking the break-in to Dr. Armistead's murder *yet*, right? Karen said you told Dr. Armistead that it was probably kids looking for drugs. But yesterday, Jess said if they were looking for drugs, they wouldn't target a psychotherapist's office when there are so many other sources for drugs in the building…"

"Hold up," Darby interrupts me and drops his pen onto his folio. "The full impact of your visit yesterday with Jess and Karen is just hitting me." He pauses and crosses his hands on his lap. "Yesterday, you're sitting in your yarn store, casually chatting with your husband's girlfriend and your boyfriend's ex-wife. The three of you were comparing notes on the murder of a marriage counselor you were all patients of." He quirks an eyebrow and smirks. His expression is a combination of amusement and shock.

I take a deep breath and let it out. "When you say it like that, it sounds a lot weirder than it actually is," I reply. "Also, Adam is my *ex*-husband, and none of us *knew* at the time that Karen is Eric's *ex*-wife, and we were discussing Dr. Armistead's *death*, not his murder. Until this morning, we believed he died of natural causes."

"C'mon," Darby pleads, still grinning. "You have to admit it's unconventional."

"Fiiine," I acquiesce with a sigh, so we can move on and get back to talking about the break-in. "It's unconventional. You know what else is unconventional? Drug addicts leaving behind a perfectly good computer they could've sold for drug money."

"Who told you what was or was not stolen from Dr. Armistead's office?"

"The person who helped him clean up the mess."

I don't think he knew Karen was there and helped Dr. Armistead clean up after the break-in.

"We're still looking into the break-in," Darby says. "It's an open case."

'It's an open case,' is cop speak for 'I'm not telling you anything, so you may as well stop asking'.

"As usual, it's been educational and delightful, Megan." Darby and I exchange a cheek kiss at the door on his way out.

"When this is settled, the four of us should get together for dinner," I suggest, referring to Darby and his wife, and Eric and me. "I promise I won't serve anything you're allergic to." I gasp and cover my mouth with my hand. Next to me, Eric stifles a laugh. "I'm sorry," I blurt out. "It was too soon and in poor taste."

"Are you sure you aren't a cop?" Darby teases. "Dark humour is a common coping strategy for cops."

"I tell her that all the time," Eric concurs.

I say goodbye to Darby, then go to the back door and put Sophie outside while he and Eric talk.

"You've been busy," Eric says after closing the door behind Darby.

"Not really." I shrug. "Most of the time information finds me, not the other way around," I clarify.

It's true. Mostly. Granted, I seem to emit an energy, telling the universe I'm open to receiving the information, but it's not like I can turn that off. And if I could, I'm not sure I'd want to.

"You can say Karen's name, you know," Eric says. "It's fine. It's not a trigger or anything. I was caught off guard yesterday, but I'm fine now."

"OK." I nod. "Now that Darby's gone, can you tell me what made you squirm when we talked about the break-in at Dr. Armistead's office?"

"That was the first I've heard about it," Eric explains. "You said it happened on Monday?"

I nod. "Right."

"This past Monday? The twenty-eighth?"

I nod again. "Right. Your birthday."

Where is he going with this?

"Do you happen to know what time it happened?"

"Lunchtime," I reply.

"Remember when I cancelled lunch with you on Monday because I couldn't get away from work?"

"I remember."

Eric and I planned to go out for lunch on Monday to celebrate his thirty-ninth birthday. We planned to go to the pub, then he was going golfing. But something came up and he couldn't leave work, so his birthday lunch became a birthday dinner, and he missed his tee-off time.

"The reason I was stuck at work was because Charmaine had a dental emergency. She broke a tooth snacking on popcorn. I had to take her place in a meeting and a conference call while Emory took her to the dentist."

"Okaaayy." I'm not sure why this is relevant to anything related to Dr. Armistead.

"Her dentist is in Harmony Hills," he explains. "I know this because I offered to have a patrol car drive her. But she wanted Emory to take her instead. She would've been at the dentist office around lunchtime."

"Do you know which dental office she went to?" I ask, starting to understand why this might be significant.

He shakes his head. "There are quite a few dental offices in Harmony Hills."

What are the odds she was at Jess's dental office in Dr. Armistead's building? Are dental offices subject to the same standards of patient confidentiality as doctor's offices?

"Would Charmaine be able to pick a lock?" I ask.

Eric nods.

CHAPTER 10

Surveying the tables and booths, I see a lot of people I know, but not the people I was hoping to see. The sign by the door says, WELCOME TO TIFFANY'S, PLEASE SEAT YOURSELF. I scrutinize the available seating and choose a booth with a relatively unobstructed view of the door so I can keep watch discreetly.

I position myself in the booth and pull out my knitting. I'm at the easy part of the sweater, working stitch after stitch in plain stockinette. I can knit without having to look down at my needles. I want to keep my hands busy, but I don't want to miss them if they show up.

"Connie!" I drop my knitting onto my lap and wave over my head to get her attention.

"Good morning, my dear!" She bends over and we exchange cheek kisses, then she settles across from me in the booth. "This is nice. We hardly ever get together for breakfast. I can't remember the last time I had breakfast at Tiffany's."

We scan the menu and discuss what looks good. Connie says she only has an hour for breakfast before she has to leave to take Archie to a physiotherapy appointment. We place our orders and sip our coffees. I knit intermittently on my sweater, and, as if on autopilot, Connie knits on a sock she keeps in her purse.

"You seem distracted, my dear." Connie puts her coffee on the table and resumes knitting. "Is it this nasty murder business with the marriage counselor?"

"Kind of," I admit. "It happened right outside Knitorious. It's almost like he *wanted* me to be the person who found him."

"Just because it happened outside your store, doesn't make it your responsibility," Connie advises. "You don't always have to fix everything for everyone. This murder has nothing to do with you. It's not your job to right all the wrongs in the world."

No, but I feel like it's my job to right all the wrongs in my little corner of the world if I can.

"It's too late now," I respond.

"What does that mean?"

I explain how Jess introduced me to Karen, and the eye-opening conversation that followed. Then I tell her about Jamila and Charmaine's furtive meetings before and after Jess and I found Dr. Armistead's body.

"I wonder if these clandestine meetings with Jamila

are related to whatever happened between Charmaine and the mayor?"

The server brings our breakfast, and I stash my knitting in my tote bag, safely away from the poached eggs. Egg yolk gets right into the fibres of cashmere-merino yarn and is harder to get out than you'd think. I speak from experience. Learn from my mistakes, people!

"Something happened between Charmaine and the mayor?" I quietly ask after the server leaves.

"I don't know the details," she whispers, leaning over her plate of scrambled eggs so I can hear her. "The mayor wouldn't tell me. Even after two margaritas, she managed to stay tight-lipped. And that's not like her."

"Then how do you know something happened?"

"Remember, I invited the book club to that impromptu meeting on Saturday night? When Eric and Archie went to the hockey game?"

I nod until I swallow a mouthful of food. "You said you'd ask the mayor if there's any truth to the rumour she isn't renewing Charmaine's mandate as police chief, and who she's considering to fill the position."

"Right. And I did. According to the mayor, Charmaine left her no choice. She said the increased murder rate in Harmony Lake is only part of the reason Charmaine has to go. The mayor says Charmaine overstepped in her role as police chief and interfered in town business. I don't know what happened, but they both want to keep it hush-hush."

"Interesting," I say.

Why would Charmaine insert herself in town business? Maybe it's revenge because she knows the mayor isn't renewing her contract. Maybe she's working on behalf of someone who plans to run against the mayor. But no one ever runs against our mayor. She's run uncontested in every election since I've lived in Harmony Lake. Unless... Could Charmaine have set her sights on the mayor's job? The mayor would not like that.

"Anyway," Connie continues, "she did confirm that she's interested in talking to Eric about becoming the new police chief. She says she's impressed by his track record and how quickly the locals warmed up to him."

"Speak of the devil." I nod toward the front door where Emory and Charmaine Solomon are stepping into the restaurant. I recognize her short, platinum-blonde shaggy pixie cut immediately.

Connie turns and looks toward the door, then turns back to me.

"Coincidence?" she asks. "Or were you hoping to run into them?"

"Yes," I reply to both questions.

The Solomons have breakfast at Tiffany's regularly. It's one of the reasons Eric and I rarely come here—he doesn't want to get stuck sitting with his boss and her husband.

I smile and make eye contact with Charmaine as she walks toward our booth, presumably on the way to an empty booth or table behind us.

"Megan! It's lovely to see you. Actually, I'm glad we bumped into you. How's Eric doing?" Charmaine and Emory stop at our booth.

"Hi, Charmaine," I reply with a smile. "It's nice to run into you too. I was hoping to ask you something. Eric is fine, if not a bit bored helping at Knitorious." We laugh. "Emory, I was sorry to hear about your friend, Dr. Armistead. It must have been quite a shock. I wanted to reach out earlier, but I was afraid it might be inappropriate given all the conflicts of interest involved."

"Thank you for the sympathy, Megan. It really is a shame. He was so young. Dr. Armistead and I were more like colleagues than friends. We've known each other for years, but in a professional capacity. Still, a shocking death is a shocking death, whether it's a friend or a colleague."

Am I the only one who notices Emory's attempt to distance himself from the victim? I understand you don't have to be friends with someone to have dinner with them. Goodness knows I hosted and attended more dinner parties than I can count with Adam's colleagues during our marriage, but I didn't intentionally distinguish them as colleagues instead of friends if someone made the assumption.

"How's Archie doing since his hip replacement?" Charmaine asks, looking at Connie.

While she updates the Solomons on Archie's recovery, Connie shifts over and taps the Tiffany-blue pleather seat, gesturing for Charmaine and Emory to join us. I follow her lead, also sliding over to create space.

"Just for a minute," Charmaine stipulates, sliding into the booth next to Connie.

"You catch up with your friends. I'll claim that table before someone else takes it and order our coffees," Emory suggests to his wife, nudging the bridge of his glasses with his index finger.

Emory is a couple of inches shorter than his wife, Charmaine, and though they're close in age, his salt-and-pepper hair and stomach paunch make him look older than his fit, carefully groomed wife. Charmaine's trendy clothing and hairstyle also contribute to the illusion. In contrast, Emory looks like someone who's dressed up for Halloween as a university professor—complete with a dark turtleneck under his tweed sports jacket with elbow patches. Whenever I see him, his hair has a windswept look, regardless of the wind situation that day.

Charmaine smiles and nods at him.

"Ladies, it was nice running into you." Emory smiles and looks from Connie to me, giving his glasses another small nudge.

"You, too, Emory," I reply.

"Take care, Emory." Connie smiles.

"I'm glad we ran into you, Megan," Charmaine says quietly, leaning across the table. "You might be able to save me a phone call. Does Adam handle criminal law?

The lawyer we have now is *meh*. We called the first lawyer who came to mind, but we'd like someone who specializes in criminal law. Also, our guy is all the way in the city, and we'd like someone closer."

The Solomon's have lawyered-up? Consciously, I smile and focus on my breath in an attempt to hide my shock. Are they being prudent, or do they have something to hide?

I dig through my bag and find my phone, then, leaning across the table toward Charmaine, I unlock the screen and open the text app.

"I'll text you Adam's number," I say quietly as my thumbs type. "If he can't help you, he'll refer you to someone who can."

"Thank you," Charmaine whispers. "Who is Eric using?"

Why would Eric need a lawyer? Oh my god, does Eric need a lawyer? Is he a suspect? He saw Dr. Armistead in passing before dinner, but not alone, and not for longer than a minute, according to Eric. They have a history of confrontation, but that was a long time ago. Dr. Armistead was dating Eric's ex-wife, but Eric didn't know about that until after Dr. Armistead died.

I shake my head and shrug one shoulder. "I'm not sure."

"Surely, Eric doesn't need a lawyer," Connie insists. "If everyone hires a lawyer, that would slow down the investigation and drag out this unpleasantness even longer."

Picking up on my surprise at the question, Charmaine lays one of her hands atop of mine. "Not because he did anything wrong," she reassures me with a smile. "Lawyers aren't only for guilty people. It's a good idea for everyone involved to protect their own interests."

I nod. I know what lawyers are for, but I appreciate Charmaine's attempt to reassure me, nonetheless.

"What do you think happened to Dr. Armistead, Charmaine?" Connie blurts out.

Thank you, Connie! I've been biting my lip on this very question since Charmaine got here. I'm scared if I ask, it might cross a line into one of the many conflicts of interest surrounding this case. I can always rely on Connie to ferret out information in a nonchalant manner.

Charmaine purses her lips and shrugs. "I'm not sure." She shakes her head. "I suspect he ate or drank something after he left our house, or somehow, someone injected him with it. Our lawyer is trying to get a detailed inventory of the contents of Mac's car. The source of the caffeine might be there. Like a water bottle or something."

Connie and I nod. "Who would want to kill him?" Connie asks, intuitively sensing what I want to know.

Again, Charmaine shrugs. "He had four ex-wives," she points out.

Unfortunately, previous experience has taught me that the spouse, or ex-spouse, is usually the prime suspect. In Dr. Armistead's case, there are four to choose from. Not including his current partner, Karen. Murder investigations are kind of like a series of nested circles surrounding the victim. The police start with the smallest circle, the people closest to the victim. They either eliminate them, or investigate them, then move outward to the next circle of people in the victim's life.

"Did Jamila lawyer-up, too?" I wonder out loud.

I don't expect Charmaine to answer me. Sometimes my thoughts escape from my mouth when I'm deep in thought.

"I don't know," Charmaine replies. "Jamila and I haven't spoken since Friday night."

Lie.

"I saw her yesterday," I volunteer. "She sold me a laptop."

"How was she?" Charmaine asks.

Her blue eyes narrow into slits as if she's trying to bring my face into focus.

I shrug. "As well as can be expected. She was in shock and sad about what happened. She didn't say much. I got the feeling she didn't want to talk about it."

"What did you want to ask me?"

"I'm sorry?" I reply, confused.

"When Emory and I got here, you said you were glad to see me because you want to ask me something."

Right! I'd contrived an excuse to talk to Charmaine if she showed up, but I didn't need it because she came to me.

"Your mouth!" I exclaim, remembering my fake

reason. "Eric said you had a dental emergency last Monday. How's your mouth?"

"It's fine now. I cracked a tooth on a popcorn kernel. Who knew one little kernel could cause such a big inconvenience? Thanks for asking. That's what you wanted to ask me about?"

"Sort of," I say. "Who's your dentist? I'm kind of in the market for a new dentist, and yours seemed to take you right away after your kernel-issue. If you're happy with them, would you mind passing along their name and number to me?"

I'm not in the market for a new dentist. I'm quite happy with the Klines, but I'm trying to determine if Charmaine was in the medical centre where both Kline Family Dentistry and Dr. Armistead's offices are located on the day and time that Dr. Armistead's office was broken into.

"I don't think I can help you," Charmaine replies. She leans forward again, and Connie and I lean forward, too, meeting her in the middle. "I assume you're trying to put some distance between yourself and the dental hygienist your ex is dating?" she whispers.

"Something like that," I agree quietly.

"I go to the same dentist. The Klines have been our dentist since Emory and I moved here."

"It was worth a try," I say, leaning back into a normal sitting position.

"I heard you and the hygienist were getting along

well," Charmaine observes. "Or is that just a rumour?"

"Oh, we do get along well," I say, setting the record straight. "I like Jess. But a few boundaries might be a good idea."

"I get it." Charmaine winks at me. "If you want to discuss boundary issues, you should book an appointment with my husband. Relationship issues are his thing."

I know she's kidding, and I laugh along with her, but maybe she's right. Maybe I should book an appointment with Emory.

CHAPTER 11

"I THINK you're overlooking the most obvious suspect," April says as we have our morning phone call while I walk home from *Tiffany's* after breakfast.

"Who?" I ask. "Only three other people were there. Charmaine, Emory, and Jamila. It has to be one of them or a combination of them."

"What about Karen?" April asks. "Maybe she was tired of being Dr Armistead's secret girlfriend, or maybe she found out he was friends with her shrink, Emory. Maybe he broke up with her. Maybe they were never even a couple. Maybe she was his stalker. Without him alive to tell his side of the story, we can't know for sure. She can say whatever she wants. There are no friends or family to confirm anything because no one knew about them."

"Darby said he found out about Karen and Dr.

Armistead's relationship when he went through Dr. Armistead's phone," I remind her. "So, at the very least, they were a couple. You're right about everything else, though. But, when and how did Karen have the opportunity to give Dr. Armistead the caffeine?"

Truth time: It would be convenient if Karen is the killer. I don't know her, so I wouldn't constantly look back in hindsight, searching for signs that she was capable of murder. Also, she's not local. I wouldn't have to live with knowing I regularly greeted her with a smile on the streets of my sweet, cozy hometown without realizing she was a monster. Collectively, the residents of Harmony Lake wouldn't have to deal with the emotional fallout of a killer living among us and blending in without being noticed. If the killer is a local resident, it could really harm our sense of trust and community spirit. And let's not forget that one of the suspects is the highest-ranking police officer in town, and another is a trusted psychotherapist—both positions of trust.

While Karen being the murderer might be the best possible outcome, if there is such a thing in a murder investigation, I don't really want it to be Karen because I don't want to believe that Eric could unknowingly marry a murderer. He'd blame himself for not seeing her for what she was. And would he ever trust his cop-instincts again? If it turns out that Karen did kill Dr. Armistead, I'm worried the revelation could unravel him.

April and I continue to talk about anything and everything until our conversation is cut short when she gets a call from an eaves trough company.

"Hey, Soph!" I lock the door behind me and crouch down to greet the happy corgi. "I'm happy to see you too."

A familiar *swoosh* grabs my attention. Pipes.

"Water," I say, looking down at Sophie. "Is something leaking, Soph? Did I leave a tap running?"

If Sophie knows the answer, she's not telling. She looks up at me with her mouth slightly open and her corgi tail wagging.

"Shoot! I hope it's not a leak," I mumble, checking the laundry room, then rushing to check the kitchen.

Nothing. Not even a drippy faucet. As I hurry toward my bedroom, the *swooshing* grows louder. It's coming from my ensuite washroom.

I burst into the bedroom, and humid, steamy air gets thicker as I get closer to the half-open washroom door. The shower is running, and Eric's phone is plugged into the charger beside the bed. Mystery solved.

Why is Eric here? And why isn't his car in the driveway? It has to be Eric. That's definitely his phone, and if a stranger were in the house, Sophie wouldn't be this calm and happy. Also, who else would come over and use the shower?

"A heads up would've been nice, Sophie," I teasingly chastise.

Sophie doesn't care. She's sprawled comfortably on the bed, ready for a nap.

It's Monday. Knitorious is closed on Mondays, and I usually run errands and do housework. So, while I'm in here, I may as well collect the dirty laundry and take it to the laundry room. I slip into the steamy washroom and find Eric's sweaty running clothes on top of the dirty laundry in the hamper. Another mystery solved; his car isn't in the driveway because he ran here.

I walk around the house, collecting kitchen linens and sofa blankets to add to the laundry pile, then put the first load in the washer.

"Another one for the pile," Eric says.

I pop my head out of the washing machine, and he drops the towel into the sink.

"Hey, handsome. What are you doing here? I thought you were going to the driving range this morning." I give in to the urge to hug him and lean into his strong, solid chest and inhale deeply. Eric always smells good, but I especially love the way he smells right after a shower.

"Change of plans," he says, then kisses the top of my head. "I met with Darby this morning instead."

While I toss a pod in the machine and turn it on, Eric asks me about breakfast with Connie and my morning phone call with April. I provide general answers to his general questions and, for now, leave out my sort-of chance encounter with the Solomons and April's theory about Karen being the prime suspect in Dr. Armistead's murder.

We move to the family room where Sophie has already positioned herself on the sofa.

"Why did you meet with Darby?" I ask.

"I told him about Charmaine's dental emergency last Monday, and he wanted to ask me a few questions," Eric explains. "And I gave him permission to search my apartment."

"Search it for what?" The panic in my voice reflects the panic in my body. "Are you a suspect?"

"For evidence." He shrugs. "And I don't know if I'm a suspect, but I'm definitely a person of interest. I saw the victim shortly before his death, the victim and I have a history of confrontation, and it's no secret that I didn't like Armistead. Darby has to eliminate me."

"Are they searching it now?" I ask. "Are they searching the store too?"

"Darby said they'd search it today and finish as quickly as they can. They're not searching the store. I can't give permission for that, and he didn't indicate he was interested in the store, anyway. I also gave him permission to search my car and left it for him. I ran ten K, then came over here to shower and change. The search was my idea, Megan. I offered."

"You offered? Why?"

"I have nothing to hide. Anyway, he'll have to search my place, eventually. Same with the Solomons and probably Jamila's place too. Today is the perfect day, so I made him a deal. I gave him permission and saved him the trouble of getting a warrant, and he agreed to do it today while both Water Street and the store are closed."

"Water Street is closed?" I ask.

My travels to Tiffany's and back didn't take me near Knitorious or that part of Water Street.

"There's a hydro crew fixing the streetlight that Armistead's car hit. They closed Water Street around it, and there's a cop detouring traffic. As far as police searches go, this is as low profile as it gets."

"Stay here until this is over," I suggest. "You have enough stuff here for at least a few days."

I wouldn't look forward to going home after people I don't know—whether they're cops or not—touched everything, opened my drawers and cabinets, and rummaged through my personal belongings. Just thinking about it makes me feel violated. Also, if anything else happens, if Eric and I are under the same roof, we might be able to alibi each other.

"Don't worry," Eric assures me. "The only caffeine Darby and his officers will find in my apartment are my coffee pods and your chocolate stash."

"I don't have a chocolate stash at your apartment," I clarify.

I don't have a chocolate stash anywhere. I tell myself if it's not in the house, I can't eat it. I don't let that stop me though. When I get a craving, I go out and buy some. Also, my best friend and her wife own a bakery, so chocolate and other sweet treats find their way to my kitchen on a regular basis, with no effort on my part.

"Yes, you do," he asserts. "I maintain it, but it's your stash. For those days when you don't feel well and complain that you have no chocolate in the house." Eric shrugs. "The stash has saved me a lot of trips to the store."

"You keep a stash of PMS chocolate for me? Eric, that's so sweet." I'm so touched I might cry.

No one has ever kept a chocolate stash for me before.

"Where is it?" I ask, nuzzling up to him.

"I'm not telling." He smiles.

"Do you have a lawyer?" I ask, changing the subject.

"I don't need a lawyer. I told you, I have nothing to hide."

"Charmaine says you should get a lawyer," I argue. "She and Emory lawyered up."

"You spoke to Charmaine?" He raises one eyebrow slightly and sits up a little straighter.

I nod. "Connie and I ran into her and Emory at breakfast."

"You went to Tiffany's?" Eric asks. "I told you the Solomons go there for breakfast. You clever little sneak. Did you run into them accidentally-on-purpose?"

How can he be so flippant? He's a person of interest in a murder investigation.

"Remember when you told me you were reprimanded for looking up Dr. Armistead?"

Eric nods.

"Charmaine would know about that, right? She's your boss, so she has access to your employee file?" I ask.

"Sure," Eric replies.

"Have you considered that Charmaine met with you at her house on Friday intentionally so she could place you in the frame for Dr. Armistead's murder?"

"Uh-uh." Eric shakes his head. "No way. Charmaine would never do that. Armistead showed up for dinner early, and we happened to pass each other at her front door. It was an unfortunate coincidence."

"Was it?" I ask. "Or did he show up exactly when he was told. Think about it. Charmaine knows you and Dr. Armistead have an unpleasant history, but she put you in a position where you could potentially bump into each other. And he happened to die shortly after."

"Coincidence," Eric insists.

Charmaine Solomon is a smart woman. You don't climb up the ranks to police chief without strategically planning your career path. I suspect Eric's chance encounter with Dr. Armistead was carefully orchestrated.

"Last Monday, Charmaine was at the medical centre where Dr. Armistead's office is located. At lunch time. When Dr. Armistead's office was broken into. She was in the building, Eric."

"You know this for sure?" Eric asks.

I nod. "She told me."

He shakes his head again. "I'm telling you, Megan, she wouldn't do that. Charmaine is totally above board. I trust her with my life."

I wish I had as much faith in anything as Eric has in the Harmony Lake Police Department and its leader.

Eric considers Charmaine a mentor. He looks up to her and admires her achievements. No one wants to believe someone they respect so highly would do something unethical and illegal.

I'm debating whether now is the right time to tell him about April's theory that Karen is a prime suspect in Armistead's murder when my phone dings.

Connie: Check your email.

I tilt the screen to show Eric the message, then I open the email app on my phone. There's an email from a generic email address I don't recognize: *truthfinder234093@freemail.com.* The subject line says, *Dr. Armistead.*

I open it, and the body of the email is a link.

"Should I click it?" I ask, looking at Eric.

"I'm not sure," he replies, "but I just got the same email."

"I'm clicking it," I say.

The link leads to a simple webpage with an alphabetized list of Dr. Armistead's patients. I scroll down to the M's and find *Martel, Adam and Megan.* It's a long list. Are these just his past patients, or are his current patients listed too? Why would someone post this?

Scrolling through the hundreds of patient names, I recognize dozens of them. I'm shocked so many Harmony Lake residents travel to Harmony Hills for therapy when Emory is right here in town. Like Adam and me, I guess they were hesitant to go to someone local and risk having their personal business become fodder for the town gossip network.

Eric mutters a curse word under his breath.

I'm sure he scrolled down the list to S and found his and Karen's names. I scroll down to S and look for his name, but there are no patients with the last name Sloane.

"You and Karen aren't listed," I observe. "But Adam and I are listed, and Jess and her ex-husband are listed."

"We're listed," he confirms. "Look under P for Porter."

"Right," I say, scrolling up to P and finding *Porter, Karen and Sloane, Eric.* "Who sent this?" I ask rhetorically.

"That's for Darby to figure out," Eric replies. "I just forwarded him the email."

Within five minutes, my phone starts dinging constantly as people all over town receive the link either from the anonymous email address or from a friend. Everyone is speculating what it could mean, who posted it, and why it was posted. Above all, everyone is shocked they recognize so many names on the list.

"Is this list even real?" I ask, dumbfounded that someone would post this and send out the link. "Why would someone do this?"

"The killer might be trying to create a distraction," Eric speculates, "or maybe someone who knows something is trying to give the investigators a clue."

"Could it be a warning?" I ask. "If the poster has this information, they might have more information, like Armistead's notes and such. Maybe this is a warning. Back off or they'll post more information. Maybe someone on the list knows something, and this is a warning to keep quiet if they don't want the notes their therapist took posted on the worldwide web for everyone to see."

"Anything is possible," Eric concurs. "The question is, who has access to this information?"

"Dr. Armistead," I reply, stating the obvious. "An assistant. Did he have an assistant? I don't remember anyone else in the office when we were his patients, but an assistant would probably have access to his files."

"Whoever provides his tech support," Eric adds.

"Jamila," I elaborate. I pause briefly and take a breath. "His girlfriend might have access to his files," I suggest delicately.

"Karen?" he asks.

I nod. "She helped him clean up his office after the

break-in, which means she had access to his physical files. Maybe she had access to his electronic files too."

Careful not to throw anymore shade on Charmaine, I silently wonder if she could've used her influence as police chief to access Armistead's files? How hard would it be to influence an officer working on the case to access them for her?

CHAPTER 12

TUESDAY, October 6th

Thanks to Darby's quick intervention, the webpage disappeared almost as quickly as it appeared. Less than an hour after I first clicked the link, it was dead.

Dr. Armistead's patient list might be erased from the internet, but it's not erased from the minds of the residents of Harmony Lake. My phone lit up all night with texts about the list, and people are still talking about it today. Some people took screen shots. The link might be dead, but I'm afraid the list will live on forever.

"So, you and your new best friend, Jess, need relationship counselling with Emory Solomon," April teases during our morning phone call.

I just told her about my plan to rope Jess into coming with me to question Emory.

"I'd rather go to therapy with you, but you're not here," I jokingly reassure her.

"I'm not sure if that makes me feel better or worse," she responds.

While April and I catch up on the last twenty-four hours of our lives, Sophie and I meander through the park across from the store. The first fallen leaves of the season crunch beneath our feet and paws. The air is crisp, and the changing leaves on the trees makes Harmony Lake even prettier and cozier than usual. Fall is my favourite season, and I bask in it every chance I get. I love our morning walks; the world is still relatively quiet, and there's something about a new day that's fresh and full of potential. Our first walk of the day is meditative and helps me get into the right headspace to tackle whatever else happens throughout the day.

"Keviiiin! I'm coming, Keviiin! Daddy's here!"

Phillip's voice jolts me out of the zone I'm in with April. Sophie and I stop walking, and I turn to see Phillip Wilde helplessly banging on the front door of Wilde Flowers.

Phillip is my neighbour. His florist shop, Wilde Flowers, shares a wall and a parking lot with Knitorious, and he also lives next door to me.

"April, umm… Can I call you back? Phillip needs help with something." We end our call, and I shove my phone in the back pocket of my black skinny jeans.

"Uh-oh, Soph!" I give the leash a gentle tug, and she looks up at me. "Let's go."

We hustle to the sidewalk and cross the street.

"Phillip, what's wrong?"

"I locked my stupid keys in the store!" He grabs the door handle and jiggles it so vigorously, the force rattles the windows of his florist shop. "Kevin's in there *alone*!" Phillip looks at me pleadingly. His eyes are open wide, and the inner corners of his eyebrows almost meet, forming an inverted V. His desperation is painful to watch. "He won't understand. He'll think I left him." He cups his hands on either side of his face and peers into the window. "It's OK, Kevin. Daddy's here. Daddy will save you."

Kevin is Phillip's chihuahua. They go everywhere together.

I copy Phillip and cup my hands on either side of my eyes and squint into the window next to him.

Granted, Kevin and I don't know each other very well, but he looks fine to me. He's atop his royal blue velvet pillow. The one with gold piping and gold tassels. Kevin is laying down with his wee head resting on his tiny paws. I think he might be asleep, but his face is so small, I can't tell for sure.

"Kevin has *terrible* separation anxiety. He won't be able to cope." Beads of perspiration dot Phillip's forehead, and his breath is fast and shallow; he's on the verge of hyperventilating.

Kevin has separation anxiety? Got it. Apparently, Kevin has the anxiety, but Phillip suffers the symptoms.

"Who has a spare key?" I ask.

"Noah!" Phillip blurts without looking away from the window.

Noah is Phillip's shop assistant and florist apprentice.

"Where does Noah live?" I ask. "I'll drive there and get his key."

"We don't have time for that. He lives all the way in Harmony Hills. Anyway, he's not home. He switched his usual day off from yesterday to today because he has an appointment this morning." Phillip looks at me. "Unless you can pick a lock, I'm throwing a brick through the window and saving Kevin."

A brick seems hasty, considering Kevin appears to be the most comfortable and content of all of us right now, but I doubt Phillip would agree.

"Ryan!" I exclaim, already pulling out my cell phone and typing a text to the local handyman-slash-locksmith.

"Good idea, Megan!" Phillip resumes watching Kevin through the window. "We're going to get you out, buddy. Stay brave. You're such a brave boy, Kevin."

I peer into the window again. Kevin is definitely asleep.

My phone dings. "Ryan's working a job in the city. He won't be back until tonight."

"Can Eric pick a lock?" Phillip asks, looking at the ground around our feet, presumably for something he can use to break the glass in the door.

"Eric isn't around. He's at the driving range, then

he's getting a haircut. He won't be back until late morning."

"Have you tried the back door?" I ask.

Phillip nods. "Locked."

Phillip paces up and down the sidewalk with his gaze glued to the ground, scouring for something to hurl through the window.

"Did you lose something, Phillip?" Jamila's gaze also scans the pavement, despite not knowing what she's looking for.

Phillip fills her in about his keys, Kevin's separation anxiety, and the downside of being someone who diligently locks his doors.

"Hang on," Jamila replies, reaching behind her head and pulling two hairpins from her chignon. Her smooth, shiny, black locks fall gracefully around her shoulders as she bends and twists the hairpins until they no longer resemble hairpins. "No promises." She crouches in front of the locked door and fiddles with the straightened hairpins and the lock. "I haven't done this in years." She looks up at us briefly. "Hopefully locks haven't changed much." More fiddling with the hairpins and jiggling the door handle. "I think that's it," she mumbles. She turns the handle, gives the door a push, and it opens.

"Wow, Jamila," I say. "That's impressive. Where did you learn to do that?"

"By-product of my misspent youth," she chuckles.

"Oh." Still shocked by Jamila's lock-picking prowess, now I'm doubly shocked by what she just said.

"I'm kidding." Jamila laughs and touches my arm gently. "My brothers were into magic, and they taught me to pick locks so I could be their magician's assistant." She shrugs. "It was fun. We used to have races to see who could pick a lock fastest." She grins nostalgically. "I usually won. Our parents hated it. We'd pick every lock in the house, and sometimes other people's locks too."

"It's amazing! Thankfully you remembered, after all these years." Unless she brushed up her lock-picking skills last Monday at Dr. Armistead's office.

"It is," she agrees. "I don't think I've picked a lock since I was a teenager."

"Oh, Jamila! Thank you! Thank you! Kevin and I are forever in your debt." A relieved Phillip appears with a sleepy Kevin in his arms.

Did Jamila pick the locks on Dr. Armistead's office door and filing cabinets? Would hiding caffeine and secretly adding it to someone's food be considered a magic trick?

"Slow, how?" Adam asks, opening the laptop.

Something's wrong with my new laptop. I tried to use it this morning to check the store email and process the online orders that came in over the weekend, but it's so slow, I couldn't finish either task and had to use my phone instead. I've brought the machine to Adam's office so he can look at it and hopefully fix it.

"Nothing loads. I can't check email or search the web. I bought a dud."

"It could be something simple," Adam says. "It was fine when you showed it to me on Sunday."

"It was fine before you installed the cyber security app-program-thingy. Could that be the problem?" I speculate.

"Let's see." He opens the laptop and types in the password.

"So, what do you think of this patient-list scandal?" I ask while we wait for whatever Adam launched to open.

"I've been getting calls all morning from people on the list. They want to know who they can sue for breeching their privacy."

"Really?" I ask, wide-eyed and wondering who called him. "Who knew the residents of Harmony Lake are so litigious."

"People are angry, Meg. They feel violated. Frankly, I don't blame them. I feel violated too. Our names are on that list."

"I know," I sympathize. "It's not pleasant, but at least whoever did it, didn't post anything else, like Dr. Armistead's notes, observations, or diagnoses."

"Do you think they have all that information?" Adam sounds concerned.

"I have no idea." I shrug. "But if they were able to

get an extensive patient list, you have to wonder what else they have access to."

"Let's hope the police find out who did it before they post anything else," Adam says.

"It should be easy for the police to find them, right?" I ask. "Computers leave digital trails? IP addresses and things like that?"

"Someone who knows what they're doing can hide their digital footprint," Adam explains. "They can use VPNs and other masking technology to make it appear as though they're posting from a different computer at a different location. They can make it look like they're anywhere in the world."

"Oh," I respond.

Adam continues to explain the different ways computer-savvy people hide their identities, locations, and crimes.

I was under the misguided impression that technology makes it *more* difficult for people to hide, but for criminals who are technically inclined, technology actually makes it easier for them to avoid detection and get away with their bad deeds.

Adam's monologue is interrupted when his phone rings. He answers the call and puts the caller on hold.

"I have to take this, Meg. It's about a case that's going to court next week."

"No worries," I assure him. "I'll leave the laptop with you. Look at it whenever you have time, and let me know when I can pick it up."

"Sounds good," Adam says.

I get up from my chair and leave his office. I close his office door quietly behind me and hear Adam resume his phone call.

When I reach the bottom of the stairs, the receptionist, Lin, is on the phone. I smile, wave, and mouth a silent goodbye to her on my way to the door.

"Megan!"

I turn back to the waiting area, and Jess is standing up, smiling at me.

"Hey, Jess! What are you doing here?" We hug and kiss cheeks.

"I'm taking my favourite lawyer out for lunch," she explains. "It's an apology lunch. Adam and I had plans last night, but I had to cancel because my youngest was in his first car accident."

"Oh no! Is he OK?"

"Adam or my son?"

Ha!

"I'm sure Adam is fine. How's your son?"

"He's OK, thank goodness. It was his first fender bender. He was more shaken than anything. My fender is the real victim here."

"That first year or so after they start driving is the most stressful year of parenting," I commiserate.

"It is. Thankfully, this is my last teenage driver. If I can get through his new-driver-phase, I'm in the clear. What are you doing here?"

"I dropped off a laptop for your favourite lawyer to look at."

"Your new laptop?" Jess asks. "The one you just bought?"

"The very same," I reply.

"We've had a stressful few days," Jess observes. "First, we found a body, then you, me, and Karen had that awkward visit, then the list was posted, and now your new computer is on the fritz! We deserve a drink."

"Isn't that how this started?" I tease. "You, me, and a couple of bottles of wine?"

"You're right," Jess replies. "We need a new vice."

"Well, if we choose chocolate, I have a lead on a chocolate stash in the apartment above the store." I tell Jess about Eric's confession that he keeps chocolate in his apartment to appease my cravings.

"He's a keeper," she replies.

"Did Adam talk to you about Thanksgiving?" I hope I'm not overstepping by asking.

"Yes! I can't wait to meet everyone. Are you sure I can't bring anything?"

After a few minutes of polite banter, where I insist she shouldn't bring anything, and she insists she should, we finally agree that Jess will bring an appetizer.

"I should go," I say, checking the time on my phone. "Eric's alone at the store."

"I wonder what's keeping Adam?" she asks. "He knows I'm here."

"He had to take a call," I explain. "I'm sure he'll be right down."

"Are you ready, Karen?" We turn toward Emory Solomon's voice.

"Karen!" Jess and I exclaim in unison as Karen puts down the magazine she was holding in front of her face and stands up.

"I didn't see you there," Jess declares, giving Karen a quick hug.

"Hi, Karen," I say, "It's nice to see you again." I look at Emory. "Hi, Emory."

He smiles and nods at me.

"I didn't see you ladies, either. I was lost in my own thoughts. It's been a rough few days."

Jess and I nod sympathetically.

Was she lost in her own thoughts? Or was Karen holding up that magazine to hide from Jess and me? Perhaps she doesn't want us to know she's a patient of Dr. Solomon, or maybe she'd like to avoid another uncomfortable conversation with her ex-husband's new girlfriend. Either reason is understandable.

"I'll see you later, I don't want to keep Dr. Solomon waiting," Karen says as she follows Emory upstairs to his second-floor office.

"What the heck?!" Jess blurts out after we hear Emory's office door close.

"I found out on Sunday. From your favourite lawyer." I tell Jess that Adam recognized Karen's photo as one of Emory's patients.

"That can't be right." Jess sounds concerned. "Surely it's a conflict of interest."

"Like Karen's personal relationship with Dr. Armistead was a conflict of interest," I remind her.

"I'd love to ask Dr. Solomon a few questions," Jess mutters, still looking up the stairs toward Emory's office.

"Me too," I respond.

I move closer to Jess so Lin won't overhear. I tell Jess I'm considering booking an appointment as an excuse to ask him about Dr. Armistead.

Jess looks at me with an expression somewhere between shocked and impressed. "He's a suspect. You shouldn't see him alone," she whispers. "Do you think we would benefit from joint therapy?" she whispers, gesturing between us.

"Totally," I agree.

"Why are you together, and what are you whispering about?" Adam is halfway down the stairs.

The crease between his brows is extra deep. He looks worried.

"Don't worry," Jess says, taking his hand. "We aren't ganging up on you."

"It's a pleasant coincidence," I add. "Jess was arriving as I was leaving."

Adam's facial muscles relax a little.

I turn to leave, and Jess touches my arm. "Leave it with me. I'll make the arrangements and text you," she says quietly, then smiles and nods.

CHAPTER 13

"DARK ROAST, DOUBLE-DOUBLE," I announce, placing Eric's coffee on the counter, then bending down to Sophie's level to give her some love.

"Thank you," Eric says from somewhere deep in the store.

This is backwards. Eric usually brings me a coffee during the day, not the other way around. This whole week has been a role reversal with him working at Knitorious while I pound the pavement trying to solve Dr. Armistead's murder.

"Hi, Megan." A chorus of slightly out-of-sync voices greets me when I stand up.

The charity knitters are here. They're seated around the harvest table at the back of the store. I thought I heard the low clicking of knitting needles, but I assumed it was psychosomatic because I associate the sound with Knitorious. Like how I occasionally think I feel my phone vibrating in my pocket even when it's not in my pocket.

"Hi, ladies," I say with a wave. "You don't usually grace us with your presence on a Tuesday."

"Well, we heard you weren't here and thought Eric could use some company," one of them replies.

"Would you like a date square, Megan?" another one asks. "I made them for Eric, but there's enough for everyone."

"On Saturday, I mentioned I like date squares. They remembered and made some. Isn't that nice?" Eric asks.

"There are carrot muffins too," Mrs. Roblin adds, nodding toward the centre of the table. "Help yourself."

"Not right now, thank you," I reply, politely declining their offers. "It's thoughtful of the Charity Knitting Guild to think about Eric and keep him company."

"It sure is," Eric concurs in a perky voice. He gets up from his seat at the table and retrieves his coffee from the counter. He flashes his fan club a wide, toothy smile. "Thank you for the pleasure of your company, ladies, but now that Megan's back, I think I'll go upstairs and phone my parents to see how their Thanksgiving preparations are coming along."

Accompanied by a chorus of "Bye, Eric," he makes a swift exit.

After the charity knitters discuss amongst themselves what a caring and doting son he is, and how proud his parents must be, they ask me if Eric phones his parents often, and when I think he might be back.

"A couple of times a week," I reply. "I don't know when he'll come downstairs. His mum is pretty chatty. He could be gone a while." I shrug. "I'm here until the store closes, so he might talk to her for the rest of the afternoon."

After reminding me to wrap and store the date squares and carrot muffins, the charity knitters decide it's time to pack up their knitting and leave.

"Is it clear?" Eric asks after he cautiously scans the store.

I nod. "I told them your mum is chatty."

"Thank you. It's not that I'm not appreciative of the knitters, they're sweet and very doting," he explains. "But there are so many of them, and they're almost competitive with their attention."

"They like you," I respond. "You seem to be one of their projects."

"I've been thinking about that list of Dr. Armistead's patients," Eric says, changing the subject. "You could be right. The list could be a warning."

"You think one of his patients knows something?"

"Possibly," he replies. "Or it could be a warning to an amateur sleuth who is snooping around and asking questions."

"Just say it. You mean me."

"I mean you."

"A warning that they'll post more information? Or that I could be next?" I ask.

"Both. Either. I don't know." Eric shrugs. "But either way do you want to risk it?"

"I've risked it before," I remind him.

"Those were my cases, Megan. I was the investigator. I had access to all the information. I have none of the information on Armistead's case. I haven't interviewed anyone. I have no sense of what kind of suspect we're dealing with, or how to gauge how much risk you're taking."

"If I back down, they win."

"And if you back down, I win because you stay alive and safe."

"I'll be fine," I assure him. "The killer's MO is feeding the victim something the victim is allergic to. I don't have any food allergies."

"That's not funny." He's not smiling. In fact, he looks dead serious.

"You always say a sense of humour helps to deal with murder."

"In general." He takes my hands. "But it's not funny when it's you."

"I'm sorry."

"I can't tell you what to do, but I'd feel better if you let this go and let Darby handle it," he says. "I know people come to you and drop evidence into your lap, but maybe this time you don't have to actively look for it."

Now is not the time to tell him about the therapy appointment Jess and I are planning.

"I want to fix this for you," I admit. "You helped me once when I was tangled up in a murder investigation, and now I want to help you."

Saved by the bell.

"Oh my, Phillip! Let me help you." I rush out from behind the counter and relieve Phillip of the huge floral arrangement he's carrying. "How did you find your way over here with this?" It's massive, I can't see through it, and I can't see around it.

"You get used to it after a couple of decades," he replies. "Full light, sweetie. Over here."

Phillip guides me to the cozy seating area and I carefully place the arrangement on the coffee table. Literally nothing else will fit on the coffee table now. I'll take them home with me tonight. They'll look gorgeous in the living room window.

"It's beautiful!" And smells delightful.

"Thank you," he replies, fussing over a few individual blooms that shifted on the short walk between our stores. "It's your October bouquet. I wanted to do something extra special after the help you gave Kevin and me this morning."

Back in January, Eric and I attended a fundraiser. It was kind of our first date. Phillip donated a year's worth of monthly floral arrangements to the silent auction, and Eric had the winning bid. So, now I get a beautiful seasonal floral arrangement delivered each month.

"I didn't do anything. Jamila saved the day," I remind him. "If anyone deserves thank-you flowers, it's her."

"She's next on my list," Phillip assures me. "Her arrangement is gorgeous. All white to match her store."

"What did I miss this morning?" Eric asks.

Phillip tells him how Jamila's latent lock picking skills saved the day, and saved Kevin's life, after he almost died of separation anxiety because he was left unattended in the shop for fifteen minutes.

"You should leave a spare key with someone nearby," Eric suggests.

"Great minds think alike!" Phillip reaches into his pocket and hands me a key on an enamel, flower-shaped key chain. "I had a spare key cut. Would you mind keeping it safe for me?"

"Of course," I reply taking the key from him. "It'll be in the cash register, under the tray."

Eric opens the till and I hand him the key. He lifts the tray, drops the key, and closes the till.

"How is Kevin? Has he recovered from being locked in the store?" I'm sure Kevin is fine. It's Phillip who might be feeling the aftereffects.

"He's emotionally exhausted," Phillip replies. "But he's a brave boy and doesn't let it show. He doesn't like to upset me. He's very sensitive to other people's feelings, you know. But I can tell he was scared."

"I'm glad you're both OK," I tell him.

"CAN YOU PICK A LOCK?" I ask Eric after Phillip leaves.

"I know how," he replies. "I haven't done it in ages though, and lock picking is one of those use-it-or-lose-it skills."

"How so?" I ask, remembering that Jamila said she hasn't picked a lock since she was a teenager, which would be at least fifteen years ago.

"It takes practice to develop the muscle memory you need to maneuver delicately around the tumblers inside the lock. And your hands learn to recognize the subtle changes that happen inside the lock. You can't see inside it, so you have to rely on the way the lock reacts to the pick."

"I didn't realize lock picking is such a subtle, sensitive skill," I comment. "Does it come in handy at work?"

"No," he replies. "We call a locksmith. Unless it's urgent, then we smash a window or break down the door because it's faster than picking the lock."

"Jamila picked Phillip's lock in about two minutes," I tell him. "She said it was the first time she'd done it in years."

"Hmmm," he replies.

I can practically see the wheels spinning inside his head.

"Hi, Darby." I put down my knitting and stand up.

Darby closes the door behind him. "Good afternoon, Megan!" he booms, surveying the store. "Are we alone? Is now a good time to talk?"

"Eric's in the back somewhere, but other than that, it's just us." I gesture for him to join me in the cozy sitting area.

I offer Darby a drink, which he declines. He opens his folio and uncaps his fountain pen.

"TWO OH NINE!" Eric bellows from the back room.

"GOT IT!" I shout back, making a note of the numbers in my planner on the sofa next to me. "GOOD JOB, HONEY!"

"Two hundred and nine what?" Darby asks.

"Two minutes and nine seconds," I clarify. "Jamila picked a lock this morning. It took her less than two minutes—at least it felt like less than two minutes—despite insisting that she hasn't picked a lock since she was a teenager. Eric is trying to beat her time. His personal best so far is two minutes and nine seconds."

"Right," Darby says nodding. "What lock is he picking?"

"I'm not sure. The back door. His apartment door. The back door at Wilde Flowers." I shrug. "He's bored, but he won't admit it. I told him to go back to work, but he insists on helping at the store until Connie and Marla are back next week. Have you had any luck finding the person who posted Dr. Armistead's patient list online?"

"Not yet," Darby shakes his head. "The suspect used an elaborate network of proxies to hide their location and identity. The cyber-crimes division has traced it from Germany to India to Mexico, to France, so far. They're still working on it, but I'm confident they'll track down the person or persons responsible."

This is what Adam explained to me earlier. The cybercriminal bounces their signal off servers all over the world, hiding their true location and the identity of the computer they use. How many people would know how to do that? Is this a skill an average computer user would have? I don't have it, but I'm neither technically inclined nor technically interested in computers, beyond how I can use them to shop online and find funny pet videos.

"I hope so," I say. "People around here are nervous. They're worried whoever has the list has other, more personal information and might post it."

Let me clarify. *Most* people are worried, but a few are *hoping* the hacker will post personal information about their friends and neighbours so they can read it.

"So, Ms. Jagger can pick a lock. That's interesting, isn't it?" Changing the subject, Darby turns to a blank page in his folio and makes a note. "Did you see this firsthand, or did someone tell you about it?"

I tell Darby about the heroic role Jamila played in

Phillip and Kevin's harrowing ordeal. "You know who else can pick a lock?" I ask.

"Eric?" Darby answers my question with a question.

"Charmaine Solomon," I tell him.

"You're telling me this like it's relevant to Dr. Armistead's murder investigation."

"It's relevant to the break-in at his office last week," I explain. "And the break-in at his office could be relevant to his murder, no?"

"We haven't found any evidence linking the two incidents."

A standard-issue cop response.

"Charmaine and Emory Solomon were in the building at the same time Dr. Armistead's office was broken into," I point out.

"Now, how do you know that, Megan?"

"Charmaine told me," I reply.

"You spoke with the Solomons about the case?"

"I spoke with Charmaine," I correct him. "We ran into each other at a local restaurant."

"Coincidentally, of course," he adds.

"Of course," I confirm.

"ONE FIVE EIGHT! WOOHOO!" Eric yells from what sounds like the parking lot.

I note the time in my planner under the last entry.

"GOT IT!" I yell in response. "YAY! YOU DID IT!"

"Well done, detective sergeant!" Darby booms.

The bass tone of his voice is so deep, it makes my insides rumble. And I don't think he was shouting.

"I'd like you to look at something for me, Megan." Darby unzips the large pocket at the back of his folio and pulls out an iPad. "A video." He unlocks the screen and taps a few times, then hands me the device.

"What am I looking for?" I ask.

"Anyone or anything you think you recognize. If you see something or someone, pause the video by touching the screen and show me."

I nod. "Got it."

Eric comes into the store and says hi to Darby. He suggests that Darby and I use his apartment and offers to stay down here and watch the store.

CHAPTER 14

THE LEATHER SOFA in the upstairs apartment wheezes when I sink into it. I tap the iPad screen, making the video footage start. It's the main entrance to the medical building where Dr. Armistead's office is located. Specifically, the area between the front door and the elevators.

According to the date and time stamps at the top of the screen, it's from the day Dr. Armistead's office was broken into. The video quality isn't great. It's black and white, grainy, and kind of far away from the people being filmed.

I tap the screen. "Here," I extend the device toward Darby and point at the image. "That's Charmaine Solomon, and her husband, Emory, behind her." The Solomons are entering the building. Charmaine cups her jaw with one hand, and Emory holds the door open for her as she enters the building.

Darby reaches over and takes a screenshot of the paused video then nudges it toward me.

"Again?" I ask.

Darby nods.

I tap the screen and watch anonymous, grainy people come and go from the lobby of the building.

"There," I tap the screen. "That's Dr. Armistead, in the lower left, leaving the building."

I pass the device to Darby and he takes another screen shot and hands it back.

"More?" I ask.

"A little more," he replies.

I tap the screen and watch the video. It's lunchtime, and the lobby is busy. After a few more minutes of watching, the video skips ahead by almost an hour. Edited by the police, no doubt.

"The Solomons," I say, tapping the screen.

This time, they're leaving the building. I hand the device to Darby so he can take a screenshot. He hands it back.

I tap the screen and watch. The video skips ahead again. "Dr. Armistead," I touch the screen to pause the video. "He's entering the building."

Darby takes a screenshot, then uses his finger to find a specific location in the footage.

"Watch this part again." He passes the device to me.

I look at the footage, searching for a familiar face. The crowd around the elevator makes it difficult to pick out specific people. It gets harder when the elevator door opens and even more people file into the lobby.

"Sorry," I say, handing the iPad back to Darby. "Nothing."

"Don't be sorry, Megan." He taps on the screen a few times then holds up a screenshot from the video footage. The screen shot has been enhanced. It's a grainy close-up of someone from the crowded lobby wearing a dark baseball cap and looking down, away from the camera. The person is wearing a dark hoodie, but the hood is down showing hair in a low chignon. A glint of light grey near the face catches my eye.

"Jamila Jagger," I say confidently. "I couldn't pick her out of the crowd in the moving footage, but I'm sure this is her."

"Why are you sure?" Darby asks.

"Her hair," I reply. "Jamila always wears her hair either in a high ponytail or a low chignon. Also, the long, thin neck. That glint on the side of her face is the light reflecting off Jamila's nose ring."

"How sure are you," Darby asks, "as a percentage?"

"At least eighty-five percent. I'd bet money on it, but not all of my money, if you know what I mean."

"Now, if I told you that I have video footage of Ms. Jagger at a different location at the same time this footage was filmed, would that change your answer? Would that make you less certain it's Ms. Jagger?"

"It looks like Jamila to me," I say shrugging, not sure what he's hoping I'll say. "Are you sure the time-stamp on the footage is correct? Is it possible the other footage and this footage have the same time stamp but are actually from different dates or times?"

"We've done our due diligence," Darby replies.

What the heck does that mean? He's confirmed the timestamps? His image forensics people said it's all good? I hate cop speak, it's so vague.

"How does Jamila explain being in two places at once?" I ask.

Darby purses his lips into a tight line.

I see what's happening. Darby doesn't know Jamila's explanation because he can't question her whenever he wants since she lawyered up. Same for the Solomons. I've probably talked to the witnesses more extensively than Darby has.

This image of Jamila is the whole point of this video footage exercise. Darby was hoping I'd pick Jamila out of the crowd but didn't want to make his focus obvious, so he also made me look at footage of the people who are easily recognizable.

"Can I see the other footage?" I ask, expecting to be told no.

Darby taps the iPad screen a few times and hands it to me.

This footage is from Bits'n'Bytes. The video quality is better than the other footage; it isn't grainy and it's in colour. Jamila sits at one of the round, shiny, white tables in the showroom, working on a computer. The computer is covered in stickers and decals, so I assume it's her personal computer and not a computer she's selling.

"It looks like she's doing administrivia," I say.

Jamila has the same bored, glazed-over look on her face that I get when I'm bogged down with administrative tasks, and last Monday was the twenty-eighth, so she could be getting a head start on her month end or quarter end paperwork.

The longer I watch the bigger the knot in my stomach gets. There's something in front of me that I'm missing. "Something isn't right, but I can't figure out what." The video ends. I look up at Darby. "May I watch it again?"

"Absolutely," he replies.

The angle of the camera also shows the front window of the store, so I'm occasionally distracted by a car or person passing by, and I'm afraid I missed something in the store because I'm watching the window. I re-watch the footage, and my sense of cognitive dissonance grows. What's wrong with this footage? What am I missing?

I ask Darby if I can have a copy to watch again later. He says no, which is what I totally expect his answer to be. He waits patiently while I watch the video one more time, trying to find the part that makes my stomach hurt.

A knock at the apartment door brings me back to the here and now. Eric opens the door just enough to poke his head inside.

"Adam's on the phone," he says looking at me. "He says it's urgent."

I pick up my phone from the coffee table. No missed calls. "My phone's here."

"He called the landline," Eric clarifies.

My heart pounds so fast and hard I can hear it. I force myself to swallow. Something's wrong. Adam hasn't called the landline at the store or the house in forever. I didn't think he even knew the phone number for Knitorious. I lunge the iPad at Darby and jump to my feet.

"Is it Hannah?" I ask, racing toward the door.

"He didn't say," Eric replies as I rush past him and run down the stairs.

"Adam? Is Hannah OK?" I inhale sharply and brace myself for his answer.

"Hannah's fine, Meg. I'm not calling about Hannah." I exhale and my shoulders drop about three inches from the tension they release.

"Why are you calling the landline? You never call the landline."

"I'm not sure it's safe to call your cell phone."

"Why wouldn't it be safe to call my cell phone?" I ask.

"Because of what I found on your computer…"

"Adam," I interrupt him. "Darby Morris is here. Should he hear this? Should I put you on speakerphone?"

"Definitely, and yes."

In the quietest whisper possible, Eric asks me if Hannah is OK. I nod. If she wasn't, I wouldn't be this calm.

"Adam found something on my computer," I say, looking at Darby. He says you should hear this. I'm putting him on speakerphone.

Darby nods. I put the call on speakerphone and hang up the receiver. Eric locks the front door and puts up the BACK IN TEN MINUTES sign. We've gotten more use out of that sign this week than the entire time I've worked here.

"We're listening, Adam," I say.

"When you dropped off the laptop, you said it worked fine before I installed the security software."

"Right," I agree, nodding, even though he can't see me.

"You were right," Adam confirms. "The security software is the reason it slowed down. The security software was trying to disarm and uninstall the spyware on your laptop. In response, the spyware was trying to shut down the security software. The battle between the two programs used up so much processing power that it brought the computer to a standstill."

I don't follow most of what he said, but I'm pretty sure the spyware is the important part.

"How did the spyware get there?" I ask.

"Someone who had access to the laptop installed it."

"I've only had the thing since Saturday. It sat, unused, at my house until this morning," I say. "The only people who had access to it are you, me, and Jamila."

Jamila!

"Listen to me, Meg."

"I'm listening," I respond.

"All your devices are connected. And Jamila had your phone when she set up the laptop, right? The spyware could be spying on all your devices. That's why I didn't text or call your cell phone. It might've tipped off whoever is monitoring you."

"Why would anyone want to monitor me? What kind of stuff can they monitor?"

I feel violated. Violated and nauseous.

"I'm not very familiar with spyware," Adam disclaims. "But they might be able to read your emails, access your passwords, read your texts. They could pretend to be you."

"Did you uninstall it?" I ask.

"Don't uninstall it!" Darby shouts, leaning toward the phone on the counter. "Don't alter the computer in any way, Adam." He looks at me. "Cyber-crimes will need to look at your computer," he says quietly. "Will you give me permission to take it?"

I nod. "Adam, Darby will pick up the laptop."

"OK," Adam replies. "Meg, listen to me carefully." He knows I zone out when he talks about tech stuff. "You need to get your hands on another computer, someone else's computer that doesn't sync with your stuff, and change your passwords. As soon as possible."

"All of them?" I ask, flipping to the page in the back of my planner where I keep my passwords.

They're encrypted in a code my friends and I made up in middle school, so we could pass notes in class without worrying about the teachers reading them if they were intercepted.

"All of them," he replies.

That's a lot of passwords.

"She can use my laptop," Eric says behind me.

"But if I suddenly stop using my devices, won't that tip off Jamila?"

We decide that Eric will create a Modern Family 2 group chat with everyone from the original Modern Family group chat except me. Then, he'll send a text explaining that my computer was hacked, and they should call me on a landline if they need me.

Darby and Adam also offer to send me occasional, innocuous text messages. I'll reply to them so whoever is watching me won't suspect I stopped using my devices because we discovered the spyware.

"Can you send me proof?" I ask Adam.

"I'll use my phone to take some photos of your computer screen, and I'll text them to Eric. I don't want to take screen shots with your laptop in case whoever is spying on you sees them."

"That makes sense," I respond. "Thank you."

"Darby, you can pick up the laptop at my office," Adam says.

"Thank you, Adam," Darby responds.

"Adam, before you go. Can they hear my phone calls? Or see my Facetime calls?"

"I don't know, Meg. Darby's cyber-crimes people will be able to tell you that."

"OK. One more thing. Jess is supposed to text me some information. Can you tell her to either call me on a landline or text Eric?"

"Sure thing," he replies.

We hang up, and I drop my weary, overwhelmed self into one of the Parsons chairs at the harvest table. While I try to process everything that just happened, Eric rubs my shoulders.

Darby sits in the chair across from me.

"Jamila installed the spyware. You know that, right?" It's a statement of fact, not a question.

"We have no evi…"

I raise my hand in a stop motion, cutting him off mid-sentence. "Don't. Just don't. No more cop speak." I lower my hand. "Jamila Jagger is spying on me, and I want to know why."

"I'll look into it," Darby says. "Leave it with me."

This could explain how someone got hold of Dr. Armistead's patient list.

"Did you find spyware on Dr. Armistead's computer? Jamila did tech support for him. She told me."

"There was no spyware on Dr. Armistead's computer," Darby replies. "Megan, why are you concerned about someone accessing your phone calls and Facetime calls?"

"I talk to April at least once a day. Every day," I explain. "We talk about everything. Personal stuff. Other people. Dr. Armistead's murder. If Jamila is listening in, she knows everything I know."

"I know it's early," Eric interjects, "but let's go home, eat pot roast, and change your passwords."

On the way to Adam's office to drop off the laptop earlier, I stopped at home and put a pot roast in the Crock-Pot for dinner. I'm glad I did. I need comfort food right now.

I nod. "I have to drop off the online orders at the post office first."

Darby leaves to pick up the laptop, and Eric insists on dropping off the online orders for me.

"I'll take Sophie with me and take her for a walk after I drop off the orders." He attaches her leash, then stands up and kisses my forehead. "Relax for a few minutes and knit. I'll be back soon."

I nod and lock the door behind them. Then I grab my keys from my bag and my phone from the counter. I leave Knitorious, lock the door behind me, and storm off in the direction of Bits'n'Bytes.

CHAPTER 15

THE DOOR IS LOCKED, and the lights are off at Bits'n'Bytes. The neon OPEN sign in the window is off. I'm not the only store owner who closed early today. I rap my knuckles loudly on the door, then on the glass window. Nothing. I peer in the window. Everything is dark. Still determined, I march up the alley beside the store to the parking lot. Empty. Jamila's car isn't here. My quest for answers will have to wait until tomorrow.

On the way back to Knitorious, I look in Jamila's window one more time and spy the green light of her security camera looking back at me. If she checks the footage, she'll know I was here. I don't want her to know that I'm on to her yet, so I unlock my cell phone and type a text to her as I walk up Water Street.

Me: Hey Jamila! I stopped by the store, but you closed early. I hope everything's OK! I'm looking for a laptop sleeve for my new computer. I'll try to stop by tomorrow and see if you have anything. Have a great evening

It's much easier to be fake-nice in a text than it is in person.

"Hi, Megan."

The key is in the lock, and I'm just about to turn it. I was seconds away from avoiding another human interaction today.

"Karen! Hi." I force a small smile, convinced this day will never end. "Are you looking for me?"

"Yes. Can we talk for a minute?" Her voice and demeanour are a combination of sad and apprehensive.

I might be having a bad day, but Karen's is worse. Dr. Armistead was murdered four days ago, and most of the world thinks she lost a co-worker, not her true love. I wouldn't switch places with her for anything in the world.

"Sure," I smile. "Come in." I lock the door behind us and gesture for her to sit in the cozy sitting area. "What brings you to Harmony Lake?" Surely her appointment with Dr. Solomon ended hours ago.

"I want to apologize to you," she says.

"For what?"

"My behaviour on Saturday when Eric showed up. I was in a bad place, and I wasn't expecting to see him..."

I touch her hand. "It's OK, Karen. I get it. I understand. The last few days have been horrible for you, and honestly, under the circumstances, I'm amazed how well you're coping. You don't have to explain."

"I don't want you to think that's who I am. I'm not like that. No matter what Eric says."

"Eric hasn't said anything," I tell her truthfully. "He rarely mentions you." I shrug.

If I wasn't so tired and frazzled after a long day, I would have stopped myself from saying that last sentence. It sounded more insensitive than I intended. I have no desire to talk about Eric with her, and I need to shut this down.

"I'm glad he's not bitter," she smiles weakly.

"Are the police keeping you apprised of the investigation?" Time to change the subject.

"Which investigation?" Karen answers my question with a question. "The break-in or Mac's murder?"

"Both," I reply.

"Not really," she admits. "I didn't have any official standing in his life. And now I don't have any official standing in his death." Karen's voice hitches on the last word, and her eyes fill with tears.

I hand her a box of tissues. She pulls one out and the tears flow. Unable to restrain myself, I put my arms around her and rub her back while she sobs on my shoulder. We stay like this for a few minutes until Sophie comes charging into the store from the back room and puts her paws on Karen's knees.

Eric's back! Thank goodness he used the back door.

"Hi, Sophie," Karen says, her voice thick with sobs. She scratches Sophie between the ears.

"I'll be right back, Karen," I say, untangling myself from her. "Sophie will keep you company."

I speed walk to the back room and close the door. Where's Eric? I check the storage room, the washroom, then look up the stairs. His apartment door is open. I'm about to go up, when he appears at the top of the stairs.

"Just getting my laptop," he says, closing his apartment door behind him. "And some chocolate from your stash. It's been one of those days. Ready to go?"

"Karen's here," I whisper when he reaches the main floor.

"Why?" he hisses, narrowing his eyes.

"She showed up unannounced. She wanted to apologize for Saturday."

"To you or me?"

"Me. I don't think she knows you're here."

"Can you tell her you have to leave?"

I shake my head. "She's crying. It's not a good idea to send her away when she's this emotional."

Eric sighs. "Are you making friends with my ex-wife?"

"Are you serious?" I ask. "You are literally best friends with my ex-husband."

"That's different. *You're* friends with your ex-husband. Karen and I are *not* friends."

"No, Karen and I aren't friends! Why would you even think that?"

"You have a way of making friends quickly."

"She's grieving for goodness' sake. Who else does

she have to cry with, Eric? It's me or Jess, and Jess isn't here," I whisper-yell.

He puts his laptop and the chocolate on the stairs and puts his hands on my shoulders. "Megan, it's not your problem that Karen agreed to be Armistead's dirty little secret instead of choosing a partner who was willing to date her publicly."

At a loss for words, I huff. Twice. "That's harsh, Eric." I huff again and throw up my hands in frustration, forcing his hands from my shoulders. "I've never seen you so insensitive. We kept our relationship a secret at first, remember? Was I your dirty little secret? I know you have issues with her but come on! Where's your compassion?"

"It's not the same, Megan, and you know it. You wanted to keep us quiet so we could get to know each other without being the talk of the town. And we kept it on the down low for a few weeks, not over a year. And neither of us was breaking any rules or professional codes of conduct."

I sigh. "It's been a long day. I don't want us to argue about your ex-wife." I'm too tired and defeated for this.

Also, I'd rather have this discussion when we can speak with our normal voices instead of whisper-yelling at each other.

"You're right." He rubs my upper arms. "I'm sorry. I'll go home and roast some vegetables for the pot roast. Do you want me to take Sophie?"

I shake my head. "No, thank you. I'll take her. I'll be home before dinner is ready."

I stand on my tippy toes and kiss him goodbye, determined not to let his unresolved issues with his ex-wife interfere in our relationship.

"Sorry about that," I say, resuming my seat on the sofa.

I offer Karen a glass of water. She declines. Sophie is half on Karen's lap and half on the sofa. Karen is stroking her, and Sophie is loving the attention.

"She's sweet," Karen comments.

"She has a calming effect," I agree.

"Was that Eric?" she asks.

I nod. "He left. He went home."

"Doesn't he live here?"

"He does. Like eighty percent of the time," I explain.

"Mac used to stay over at my house all the time. A lot of his stuff is still there. I don't know who to give it to."

"I'm sure if you ask Darby, he can help you with that."

"I'll do that."

"Karen, remember when you told me whoever turned over Mac's office didn't take anything? Do you believe it was a crime of opportunity, and they were looking for drugs? What do you think they were looking for?"

"I have no idea, but they probably got frustrated trying to find it. I jokingly told Mac that's why they tossed his office, because they were frustrated with his horrible filing system." She chuckles under her breath. "On the surface it looks organized, but inside those drawers are a mess. Well, they *were* a mess. After the break in, I helped him organize it properly. I doubt he would have maintained it, though."

"A mess how?" I ask.

"Take the O-P drawer for example. It wasn't just for patient files. Anything starting with those letters was in those drawers. P for phone bill. P for property taxes. O for owner manuals. Then within each file everything was misfiled. The latest phone bill might be filed in the phone bill folder, but it more likely landed in one of the five files around the phone bill file. You see what I mean?"

"I do." I nod. "He could've used an assistant to keep him organized."

"I suggested that," Karen says. "But he said he didn't have enough work to keep an assistant busy. Almost everything is electronic now. Patients don't have paper files anymore. And his electronic files were way more organized than his paper files."

She could only know that if she had access to his electronic files.

Darby said no spyware was found on Dr. Armistead's computer, but I wonder if they searched Karen's computer. She said Dr. Armistead stayed over at her house regularly. Maybe he used her computer while he was there.

Karen tells me a few stories about her and Dr. Armistead. Their first date, practical jokes they played on each other, and how good he was at making her laugh. Now that her mood has improved, and she's not crying, I think it's safe to send her out into the world.

"It's been nice talking with you, Karen, but I have to get Sophie home for dinner," I say as I stand up and brush some corgi hair from my lap.

"I'm sure you want to get home to Eric," she says. "It's OK, I'm not angry or bitter anymore. You're really nice. I hope you and Eric are happy together."

She's not bitter *anymore*!

"Thank you, Karen. That means a lot coming from you."

"We were a bad match from the start," she explains.

"That's too bad," I sympathize. Please don't let this be the beginning of a long post-mortem discussion of their marriage.

"I hated that he was a cop," Karen says. "It's not a job, you know, it's a lifestyle." It sounds more like a warning than a statement of fact.

I nod. "I know. My ex-husband was a workaholic."

"Well, I'm happy you got a different version of Eric."

What a strange thing to say. Deep breath. Give her some grace, Megan, her world imploded this week, and her life partner was murdered.

"How do you know what Eric is like now? You haven't spoken to him since you split."

"He walks your dog, he helps in your yarn store, he sees you during the day, and he even keeps a stash of PMS chocolate for you. The Eric I was married to didn't do those things."

She overheard me tell Jess about the chocolate stash. It didn't occur to me that Karen heard us talking while she waited for Emory. In my head, I quickly replay Jess's and my conversation, making sure we didn't say anything about Dr. Armistead's murder. I'm sure we didn't mention it until Karen and Emory were in his office.

"Karen, you know that Mac was at the Solomon's house for dinner the night he died, right?"

She nods. "I know. That's why I met with Emory today. He told me about the last few hours of Mac's life."

"That was nice of him. Is today the first time you met Emory?"

She nods again. "Yes. I got his contact information from Mac's address book. He told me he was having dinner at his friend Emory's house."

Dr. Armistead told Karen that he and Emory were friends, but Emory insists they were just colleagues.

Adam is sure he's seen Karen in the reception area waiting for Emory, but she says today is the first time she met him. I believe Adam over Karen.

Who is Karen trying to protect with her lie? Herself, her dead boyfriend, or Emory? And why?

What else is she lying about?

CHAPTER 16

"How can we be sure your landline isn't bugged?" April asks when I explain why I'm calling her from the landline at the store this morning.

"Only customers and telemarketers call the landline. Would it even occur to someone to hack a landline nowadays?"

"Well, if it is bugged, we can always use smoke signals. Or two tin cans and a long piece of string."

"How about two tin cans and a piece of yarn?" I ask. "Would that work? Between the store inventory and my personal stash, I might have several thousand kilometres of the stuff."

I tell April about my long, hectic day yesterday. "I'd send you a pic of the beautiful floral arrangement Phillip made, but I'm avoiding my phone until I know for sure it's not spying on me."

"I will never buy another thing from Jamila Jagger again!" April declares angrily.

"I don't think I will, either," I concur. "The worst part is, now the police have the laptop, and it's stuck in evidence. By the time I get it back, laptops will probably be a thing of the past."

"I'm glad she wasn't there when you went to Bits'n'Bytes last night," April says. "If you confronted her and she's the killer, she might have snapped and killed you too."

"I know," I admit. "I realize that now. I felt angry and violated at the time. I didn't think it through. I won't go back unless someone is with me. That way if she snaps and goes homicidal, whoever is with me can escape and make sure she's held accountable for killing me."

"That's funny, not funny, Megapop. Death jokes are only funny when they're about bad people or people we don't love."

"Sorry, not sorry," I say.

"*Are* you and Karen friends?" April asks after I tell her about Karen's surprise visit and the whisper-yelling argument Eric and I had in the back room.

"No," I state firmly. "She lied to my face. I can't be friends with someone who lies to me. And it was a risky lie. She knows Harmony Lake is a small town, and everyone knows everyone else. She knows there's a high likelihood someone I know has seen her at Emory's office. Also, she has a habit of steering our conversations toward Eric, and I don't want to talk about him with her. Or about her with him."

"Do we hate her now?" April asks.

"No." I reply with a sigh. "We don't hate her, but we don't trust her."

"Got it."

"Is everything OK with you and Eric after the whisper-yelling argument?"

"Totally," I assure her. "We talked after dinner while I changed my passwords. Karen's sudden appearance in Harmony Lake rattled him. The Karen he knows is spiteful, and he's afraid she'll try to sabotage our relationship. We're on the same page now. He promises to trust my judgement about dealing with his ex-wife, and I promise not to befriend her and invite her to Thanksgiving dinner."

I came to the store early to phone April. To give us some privacy during our call, Eric stayed home. He says he'll clean out the shower drain, vacuum the dryer vent, and put the winter cover on the air-conditioning unit. Despite reaching the fix-stuff-around-the-house level of boredom, he still insists on using his time off to help me at the store. I think what he's really doing is avoiding work because it's too difficult for him to watch someone else investigate a murder that happened on his doorstep—literally and figuratively.

While I putter around the store before it opens, April and I talk, and talk, and talk until my cell phone dings.

"It's Jamila," I say, picking up the phone.

"Sneaky computer hacker," April says. "What does she want?"

I read Jamila's text out loud.

Jamila: I have loads in stock. Come by whenever.

"Loads of what?" April asks.

I tell her about the text I sent to Jamila when I realized she would see me on her camera footage banging on her door like a crazy woman.

"But you won't go alone, right?" she reminds me.

"Right," I agree. "I promise."

Me: Great! I'll stop by later this morning.

"GOOD MORNING, LADIES!" I smile at Mrs. Roblin and Mrs. Vogel. The rest of the Charity Knitting Guild files into the store behind them. "I wasn't expecting you until this afternoon," I remark.

The charity knitters come by the store on Wednesday afternoons to knit, plan their projects, and order yarn for upcoming charity knitting endeavours.

"We thought Eric was working," Mrs. Vogel says while Mrs. Roblin stands next to her, craning her neck and surveying the store for any sign of Eric.

"He'll be in later this morning," I advise them. "But you're welcome to stay. I'll put the kettle on."

"It's OK, Megan. Don't go to any trouble. We'll come back at our usual time." Mrs. Roblin smiles at me. "He's not here, ladies," she tells the rest of them as she turns back toward the door. I hear a faint chorus of disappointed groans as the group of knitters turns and files out of the store.

"I think Eric is more popular than us," I say to Sophie after the door closes behind them. She sits at the door patiently, staring and waiting, hoping her friends will come back. "They'll be back later, Soph. Try not to take it personally." The last sentence was for both of us.

To distract Sophie from feeling dejected, I convince her to follow me into the kitchenette where I give her some dog treats even though it isn't snack time. I put the last treat on the floor and, like one of Pavlov's dogs, rush back to the store when the bell over the door jingles.

"Good morning, my dear," Connie sings.

"Good morning," I say, hugging her. "This is a nice surprise."

"Did I just see the back ends of the charity knitters marching down Water Street?" she asks.

I nod.

"It's not like them to congregate this early in the day. What's going on?"

I tell Connie about the group's shared disappointment that Eric isn't here.

"Yes, I hear they're fond of him," Connie says. "Apparently, he's very charming and attentive to them when they're here." She sits on the sofa and opens her knitting bag. "He's a novelty. It'll wear off."

"It'll have to," I agree. "He's going back to work

next week. Eric working here is good for business, though. So far, this is the busiest October we've ever had, and most of the sales happen when Eric is here alone. How's Archie doing?"

"His recovery is going very well, and he's ready to spend a few hours alone," Connie explains. "I thought I'd visit you for a while and tell you some gossip."

The book club calls the intelligence they gather "gossip".

"Oooh," I say, joining her on the sofa. "What kind of gossip?"

"The mayoral kind," Connie discloses. "The mayor brought Archie a care package, and the three of us had a chat."

"Did you ply her with margaritas?" I ask.

"Margaritas are for book club meetings only," she reminds me. "We had gin and tonic. One each."

"Right," I say, nodding.

"Anyway, the mayor has had a change of heart. She's renewing Charmaine's mandate. If Charmaine wants it."

"That's an about-face," I comment.

"Yes, it is," Connie agrees. "Especially when you consider how insistent she was when she told me Charmaine had to go."

"Did she explain her change of heart?" I ask.

"Nope," Connie replies shaking her head. "She said it was all a big misunderstanding, and everything is fine now."

"Interesting," I say.

At least Eric doesn't have to feel conflicted anymore about whether he wants to be considered for Charmaine's job.

Sophie joins us on the sofa while Connie and I knit together for a while. She knits on a shawl she's making for a friend, and I work on my sweater, until Connie packs up her knitting and announces she's going down the street to Artsy Tartsy to visit Marla and Tamara before she has to get back to Archie.

Almost as soon as she leaves, Eric and Adam enter the store. Together.

"Double trouble," I say, taking the coffee Eric hands me. "Thank you." I immediately crack the lid and inhale the glorious maple-pecan aroma.

They're deep in conversation about something sports related, so I sit on the sofa and knit while I wait for them to finish. As they talk, Sophie approaches Eric, then Adam, and instinctively they each bend down to rub her. Watching them gives me an idea for an experiment. If sales are good with one hot guy in the store, would sales double with two attractive men?

"Meg, did you hear me?"

"I'm sorry, I was distracted." I put down my knitting and look at Adam.

"This is Hannah's old laptop. It was in her bedroom at my place. I thought you could use it at the store until the police return yours."

"Thanks," I say. I take the laptop to the counter and plug it in. "Why are you two together, anyway?"

"We ran into each other at Latte Da," Eric explains.

"I was on my way here to give you the laptop and check your other devices."

"Right, I almost forgot," I say. "Here's my phone." I unlock the screen and hand it to him, then reach into my bag, pull out my tablet, and put it on the counter.

Adam called me at home last night and offered to check my other devices for spyware. I'd already looked and didn't find anything, but a second set of eyes can't hurt, so I took him up on his offer.

"I don't see anything on your phone." He hands me the phone, and I unlock the tablet for him.

I sip my coffee and wait for his verdict.

"Nothing," Adam declares, placing the device on the counter. "But I'm not familiar with spyware. For all I know, she only had to install it on one device. Also, your emails, texts, and photos automatically sync to all of your devices, so she can see those even if they don't happen on your laptop."

"Got it," I say. "Thank you for checking. I won't use my phone or tablet until Darby tells me it's safe." I rub my hands together and flash them a wide smile. "Who wants to come with me to visit Jamila?" I ask as if it will be fun. It won't.

"I can't go with you," Eric replies. "I'm not on duty, but I'm still a cop. Jamila has a lawyer. It could look like I'm trying to question her without her lawyer present."

I nod and look at Adam.

"If I say no, will you go alone?"

I nod.

"Fine. I'll go. But I want it on the record that I don't think it's a good idea, Meg."

"Duly noted," I say. "Do you still have the photos of the spyware on your phone?"

Adam nods.

Armed with my cell phone and coffee, I open the door and gesture for Adam to leave ahead of me.

"Please be careful," Eric says.

"Always," I respond. "You won't be alone long. As soon as your fan club hears I've left, and you're here alone, they'll rush over." I grin at him and leave.

CHAPTER 17

"I AGREE WITH YOU, but Darby says there was no spyware on Dr. Armistead's computer," I say to Adam on the walk to Bits'n'Bytes.

"I don't buy it," he says. "Maybe she was able to remove the spyware remotely, without getting her hands on his computer," he suggests. "It makes perfect sense. Jamila admits she provided tech support for him, and she installed spyware on your computer, which means she's capable of installing it on his. And she was one of the last people to see Armistead alive. What do you think she found on his computer?"

"Other than his patient list, I don't know," I say.

"Before I forget," Adam says, snapping his fingers, "Jess asked me to tell you she'll see you at noon tomorrow, and she'll meet you there. She said you'll know where 'there' is."

"Tell her thank you, and I'll see her tomorrow."

"Do I want to know where you and Jess are going?" he asks cautiously.

"Ask Jess," I reply.

"I did. She said it's a surprise."

I get the feeling Jess likes to keep Adam guessing. I'm not sure if it's a quirky part of their dynamic, or if it's mean, but either way it's none of my business.

"It's not my place to tell you if she won't," I say.

Talking about Jess makes me think of the medical centre where she works, which makes me think of Karen. I stop walking and open my phone. I find the photo of Karen that I sent to April and hold it up to Adam.

"Are you sure this is the same woman you've seen waiting in the reception area for Emory?"

He looks at my phone. "Positive. I already told you I'm certain it's her."

I nod. "I believe you, but I have to double check because Karen told me yesterday was the first time she met Emory."

"Does she have a twin?" Adam asks.

The question catches me off guard. I'm about to say no but realize I have no idea. I know literally nothing about Karen except what she disclosed the two times we met.

"I don't think so," I reply hesitantly.

"Then it's her."

"OK," I say, and we resume walking.

"Emory's office is directly across the hall from

mine," Adam explains, "and he doesn't use it very often, so when he has a patient, I notice. Unless I'm on the phone or with a client, I keep my door open—the air circulation is awful in those old Victorians—and I tend to notice the few times he comes and goes from his office."

"Does he work part-time? Or does he divide his time between multiple locations?" I wonder out loud.

"I don't think he has many patients," Adam replies. "We have an office lunch once a month, and at one of the lunches, he mentioned how challenging it is to build a practice in a small town. He said no one wants to be seen entering or leaving their therapist's office. He said people in Harmony Lake go to Harmony Hills for therapy. He hoped setting up an office in a building with other professionals would help him grow his practice because his patients would blend in with everyone else's clients."

"That's exactly why we went to Dr. Armistead in Harmony Hills," I remind him.

"I know. I didn't tell him that, though."

"Well, I'm sure he knows since Dr. Armistead's patient list was posted online."

Adam holds the door, and I enter Bits'n'Bytes first.

Jamila pops her head out of the back room. "Just a sec," she says with a smile.

"You don't have to say anything," I tell Adam quietly. "I just need a witness in case this goes off the rails."

He nods.

Jamila comes out of the back room with a stack of laptop sleeves and places them on the shiny, white table closest to Adam and I. "Hi guys," she says cheerfully.

"Hi, Jamila," Adam and I say slightly out of sync.

"All of these will fit your new laptop," she says, unstacking the sleeves and laying them next to one another.

"Actually, I think I've changed my mind about the laptop sleeve," I say. "I'd like a refund instead. And an explanation."

"A refund?" Her eyes are wide, and the inner corners of her eyebrows are squeezed so tightly together they almost meet in the middle. "I don't understand. Is there something wrong with the laptop?"

"It doesn't work," I explain. "It's super slow because the cyber security program we installed conflicts with the spyware you installed."

For a nanosecond, panic flashes across Jamila's face before it's replaced with mock concern. "Spyware? What are you talking about? I would never install malware on a computer." On the outside, her demeanour is calm, but I'm sure her insides are hectic.

"Yes, Jamila, you did. And you've been caught, so you may as well admit it."

"Hah," Jamila replies breathily and haughtily puts her hands on her hips. "Where's the computer? Let me see it." Her tone escalates from calm to defiant.

"The police have it," I explain. "I d…"

"YOU CALLED THE POLICE?" she shouts, going from defiant to full panic in the space of four words. "OH. MY GOD. Is that why HE'S here?" she points at Adam. "You brought a lawyer? What… Are you going to sue me?"

"I'm not going to sue you, Jamila," I say, trying to sound reassuring so she'll calm down. "Take a deep breath and lower your voice."

"You're not going to sue me, but you brought a lawyer? Really?"

"Well, I guess *technically* I brought a lawyer, but he's not here *as a* lawyer. He's here because he found the spyware and has proof," I explain. "And I didn't call the police, Detective Morris happened to be with me when I found out about the spyware."

Jamila drops into one of the shiny white chairs and covers her face with her hand. "OHMYGOD this is why my lawyer keeps calling me. The police KNOW." Her shoulders heave.

"Jamila, if your lawyer is trying to reach you, you should call them back," Adam advises, but I'm not sure she hears him through her sobs.

I walk behind the white shiny counter and poke my head in the back room. I find a box of tissue and drop it on the table in front of Jamila, then collapse into the chair across from her. If I'd accepted Adam's offer to find a new laptop for me, we wouldn't be here right now. If only I had a time machine.

"Why are you spying on me?" I ask. "Are you running an identity theft scam or something?"

"No, of course not." She uncovers her face and dries her eyes with a couple of tissues. "I had no choice. If I didn't install the spyware, I would have gone to jaaaai-il." The word jail evolves into a loud sob, and she's crying again. Full on crying. Ugly crying.

"Jail?" I ask. "Who would put you in jail? And why?"

"Charmaaaaaiiiine," she wails, then starts to hyperventilate, inhaling sharply after each syllable. "Be... cuz...of...the...may...yer."

"Deep breaths, Jamila." I exaggerate my own breathing hoping she'll copy me, like I used to when Hannah was a toddler having a tantrum.

"Jamila, do you want to talk to your lawyer before you say anything else?"

What did Adam just say? I look up at him and give him the stink eye. "Really?" I mouth.

"I'm an officer of the court, Meg," he reminds me, throwing up his hands.

I turn to Jamila and resume my exaggerated breathing. To my relief, she synchronizes her breathing with mine.

"Go in the back and get Jamila a glass of water, please," I instruct Adam.

This is the first time I've seen Jamila react strongly to anything. When I saw her the day after Dr. Armistead's death, and again yesterday when she picked Phillip's lock, she was cool, calm, and collected. And those were stressful situations.

By the time Adam returns with a bottle of water he found in the fridge, Jamila's breathing is back to normal, and she's able to speak.

I call upon my calmest, most reassuring voice. "Jamila, what's going on with you, Charmaine Solomon, and the mayor?"

"Jamila," Adam starts.

Jamila interrupts him before he can continue. "It's OK, Adam, I don't want to call my lawyer." She looks at me. "About two months ago, the mayor came to see me. She told me some town residents are plotting to get her out of office. She said they're frustrated by her support of the big-box policy, and they plan to have their members run for council positions in the next election and nominate a candidate to run against her in the mayoral race. She said if they succeed, and enough of their candidates get elected, they could reverse the big-box policy."

"OK." I shrug. "This isn't news, Jamila. The town has always been divided about the big-box policy."

Harmony Lake has a policy against big-box stores and restaurants. Our quaint, family-owned businesses and restaurants are what makes our tiny town so intimate and cozy. We have no drive-thrus, no neon signs advertising corporate logos or businesses, and no multi-level parking lots. None of the corporate landscape commonly found in cities and suburbs. Tourists come to

Harmony Lake to escape from that and immerse them-selves in our small-town charm.

Our mayor is a loud advocate for the big-box policy. She wants to keep Harmony Lake cozy and friendly. Not everyone agrees with her. Some residents–particu-larly the ones who would benefit from selling land to big corporations–claim the big-box policy limits Harmony Lake's potential and stops progress. Every few years, the big-boxers push to have the policy reversed, but they never win.

"This is different," Jamila sniffles. "She said Electric Avenue is funding them. In exchange, if the big-boxers win, Electric Avenue will get first refusal on a location in Harmony Lake. Megan, I can't compete with Electric Avenue. It's a big-box computer and electronics retailer. I can't offer all the products and services they offer at discount prices. It would kill my business. I've spent twelve years building Bits'n'Bytes. If Electric Avenue comes to town, I'll end up wearing one of their orange and grey uniforms, working for minimum wage, and hoping for enough hours to pay my bills."

Oh my. If this is true, and the big-boxers have found themselves a corporate sponsor, they're really upping their game. They'd have money to pay for campaign advisors and PR people. More residents might start to take them seriously.

"Why did the mayor tell you this?" I ask. "What did she want from you?" Our mayor is sweet and grand-motherly, but she's also savvy. She hasn't been mayor for over twenty years for no reason. She knows how to play local politics to win.

"She gave me a list of big-boxers and asked me to hack their computers, so she could monitor their plans and progress."

"That was a big ask," I comment, shocked.

Jamila nods. "Some of them were my clients. Local business owners and farmers on the outskirts of town. It would be easy for me to access their computers."

Adam shifts awkwardly in the chair beside me. I can't expect him to sit here and listen to Jamila confess to committing a crime. It would put him in an awful position. I pretend to check the time on my phone.

"Adam, it's getting late. I appreciate you coming with me, but I know you have a meeting to get to. You should go. I'll text you if I need those photos."

He practically leaps out of his seat. "Are you sure, Meg?" He already has one hand on the door.

I nod. "Totally. I'll talk to you later."

I wait for the door to close behind him, then ask Jamila, "So, you did what the mayor asked?"

She nods. "I sure did. I felt sneaky and dishonest the entire time, but I did it."

"I'm guessing Charmaine found out?"

"A few weeks ago," Jamila confirms. "One of the people I was spying on realized what was happening. He went to Charmaine. He wanted to press charges." Jamila starts crying again and takes a moment to collect herself. "Charmaine confronted me, and I admitted everything. She told me she wouldn't charge me but said I owe her."

"And she made you hack into Dr. Armistead's computer?" I probe. "And post his patient list online?"

"No." She shakes her head. "That wasn't me. I don't know who did that."

Then who the heck was it?

"What did Charmaine ask you to do?"

"Nothing until a few days ago when she told me to spy on you," Jamila replies.

"Just me?" I ask.

"So far." She blows her nose. "She saw us talking at the pub on Friday night. Remember when I stopped by your booth?"

I nod. Of course, I remember. I wasn't *that* drunk. I was tipsy.

"Well, I was pretty excited about selling you a computer, and I told her about it. She was happy for me. The next day, after she found out Dr. Armistead died and you found his body, she came to the store to see me. She told me to spy on your computer. She said you have a habit of inserting yourself in police investigations. She said people confide in you. She wanted to know immediately if you found out anything about Dr. Armistead's death."

"I see," I respond.

So far, Jamila's story sounds plausible. When we spoke at the pub, Jamila mentioned she was waiting for the Solomons, so it's possible they showed up while

Jamila and I were talking. Also, Charmaine was at Bits'n'Bytes the following day when I came to see the laptop Jamila picked out for me.

"When I left the pub on Friday, I saw you and Charmaine speaking in the alley beside the pub. What were you talking about?" I ask.

Jamila's shocked expression tells me it was definitely them, and she had no idea I saw them. She inhales deeply.

"Charmaine took me aside to tell me she confronted the mayor about getting me to spy on the big-boxers. She said the mayor denied it, but Charmaine wouldn't let it go. Eventually, the mayor told Charmaine her mandate as police chief will not be renewed. Charmaine tried to blackmail the mayor to renew her mandate."

"Why would Charmaine tell you that?" I ask.

"Because, according to Charmaine, if her mandate as chief isn't renewed and she loses her job, she's taking the mayor down with her. She'll expose everything."

"Including you," I point out.

"Including me," Jamila confirms. "Charmaine suggested I get a lawyer and prepare to ask for immunity in exchange for giving evidence against the mayor."

I can't fathom that my lovely little town is a hotbed of corruption and lies.

"Today, someone close to the mayor told me she changed her mind. She plans to renew Charmaine's mandate as police chief, after all."

"Charmaine won," Jamila observes, seemingly unaffected.

"So did you," I point out. "I'm sure neither of them will want anyone to know about you spying for them."

"But you know," Jamila says. "Are you going to tell?"

"I have to think about it, but I doubt it. I love this town, too, and we don't need a scandal like this."

I dare not say yes for fear of Jamila coming unhinged. I'm alone with her, and while I'm confident I would put up a good fight, I'm not certain I'd win.

"Thank you, Megan." Her eyes fill with moisture.

"Why did the Solomons invite you for dinner? What happened that night?"

Jamila shrugs one shoulder. "To make it an even number. Charmaine's funny like that. Also, I might be the only person in Harmony Lake who knows Mac. Except for all his patients."

"Have you ever met Dr. Armistead's girlfriend?" Let's toss it out there and see what happens.

"He had a girlfriend?" She shakes her head. "He never mentioned her."

I can't tell if she's lying or not. My phone dings.

Eric: Darby says it's safe to use your phone. Text me back so I know you're OK.

I type a quick reply thanking him and assuring him I'm fine.

"I have to go," I say, standing up and moving toward the door. "But I have one more question. Did spying on the big-boxers yield anything? Did you find proof they're launching a campaign and have the support of Electric Avenue?"

"No," Jamila replies, shaking her head. "But that doesn't mean it isn't true. I only spied on a few of them." She stands up and steps toward me.

I open the door, and step outside, determined to keep a safe distance from her.

"Megan, please don't tell anyone," she says before I let go of the door.

CHAPTER 18

"Hi again, ladies." I smile and close the door behind me. "Hey, Soph! Who's a good girl?" I bend down and give her a quick rub.

"You're back!" Eric says, getting up from his centre seat on the sofa and stepping around the knitters on either side of him. "How'd it go?"

I nod. "Good." My voice is too cheery and higher pitched than usual. I'm sure my anxiety is obvious to him.

"Cannelloni, Megan?" A charity knitter gestures to the plate on the table in front of her.

"No, thank you," I reply, smiling.

"I made them for Eric's lunch," she explains.

"That's sweet," I respond. "I'm glad he won't starve in my absence." I mean it sarcastically. Eric is a fully grown adult who's more than capable of feeding himself.

The sarcasm is lost on the knitters who tell me they don't mind at all, and it's a pleasure to cook for someone who appreciates it.

They bring him food every day. Sometimes multiple times each day. The fridge in the kitchenette is full. It will take hours to dispose of the leftovers and wash the containers.

"I'm glad you're here," he says slowly, like he's trying to figure out what to say next. "I need to talk to you about that order you placed. You know the order with that yarn place?"

I nod, realizing he's trying to separate me from the highly perceptive charity knitters without alerting them that something is up. "Right. The order."

Eric turns to his fan club. "Ladies, will you excuse us for a moment? There's a problem with a yarn order, and I need to talk to Megan about it in the back."

"What kind of problem?" Mrs. Roblin asks.

"They have no record of my order," I reply, making it up as I go along. "It's an order for limited edition colours. If we don't straighten it out today, we won't get *any* of it."

"Why didn't you say it's an emergency?" Mrs. Vogel asks, standing up and dropping her knitting where she was sitting. "You two go." She brushes us away with her hand as she walks toward the counter. "We'll keep an eye on the store. You get us some of that yarn!"

Eric closes the door separating the kitchenette from

the store, and I sit on the stairs that lead to his apartment.

"What's wrong?" he asks. "I've never seen you this flustered."

I take a deep breath, collect my thoughts, and try to figure out where to start.

"First of all, is Karen a twin?"

"No," he replies, confused. "She has a brother, but he's two years older than her." Short pause. "Why?"

"Unless she's a twin, it's not relevant. It was just something Adam said." I shake my head. "Next," I continue, "have you thought anymore about Charmaine's job? How attached are you to maybe becoming the next chief of police?"

Eric shrugs. "I haven't really thought about it. Armistead's murder and your laptop issues have kept me preoccupied. Why?"

I tell him what Connie told me about the mayor changing her mind and deciding to renew Charmaine's mandate as chief. Then I tell him about my conversation with Jamila.

"Adam just left you there? Alone with her?"

Of all the bombshells I just dropped, this is what he chooses to focus on? Really?

"I told Adam to leave," I explain. "There's no way Jamila would have talked with him there. She was already scared he was there because I want to sue her."

I believe part of the reason people confide in me is I don't have a stake in their story. I'm not a cop, a lawyer, or anyone else who's officially interested. I have no agenda or code of conduct to follow, except my own moral compass. I'm a neutral third party to whom they can unburden themselves.

"You told her you wouldn't go to the police with any of this?" he asks.

"I only said it to keep Jamila on an even keel. I texted Darby on my way here and asked to meet with him."

Eric nods and takes my hand. I scoot over so he can sit next to me on the narrow stair. "You did the right thing. I'm glad you got out of there safely. Did Darby text you back?"

"Not yet," I reply.

"Do you think Jamila is telling the truth?" he asks.

That's a big question.

I take a deep breath. "I believe parts of her story are true," I reply. "I believe Charmaine told her to spy on me, and I believe Charmaine found out Jamila was caught spying on someone else. I'm not sure I believe her when she said it wasn't her who accessed Dr. Armistead's patient list and posted it online. The mayor's sudden change of heart about renewing Charmaine's mandate makes sense if Charmaine blackmailed her."

Shaking his head, Eric looks at me. "I can't believe Charmaine would conceal a crime and blackmail the mayor and Jamila." His eyes are heavy with sadness. "The Charmaine Solomon I know wouldn't do that."

"It sucks when people disappoint us," I sympathize.

Eric wraps his arm around me, and I rest my head on his shoulder. We stay like this until my phone dings.

"Darby?" he asks.

I nod. "He'll come by as soon as he can."

"We should get back to the store," Eric reminds me.

"I know," I sigh. "You have cannelloni to eat, and I have to find some limited-edition yarn to order, or the charity knitters will never stop asking me about it."

Before Eric takes Sophie for her midday walk, he drops several fake hints that he won't be around the store much this afternoon. That's all the charity knitters need to hear to convince them that it's time to pack up their knitting and convene today's meeting.

Phillip walks past the store window with Kevin perched in the crook of his arm. Watching them go by, I get a tight knot in the pit of my stomach. It reminds me of the knot I had yesterday when I watched the security camera footage with Darby. I hope he brings it with him today, I'd like to have another look at both the footage from the medical centre and Bits'n'Bytes.

"I was just thinking about you," I say when Darby enters the store.

"I'm flattered," he replies, placing his folio on the counter. "Were you thinking anything in particular?"

"Just that I hope you bring the video footage with you today so I can watch it again."

"Great minds think alike, Megan" he says with a wink, tapping his leather folio.

While I re-watch the security footage, Darby reads something on his phone and eats a few of the left-over date squares that one of the charity knitters made for Eric. I still can't pinpoint what triggers my Spidey sense when I watch it.

Feeling frustrated that I *can't* figure it out, while at the same time obsessed with watching the footage because I *want* to figure it out, I lock the screen and close the flap on the iPad case.

"I need a break from this." I hand the iPad to Darby.

"No problem," he replies. "So, you paid a visit to Ms. Jagger?"

I'm about to tell him about my conversation with Jamila when Eric and Sophie return from their walk. Sophie rushes over to Darby and puts her two front paws on his knees. He rubs her and says nice things to her. Sophie and Darby are like two old friends who hardly see each other. Except they're like this every time they see each other which, lately, is frequently.

When the corgi finally agrees she has been sufficiently acknowledged by all who are present, I tell Darby about my visit to Bits'n'Bytes. At first, I don't mention that Adam was there. He wasn't actually present for Jamila's confession, and he doesn't need the hassle of another police interview. But then I remember

Jamila has security cameras in her store, and if the police check, they'll see exactly who was there. It would look suspicious if I don't mention Adam, so I include him.

"Can you arrest her?" I ask, when my story is complete. "She admits to installing spyware on my computer and spying on other people's computers."

"As usual, Megan, our conversation has been very enlightening," Darby replies, completely ignoring my question.

"Will you at least question the mayor? And Charmaine?" I ask. "I know she denies it, but it's too much of a coincidence that Jamila was cyber-spying on so many people yet insists it wasn't her who posted Dr. Armistead's patient list online. It has to be connected. All of this somehow ties back to Dr. Armistead's murder. I just know it."

"We're looking into it."

Cop speak: lots of words but no actual information.

"Of course, you are," I say with a frustrated sigh, knowing full well that this is a one-way conversation. Darby's here to get information, not give it.

When Darby leaves, I stomp up the stairs to Eric's apartment and make lunch. Open-faced roast beef sandwiches with the leftover pot roast and gravy we had for dinner last night.

We're eating at the harvest table in the store when, for the first time since we've known each other, Eric doesn't finish a meal.

"I can't do it." He drops his fork and knife in defeat and pushes his plate away. "The knitters keep bringing me food. They go to so much trouble cooking for me, and it makes them so happy when I eat what they make that I feel guilty if I don't. I'm full all the time. I forget what hunger feels like. It's like they're determined to fatten me up, and they're aggressive about it."

"It's more likely they're following the old adage, the fastest way to a man's heart is through his stomach," I tell him.

"Actually, the fastest way to a man's heart is through the fifth left intercostal space, midclavicular line," Eric informs me. "I learned that at an autopsy I attended."

Welcome to our mealtime banter! Eric explains the most efficient methods of murder, and I explain the difference between worsted weight and fingering weight yarn. Spoiler alert: It has nothing to do with weight at all, but with diameter. The real mystery is why we aren't invited to more dinner parties.

"They mean well," I remind him. "I can put up a sign, NO OUTSIDE FOOD OR DRINKS IN THE STORE, and can take it down when you go back to work."

"No," he replies. "You're right, they mean well. And it took so long for people around here to accept me, I don't want to ruin it."

The women have certainly accepted him, that's for sure.

While Eric sits and contemplates his distended belly, I stack the dishes and cutlery and take them back upstairs. When I re-enter the store from the back room, I'm looking down at my dishpan hands and massaging lotion into them.

"I don't think you should be here," Eric says, his voice low and monotone.

Who is he talking to? I look up.

"Hi, Charmaine. What are you doing here?"

"Hi, Megan," Charmaine greets me, looking past Eric and ignoring his words of caution. "I was hoping to speak to you." She glances at Eric, then back at me. "Alone."

I'm looking at Charmaine, and Eric is between us shaking his head with his arms crossed in front of his chest.

Right now, I don't trust Charmaine Solomon as far as I can throw her. She's obviously here because Jamila told her about our chat at Bits'n'Bytes this morning. Is she here to find out information? Or feed me information that supports her version of events? Let's find out.

CHAPTER 19

"WE CAN TALK," I tell Charmaine, "but not alone." I gesture for her to take a seat at the harvest table.

"Fine," she agrees. "But can we put our cell phones on the table, face up?"

I swear I hear a low growl emanate from Sophie when Charmaine walks past us. Sophie never growls. I look down at the corgi sitting next to me, and her upper lip is curled, revealing her tiny, sharp teeth as her steady gaze follows Charmaine.

I place my phone in the centre of the table. Charmaine places her phone in the centre of the table. We both look at Eric. Reluctantly, he places his phone on the table.

"I'll lock the door," he mutters.

Charmaine's eyes scan the ceiling and corners of the store.

"No cameras," I assure her.

"Just checking." She smiles.

It dawns on me that Charmaine has never been to Knitorious. She's not a knitter, and she doesn't crochet. There's no other reason to come here. Although there are people who occasionally stop in to visit Sophie, Charmaine isn't one of them.

"What do you want?" I cut to the chase.

"I heard about your conversation with Jamila this morning," Charmaine starts. "I want to explain a few things."

I bet she does.

"Jamila…misunderstood me. I didn't ask her to put spyware on your computer or to do anything malicious to your computer," Charmaine explains. "I asked her to talk to you and try to find out what you saw when you found Dr. Armistead on Friday night." She pauses, waiting for me to tell her what I saw on Friday night. I don't take the bait and stay quiet. She continues, "Somehow, Jamila interpreted that as me wanting her to monitor your correspondence and report back to me."

"I see," I reply. "I appreciate you clarifying that, Charmaine. Did Jamila also misunderstand you when she hacked into Dr. Armistead's computer and accessed his patient list?"

"I don't know what you're talking about, Megan," she replies matter-of-factly.

"Is the part about the mayor and the big-boxers true?" I ask.

"As far as I know, yes," Charmaine replies. "The

mayor coerced Jamila into doing some…questionable things to protect her small business. However, I don't know if the story the mayor told her is true or if she made it up to manipulate Jamila."

"Either way, it's illegal," Eric points out. "You had a duty to act on that information, Charmaine."

Charmaine turns to Eric. "I did act on it," she replies. "I'm conducting an investigation into Jamila's allegations against the mayor, and the allegation against Jamila for spying on computers. The investigation is ongoing."

"Let me guess, the investigation will remain ongoing as long as the mayor renews your mandate?" Eric asks.

"That depends," Charmaine replies. "I think we can all agree the last thing this town needs is a scandal. Especially one that would destroy the confidence the townspeople have in their local government and their local police force."

She makes a good point. If the office of the mayor and the office of the police chief implode under the weight of this scandal, the big-boxers could use it to their advantage and possibly gain enough support to get one of their supporters elected.

"You know how to make this go away, right?" I ask.

"Enlighten me," Charmaine crosses her arms in front of her chest.

"Solve Dr. Armistead's murder," I reply. "That's all anyone cares about. The break-in at his office, his patient list appearing online, and the spyware on my computer are only being investigated because they could be connected to his murder."

Charmaine takes a deep breath and uncrosses her arms. "We know who killed him, but we can't prove it."

"We?" I ask.

"Emory and I."

"Who did it?"

"The girlfriend," Charmaine replies.

"Karen?" I ask.

Charmaine nods. "Karen." She lets out an audible sigh. "We invited him for dinner on Friday to warn him." Charmaine closes her eyes and rubs her forehead with her hand like she has a headache. "I can't say anymore. It would compromise my husband."

I shrug. "It's up to you." I refuse to beg her. She came to me, after all. I start to get up.

"Karen is a patient of Emory's," she explains.

I sit down again. "I know," I say.

Charmaine looks at me shocked. "How do you know?"

"People I know who work at his office have seen her coming and going from appointments for months."

"Well, Emory didn't know she was Mac's—er, Dr. Armistead's girlfriend until recently. He only knew Karen was in a relationship with someone who was breaking their professional code of ethics by dating her. He wouldn't have kept her on as a patient if he knew it was Mac."

"OK." I shrug at her justification of her husband's actions, or inaction, depending on your perspective.

"Karen wanted Dr. Armistead to go public with their relationship. Recently, she gave him an ultimatum. They go public, or she'll end their relationship. He chose to end it. Karen didn't take it well. As she came more unravelled, she said things in her sessions with Emory that made him realize her boyfriend was Dr. Armistead. She also said things that convinced Emory that Dr. Armistead was in danger."

"Then Emory should have reported it," Eric interjects. "Therapists are mandated to report if they believe their patient is a threat to themselves or others."

"Emory said the threats weren't specific enough to report, and when he probed Karen further about the threats, she retracted them."

"So, he broke Karen's confidentiality and told Dr. Armistead about the threats?" I ask, skeptical.

"Emory believed he could get the point across without actually breaking the rules," Charmaine explains.

"Hypothetically?" I ask.

"Exactly," Charmaine replies, obviously relieved she doesn't have to explain further.

I was married to a lawyer. Adam and I used to speak hypothetically when he wanted to talk about a case, or vent about a client, without breaching attorney-client privilege. He'd use hypothetical clients and hypothetical scenarios, and in return I'd ask hypothetical questions and provide hypothetical support and suggestions.

"Did Dr. Armistead pick up on the hypothetical references?" I ask.

"We couldn't tell."

"Why did you invite Jamila to dinner?"

"To be a witness," Charmaine replies. "If Emory was accused of breaking patient confidentiality, Jamila would be able to confirm that Emory never referred to Karen or anyone else by name."

I'm dubious. Her explanation doesn't sit right with me. It's too convenient.

"How and when did Karen give Dr. Armistead the caffeine?" I ask.

"That's the missing piece. It's the one thing we can't figure out, and why I was hoping to find out from Jamila what you saw that night."

I shrug one shoulder. "I didn't see anything. It was dark. I was drinking. Is that all you want from me?"

"I'm hoping to convince you not to talk to the police about your conversation with Jamila today."

There it is. Of everything Charmaine said, this is the one thing I'm certain is true.

"You're too late," I respond.

The realization she told me all this for nothing hits Charmaine immediately, and the look on her face is priceless.

She must be desperate. Eric is a cop for goodness' sake. An honest one. Even if I agree to keep quiet, there's no way he would. Unless she thought we could convince him together. Peer pressure.

"Then I should tell you that before she called me, Jamila panicked and erased the video footage of your visit to the store today," Charmaine says. "She plans to tell her lawyer and the police that you were never there. It will be your word against hers."

Even without sound, the footage wouldn't have looked good for Jamila, her panic attack and hyperventilating could be incriminating.

"I think you mean it will be Jamila's word against *ours*," I clarify.

The colour drains from Charmaine's face and her jaw drops. "Who else was there?"

"Adam." I don't mention that he left before Jamila said anything self-incriminating.

"She didn't mention that." Charmaine looks stunned.

"I'm sorry I couldn't be more help." I stand up and push my chair in. We're done here. "I have an appointment with your husband tomorrow. I decided to take your advice and see if he could help me with my boundary issues. Given the circumstances, perhaps I should cancel it."

"On the contrary," Charmaine says, while in one fluid motion, she grabs her phone from the table, slips her purse onto her shoulder, and stands up. "I think it would be good for you two to talk."

And without another word, Charmaine Solomon strides to the door, unlocks it, and leaves.

For a while, neither Eric nor I say a word. Silently and separately, we putter around the store, tidying shelves and doing odd jobs while we process everything Charmaine said. Every so often we look at each other with an expression of shock and disbelief, and occasionally, one of us will open our mouth, then close it, and shake our head without saying anything.

"I feel like such an idiot." Eric finally breaks the silence. "How did I not see she's a corrupt, dirty cop?"

"She has everyone fooled," I assure him. "And I'm sure she wasn't always like this."

"You have an appointment with Emory tomorrow? Since when?"

"Since yesterday," I explain. "Jess and I are going together. Under the guise of blending our families and respecting each other's boundaries, or some such thing. It's not a real therapy session, it's an excuse to talk to him about Dr. Armistead."

"Are you still going?" he asks.

I can tell he'd prefer I don't.

"I think so. I want to talk to him. I'll only go if Jess goes. I won't go alone." I'm not sure how to ask my next question, other than carefully. "Do you believe what Charmaine said about Karen?"

"About her being a threat to Armistead?" he asks.

I nod. "Do you think Karen could kill someone?"

"No," he replies without hesitation, shaking his head. "I'm not Karen's biggest fan, but she's not capable of murder. The Karen I know holds a grudge. If she killed him, she wouldn't be able to punish him anymore, and punishing the target of her grudge is how she works through her anger. I believe she'd give him an ultimatum, though. She loves ultimatums."

I'd like to talk to Karen again, but she's already lied to me.

I don't know who to believe.

CHAPTER 20

"Sophie actually growled?" April asks through the speakers in my car. "I've never heard her growl. Ever."

"I know, right?" I agree. "Sophie's a lover, not a growler. Aren't you, Soph?"

I glance at the corgi next to me on the passenger seat. She looks at me briefly, then turns her attention back to watching the world pass by the car window.

April tells me her brother and his family are coming to stay with her parents, and she's coming home to Harmony Lake. She hopes to leave tomorrow.

"Good!" I say. "I miss you! And it means your dad's recovery is going well."

"I've been here a whole week. I'm ready to come home. I miss you guys, and I need a break from hearing about the stupid eaves troughs!"

"Didn't you get them fixed?" I ask, pulling into the parking lot behind Knitorious.

There's an unfamiliar car in the corner of the parking lot. Who would be here this early?

"I did," April replies. "Now he's obsessed with climbing up there and looking for himself. He says he wants to make sure 'they did a proper job and didn't cut any corners'," she says, mimicking her father's voice. "My brother's kids have a drone. They're bringing it with them to take pictures of the eaves troughs and shut him up."

"You're a patient daughter," I commend her.

The driver's side door of the unfamiliar car opens, and Karen Porter steps out.

"Uh-oh," I sigh.

"What is it?"

"Karen's here. She's waiting for me in the parking lot, and now she's walking toward me."

"What does she want now?" April asks rhetorically.

"I'm about to find out. I have to go. I'll call you back."

"Call me as soon as she leaves so I know you're OK," April says.

We end our call, and I step out of the car, then help Sophie to the ground.

"Hi, Karen," I say when she gets within a few feet of my car.

"Hi, Megan." She bends down. "Hi, Sophie."

Sophie trots over with her bum wagging, and Karen

rubs her. Sophie's enthusiastic approach to Karen is a stark contrast to yesterday when she didn't go near Charmaine.

"Are you looking for me?" I give Sophie's leash a gentle tug, and she trots back to me.

"Yes," Karen replies, standing up. "I would've phoned or texted first, but I don't have your number."

And you're not getting it.

If Karen really wanted to call first, she could look up the store number, send an email through the store website, or ask Jess to reach out to me.

"What can I do for you?" I ask, ignoring her comment about my phone number.

"Jess mentioned that you have a history of getting to the bottom of things. She says you've even helped solve a few murders."

"OK." I shrug, neither confirming nor denying anything.

"She said if I know anything about Mac's death, or his life, that I haven't been completely forthcoming about, I should tell you. She said you might be able to help figure out who killed him."

"Are there things you haven't been forthcoming about, Karen?" I ask.

"Yes," she says quietly. "But I'm scared. Scared what I know might give people the wrong impression of Mac and scared I could get in trouble for not speaking up sooner. I hoped the police would find a smoking gun—

metaphorically—and I'd be able to keep Mac's secrets to myself."

"Sophie and I are going for our morning walk. Would you like to join us?"

Karen nods, letting out an audible sigh of relief.

Just in case Charmaine is right about Karen being a killer, I keep our interaction as public as possible. A walk in the park by the lake is public enough for someone to hear me scream, but private enough for us to talk, as long as we keep an eye on our surroundings for nosy neighbours.

"The Solomons claim you killed Dr. Armistead," I say bluntly.

Karen stops walking and looks me in the eye. "I didn't."

"Why would they suspect you?"

"Because I was his partner," she surmises. "You know how cops think. They always suspect the victim's spouse or partner. The police ruled out Mac's ex-wives, so I guess I'm the next logical candidate."

She's right. The police always start with the people closest to the victim. To be fair, statistically the murderer is usually the spouse or someone closest to the victim.

"Why did you lie to me about how long you've known Emory?" I ask.

"How do you know I was lying?"

"Harmony Lake is a small town, Karen. I know

everyone who works at his office. You've been visiting Emory regularly for months."

"You're right," she fesses up. "I've been his patient for almost six months. When I started going to Emory, I didn't know that he and Mac knew each other. But I was careful, just in case. I never used Mac's name. I talked about our relationship and my frustration with keeping it secret, but I never used names."

"Then how did Emory figure out Dr. Armistead was your boyfriend?"

Karen shrugs and shakes her head. "He must've used context clues. I was careful to never use Mac's name, but over the course of my sessions, it's possible I disclosed enough other non-identifying information for him to figure it out."

A gang of determined speed walkers marches toward us, and we stop talking. Karen looks pensive as we step off the path to make way for them.

"I'm so stupid," she says after the walkers have passed, and we're back on the path. "I didn't realize it at the time, but I did give him information. I mentioned that Mac was married four times. I mentioned I work in the same medical centre as my boyfriend and that we both work in Harmony Hills." She looks at me with wide, wet eyes. "I told Emory everything he needed to figure out who I was dating."

"Emory didn't confront you when he realized you and Dr. Armistead were dating?" I ask.

"No, and now that I think about it, he mined me for information."

"That's awful," I say. "Not to mention unprofessional."

"There's more," Karen says quietly.

"I'm listening."

"You know the break-in at his office? The one on Eric's birthday?" she asks.

She has a knack for bringing Eric's name into conversations that have nothing to do with him.

"I remember," I reply.

"That wasn't the first time Mac's office was broken into," Karen discloses. "He usually brought his lunch from home and ate at his desk, but on Mondays he ran errands. You know, the bank, the dry cleaner, stuff like that. Well, two Mondays before the break-in, he came back from his usual errands and was convinced someone had been in his office while he was out. He was sure of it."

"Why did he think that?"

"Because the door was unlocked. He insisted he locked it and checked it before he left. He stayed at the office late that night looking through every drawer, looking for whatever could've been stolen. Nothing was missing. I didn't think anyone had been in there. I told him if it was a robbery, they would've at least taken his laptop. I assumed he was mistaken about locking the door."

"But you no longer think he was mistaken," I clarify.

Karen nods. "About a week later, Mac found spyware on his computer. He was sure whoever broke into his office that day installed it."

This revelation makes me stop dead in my tracks.

"Did he check the security footage from the lobby?"

"He tried," Karen replies, "but the property manager wouldn't show him the footage unless he had a police report for the break in."

Darby can access that footage. I need to see that footage.

"Did he uninstall the spyware?" I ask.

"He disabled it," she claims. "He wasn't super techy, but he was techy enough to do that. He said he wanted to keep it in case it was evidence."

"But Darby said there was no spyware on Dr. Armistead's computer." I'm so confused.

"There wasn't," Karen concurs. "Not on the computer in his office. The computer with the spyware is in the trunk of my car. I brought it with me today. After Mac found the spyware, he brought the infected laptop to my house and took his home laptop to the office instead. Both laptops look almost identical."

This makes sense.

"So, if the first break-in was to install spyware on Dr. Armistead's computer, was the second break-in to remove it?" I think aloud.

"Mac thought they were looking for a paper file," Karen replies.

"What paper file?" I ask.

"Mine and Eric's."

I look at her confused. "I don't understand."

"This is the part that makes Mac look bad," she admits. "When we started dating, Mac deleted mine and Eric's patient file from his computer and his backups. He wasn't supposed to do that."

"So, if anyone accused him of dating a former patient, there would be no patient record to prove it," I theorize.

"Right," Karen confirms. "The notes from our sessions are gone, but for whatever reason, our names still appeared on his patient list. I realized this when Mac's patient list was posted online."

I can see why Karen is worried about Dr. Armistead's reputation. He was shady. He dated at least one former patient, tried to bribe a police officer, and erased patient records. And these are just the things I know about.

"The hackers found you on the patient list, but couldn't find any notes with dates that would prove *when* you and Eric were Dr. Armistead's patients."

"Exactly." She sounds excited and relieved that I'm following along. "Mac thinks they were looking for a paper file when they broke in the second time. But there isn't one. He hasn't kept paper files for patients for years."

"Wow." I sit my shocked self on the next park bench we encounter. "Karen, as long as you have that computer—the one with the spyware—you're in danger. You need to give it to Darby."

"I know." She sits down next to me. "That's why I brought it today. But if I'm charged with obstructing justice, or whatever, I could lose my licence to practice as a chiropractor."

All these professional licences and professional codes of conduct really complicate things.

"Solving the murder is Darby's biggest priority. If you're telling the truth, I'm sure we can convince him to overlook you hanging onto the laptop."

"I am telling the truth, Megan."

"I want to believe you, Karen. But you've lied to me before, and everyone's version of the truth is different. It's hard to know who to trust. But the laptop will help prove your version of events," I tell her.

Karen inhales deeply, then lets it out. "OK."

Before she can change her mind, I pull out my phone and text Darby. I tell him it's urgent, and we have evidence. He replies immediately that he's on his way to Knitorious. I tell him to meet us in the parking lot and keep an eye on Karen's car. Then I text Eric to warn him his ex-wife is here. He thanks me for the warning and asks me to text him when the coast is clear.

On the walk back to the store, I ask Karen if Dr. Armistead had any theories about who broke into his office and who put the spyware on his computer.

"The lady who did his tech support. Her name starts with J."

"Jamila?" I ask, hoping I'm not leading the witness.

"That's it!" She points at me. "Her last name is Richards or something. Same as one of the Rolling Stones."

"Jagger?" I suggest, filling in the blank for her.

"Yes. Jamila Jagger."

"Why did he suspect her?" I ask.

"She saw us at the movies together a month ago," Karen explains. "Mac and I were waiting in line at the concession stand. We were hugging and kissing while we waited our turn. When we turned around with our popcorn, Jamila was in line behind us."

"Are you sure it was her?"

"That's how Mac introduced me to her. They were friendly and spoke for a minute. It was disappointing because we went to a theatre in the city so we wouldn't be seen by anyone we know, yet there she was."

I stop walking and open my phone. I find Jamila's Facebook page and Karen confirms Jamila is the woman they saw at the movies. We start walking again.

"Why did Mac go to the Solomon's house for dinner the night he died?" I ask.

"Apparently, the Solomons might be moving away from Harmony Lake," Karen replies. "Charmaine's contract is almost over, and she isn't sure if she wants to renew. Emory approached Mac and asked him if he wanted to purchase Emory's practice. The Solomons invited him for dinner to talk about it."

I don't bother telling Karen the truth about Charmaine possibly not having a choice about whether to stay on as chief of police in Harmony Lake.

"Did Dr. Armistead know Jamila would be there?" I ask.

"Jamila was there?"

I nod. "Yes, she was."

"If he knew she would be there, he would've told me," she insists.

We're about to cross Water Street, and I can see Darby standing in the driveway that leads to the parking lot. This is my last chance to ask Karen anything. As she's about to step off the curb, I grab her arm.

"Karen, did you give Dr. Armistead an ultimatum? Did you threaten to end the relationship if he didn't make it public?"

Karen looks at me, then at her feet. She looks up at me again and nods. "I didn't mean it. I said it out of frustration." Her eyes fill with tears. "He was so stressed and anxious after we saw Jamila at the movie theatre. I mean, we were always careful, but after we ran into her, he wanted to be even more careful. Do you know how hard it is to have a relationship and pretend you hardly know each other?"

I shake my head. "It must be awful," I sympathize.

"It is," she nods. "To answer your question, yes. I

gave him an ultimatum, but I regretted it immediately and took it back. I was committed to making our relationship work. We were planning to travel to Europe together next year. For at least part of the year, we would be a normal couple and not have to worry about Mac losing his job because he loved me."

We cross the street and Sophie speeds up, straining the leash when she sees her long-lost friend, Darby, waiting for her.

CHAPTER 21

"IT MAKES SENSE, RIGHT?" I ask April, as I flip the CLOSED sign to OPEN and unlock the door.

"Let me get this straight," she says through my AirPods. "Jamila saw Dr. Armistead and Karen at the movies and was so determined to prove their relationship was illicit, she hacked into his computer and accessed his patient files. Have I got it right, so far?"

"Yes," I say as I tidy shelves of yarn.

"But how would Jamila know it was a secret relationship? And how would she know Karen was a past patient?" April asks.

"Good questions," I reply. "I don't know the answers, but I have a theory. Jamila did tech support for both Emory and Dr. Armistead. I think it's possible that when Dr. Armistead introduced Karen and Jamila at the movie theatre, Jamila recognized Karen's name. For all we know, she snooped through patient files when she was on their computers. Also, Jamila might have picked up on the tension when Dr. Armistead and Karen realized they'd been seen by someone who knows one of them."

"OK," April cedes. "That makes sense, but *why* would Jamila want to expose them? Their relationship has nothing to do with her. Why would she go to so much trouble and take on so much risk to prove Dr. Armistead was dating a patient he shouldn't be dating?"

"Money," I reply. "Jamila told me she's struggling to compete with Electric Avenue and the other big-box retailers out there. She's terrified they'll run her out of business."

"So, you think she was going to blackmail him?"

"Precisely," I reply, retrieving the duster from the back room and dusting the shelves in the bulky yarn area. "But Dr. Armistead found out she hacked his computer and had proof. She broke into his office last week to find the proof and destroy it. But he hid the laptop with Karen. Maybe he threatened to expose Jamila, and she killed him."

Just like he exposed Eric for looking him up on the police database.

"If you're right, Jamila's dinner invitation on Friday night was very convenient. Too convenient," April points out.

"It was," I agree. "I wonder if Charmaine or Emory mentioned the dinner in front of her, and Jamila invited herself or dropped hints that she'd like to attend?"

"Jamila's not a pushy person, that doesn't sound like something she would do," April responds.

"Neither does cyber-spying or erasing security camera footage and denying I was at her store," I remind her.

"Touché," April concedes. "Did you tell Darby your theory?"

"The short version," I say. "He was in a hurry to get the laptop to the cyber-crimes division. He drove Karen and the laptop to the Harmony Lake Police Station and said we'll talk when he drives Karen to pick up her car after she gives a statement."

April updates me on the logistics for her return trip to Harmony Lake. She's leaving tomorrow as soon as her mother gets home from the grocery store. On her way, she'll pick up Hannah and Rachel in Toronto and bring them home for Thanksgiving weekend.

"Thank you for picking up the girls!" I'm so happy I don't have to make the nine-hour round trip tomorrow. "Adam and I will take care of driving them back on Monday so you can stay home and enjoy the day off with T."

While April and I talk about the latest episodes of our favourite shows, I put the duster away and take out my knitting. I'm determined to make some progress on the sleeves of my new sweater. I was hoping to wear it to Thanksgiving dinner on Sunday, but I'm not sure I'll be able to finish it by then.

As I knit mindlessly and chat with my best friend, I look out the front window. A familiar, powder-blue PT Cruiser drives down Water Street. Connie. She drives the only powder blue PT Cruiser in town.

Connie!

Oh my god, that's it! I have to phone Darby.

"April, I have to go. I found a hole in someone's alibi. I'll call you later."

I text Darby, telling him it's an emergency. Again. This is the second emergency text I've sent him today, and it's still morning. I send a follow-up text, reminding him to bring his iPad.

"ARE YOU SURE ABOUT THE TIMING?" Eric asks when I tell him how seeing Connie drive past the store this morning, and Phillip walking on the sidewalk with Kevin yesterday, jogged my memory about the security footage Darby showed me.

"Well done, babe!" He grins proudly. "Maybe we should switch roles. I'll run Knitorious, and you find the bad guys."

Impressing a professional investigator makes me proud and a little smug at the same time.

"The charity knitters would love that," I respond, not joking.

Just as I finish telling him about my early morning conversation with Karen, and my theory on how and why Jamila killed Dr. Armistead, Darby walks into the store.

"You're here!" I say, eager to show him what I figured out before I have to leave to meet Jess at Dr. Solomon's office at noon.

"You beckoned me, Megan, and here I am," Darby teases. "I have a couple of things to mention."

I try not to let his serious tone kill my positive vibe.

Darby bends over to greet his favourite corgi and speaks as he rubs her. "Ms. Jagger denies your version of events yesterday. She says you did not go to Bits'n'Bytes, and she provided video footage of the store at the time in question. It's almost an hour of an empty store."

"Charmaine told us Jamila erased the footage," I tell him coolly. "Adam can verify most of my version of events."

"*Charmaine* told you?"

"Oh right, we haven't told you about that. Charmaine was here yesterday. Can we bring you up to date later? I have an appointment at noon, and I want to show you this before I leave."

Darby tells me he's waiting for the property manager at the medical centre to call him back about the security footage from the first suspected break-in at Dr. Armistead's office; the one Karen told me about this morning. The one Dr. Armistead suspected was when Jamila installed the spyware on his computer.

I think I might know how to get the footage without waiting for the property manager to call back, but I don't mention it to Darby because I don't want to give him a chance to tell me not to do it.

Darby unlocks his iPad and opens the video footage from Jamila's store. The footage that disputes the medical centre footage showing her—well, someone who looks exactly like her—arriving at and leaving the medical centre during the same time frame.

He hands me the device, and I place it on the harvest table where we can all see it. I tap the screen and the video starts. Jamila is sitting in her store working on her sticker-covered laptop.

Excitedly, I bounce on the balls of my feet waiting for the first thing I remember to appear on the screen. This must be how Sophie feels when she's so excited she tippy taps her little paws.

I tap the screen.

"There!" I yell in the same voice I'd use to yell, "Bingo!" if I'd just won the jackpot, and if I played bingo,

"That man on the sidewalk is my neighbour, Phillip Wilde." I look at Darby. "You remember Phillip, right?" Phillip and Darby met in the summer when Phillip was a witness to my "car accident" as we call it.

"I remember Mr. Wilde," Darby agrees. "That looks like him and his little dog, Keith."

"Kevin," Eric and I correct him in stereo.

"Sorry. Kevin," Darby acknowledges, looking at me blankly.

"If this footage was filmed on Monday September twenty-eighth, at lunchtime, Phillip can't be there," I insist.

"Why not?"

"Because Noah is off on Mondays, and Phillip and Kevin are alone in the store. Phillip brings his lunch from home on Mondays. He only leaves the store to take Kevin outside for quick washroom breaks. Phillip would *never* wander this far down Water Street on a Monday."

"Maybe last Monday was different," Darby suggests.

I shrug. "You should ask Phillip, but I doubt it."

Fine, if he doesn't like my Phillip-evidence, I'll show him the next one. When he sees all three, he'll have to be convinced. I tap the screen again and the video resumes.

I hover my finger over the screen when I sense the next thing is about to happen.

"Connie!" I shout, tapping the screen.

"Connie?" Darby asks.

"Connie," I confirm. "In the powder-blue PT Cruiser." I point to the car on the screen. "There's *no way* Connie drove past Bits'n'Bytes on Monday September twenty-eighth at lunchtime." I shake my head. "It's not possible."

"Because?" Darby asks.

"Because that was the day Archie had hip replacement surgery. Connie was at the hospital in Harmony Hills. All Day. The next time she drove on Water Street was Thursday of that week. Thursday was October first." I point to the paused image of Jamila on the screen. "Look how focussed Jamila is on her computer. She was probably doing her month end or quarter end books, because this was probably filmed on the first, not the twenty-eighth."

"What else have you got?"

Why isn't he impressed? I tap the screen and wait. Again.

"That's me!" I tap the screen, and point to my black, crossover SUV. "That's my car. I wasn't there on Monday the twenty-eighth."

"Are you sure?" Darby asks.

"Positive," I reply, nodding. "The twenty-eighth was Eric's birthday. We planned to go out for lunch, but Charmaine had a dental emergency and Eric had to stay at work. We changed our lunch plans to dinner plans, and I went to the hospital to visit Archie and Connie. Connie and I had lunch together at the hospital cafeteria." I raise my index finger and signal for Darby to wait.

I retrieve my wallet from under the counter and pull out the pile of crumpled receipts I habitually stuff in the part of the wallet where paper money used to go when paper money was a thing. One by one, I smooth out each receipt, and a surprise ten-dollar bill, until I find one of the receipts I'm looking for. "My parking receipt from the hospital. Note the date and times." I hand him the receipt and continue uncrumpling. "And the receipt for lunch in the hospital cafeteria." I press the paper against the table with my palm to make it as readable as possible. "I paid for both meals." I hand it to him. "The hospital should have video footage of Connie and I coming and going from the hospital parking lot."

Finally, Darby cracks a small smile. "Thank goodness you're a receipt hoarder, Megan." His smile grows into a wide grin.

"Is this enough to prove Jamila wasn't at her store doing paperwork when Dr. Armistead's office was broken into?" I ask, hopeful that it is.

Eyes wide, Darby nods. "Definitely."

It also proves Jamila is good at altering video footage. So good, she was able to fool the cyber-crimes people.

Jamila is full of surprises: picking locks, altering security video, what other secret talents does she have?

CHAPTER 22

Jᴇss ɪs ᴡᴀɪᴛɪɴɢ outside when I arrive, and we go in together.

"Hi, Lin," we say simultaneously.

We exchange pleasantries with Lin and discuss our Thanksgiving dinner plan this weekend. Lin is part of my extended, non-traditional, modern family. Her partner is Ryan, Archie's son.

We remind Lin we're here to see Emory, not Adam, and she hands Jess and I each a clipboard with a pen tethered to it.

"Fill these out," Lin instructs. "When you're finished, bring back the clipboards and pens but keep the forms. You'll give them to Dr. Solomon."

Jess and I sit side by side on the leather sofa in the seating area and fill in our New Patient Information forms.

"I don't know how much information I want this guy to have," Jess mutters without looking up from her form.

"I know," I agree. "I think I'll put the information he already knows or is easily searchable and leave everything else."

I release the form from the clipboard and offer to take Jess's clipboard and pen back to Lin. She hands me her clipboard, and I hand her my completed form to hold until I get back.

"You didn't write penicillin in the allergies section," Jess chides.

I'm allergic to penicillin and all the other "cillins." My allergy first showed itself when I was fifteen years old and had strep throat. Our family doctor prescribed penicillin, and I ended up in the emergency room with anaphylactic shock.

The doctor told my parents anaphylactic shock is extreme for a first reaction, and they told him it was because I was an overachiever. I survived, obviously, and I should wear a medic alert bracelet, but never do.

"Why does a psychotherapist need to know I'm allergic to penicillin?"

"In case something happens while you're here and you need medical attention. He would notify the first responders or whoever treats you," Jess lectures. "It can't hurt to include it. I'll write it in for you."

Despite my inner voice telling me it's not a good

idea, I let Jess take one of the tethered pens and add my penicillin allergy to the form.

"I can't believe you remembered my penicillin allergy," I say, impressed. I can't even remember what I had for dinner last night.

Jess shrugs. "I've been cleaning your teeth every six months for seventeen years. I check your patient information before each visit in case anything has changed. It's burned into my brain now. Like the pit that could turn into a cavity that we're keeping an eye on in your forty-seven."

In response to my blank stare, Jess explains that forty-seven is one of my molars, and it has a pit that attracts bacteria and could become a cavity.

"Fascinating," I respond, not fascinated.

"Did Karen get in touch with you?" Jess asks when I return from Lin's desk. "She knows more than she lets on. She won't talk to the police, so I suggested she talk to you. I hope you don't mind."

"She was at the store this morning," I reply.

In hushed tones, I tell Jess about the evidence Karen had in the trunk of her car and the highlights of our conversation.

"Did Darby get the security footage from the first suspected break in?" Jess whispers.

"He's waiting to hear from the property manager," I explain. "Karen said Dr. Armistead tried to look at it, but the property manager wouldn't show it to him without a police report."

"Leave it with me." Jess winks. "I know the property manager. Our daughters are best friends. I might have some pull." She counts silently on her fingers. "Two weeks before the twenty-eighth was the fourteenth, right? Is Karen sure about the date?"

This is exactly what I was hoping to hear. I planned to ask Jess if she could get her hands—or eyes—on that footage, but she beat me to it by offering.

"She says it was definitely Monday because Dr. Armistead always ran errands at lunchtime on Mondays."

Humans are creatures of habit. We find comfort in the familiarity of routine. It's scary how easy it is for a someone with evil intentions to use our innate inclination toward the familiar against us.

"Good afternoon, ladies."

Emory's voice shocks us out of our huddle.

"Hi, Emory." I extend my hand and he shakes it.

His hand isn't big, but it's meaty. His grip is warm and confident.

"Nice to see you again, Megan." He moves his extended hand toward Jess. "Ms. Kline." He smiles.

"Please call me Jess." She flashes a wide smile and shakes Emory's hand.

We follow Emory up the curved staircase and down the hall. His office is across the hall from Adam's. We're brought to a halt briefly in front of Adam's open door while we wait for Emory to open his door. Jess and I smile and wave at Adam, who looks up at us with a series of micro expressions ranging from shock, to confusion, then dread. Emory gestures for us to enter his office ahead of him.

"Make yourselves comfortable," he instructs.

We sit next to each other in the middle of the simple beige sofa. He sits across from us in a wing chair, and we sit in silence while he peruses our New Patient Information Forms.

"What brings you here today?" he finally asks, smiling over his glasses, then nudging them with his index finger.

"Well…"

"We're hoping…"

Jess and I speak at the same time.

"You first," I say to Jess.

"No, you," she insists in response.

"Actually, it was your wife's idea," I tell him. "She said you know a lot about boundary issues."

"What she said." Jess laughs and jerks her head toward me.

Jess and I take turns explaining our unconventional and slightly complicated relationship situation to Emory. How we know each other, and how we each know everyone else in our modern family.

"We're trying to blend our families, be friends with each other, and respect everyone else's relationships," Jess summarizes.

"I'm tempted to draw a chart," Emory remarks.

"A chart *would* save time," I admit, "and give you something to refer to."

"And it's not just personal relationships," Jess adds. "We have a slew of professional relationships to deal with too." She shrugs. "Sometimes we find out things about each other we shouldn't know or would rather not know."

"Exactly," I agree, taking the baton from Jess. "For example, Jess and I recently learned someone we know uses information they learned in a professional capacity to their advantage."

I'm making this up as I go along. The only person Jess and I suspect may have done this is Emory, when he found out about Karen's relationship with Dr. Armistead.

"And we can't agree on the best way to deal with it," Jess adds, reclaiming the baton. "As a professional myself"—she clutches her hand to her chest—"*I* think there should be zero tolerance for trusted professionals ignoring their professional codes of conduct and acting in their own self-interest."

Jess assumes the role of bad cop in our make-believe scenario.

"And *I* think just because someone does something that appears unethical doesn't mean it's not justified. I think we should give our...friend the benefit of the doubt and ask them why they did what they did," I argue, trying to convince Emory that I'm sympathetic.

I'm worried our conversation sounds rehearsed, but I swear we're improvising.

"How do we resolve this?" Jess asks, dramatically throwing her hands in the air. "What would you do, Dr. Solomon? If you were, say, stuck between a patient and a professional colleague, for example? Would you break the patient's confidentiality and tell your colleague, or would you honour your duty to your patient and not let your colleague know you have personal information about them?"

We both look at Emory, smiling and waiting to hear his position on our hypothetical ethical dilemma.

"I'd need more information before I could answer," he replies. "It would depend on what profession we're talking about and the nature of the situation ..."

A ringing phone interrupts his response.

"I'm sorry," Jess says looking at her phone. She looks at me. "It's the insurance company. About the accident. I have to take this. Do you mind?"

"Of course not." I wave her toward the door. "Good luck."

Jess leaves the office without closing the door, intentionally I'm sure. Emory stands up and closes the door.

Alone with Emory, I remind myself Jess is right outside and will hear me if I need to be heard. Assuming I can make noise. I look at the throw cushions that line the sofa on either side of me. If he smothers me with a pillow, I won't be able to scream.

Stop it, Megan! No one is going to smother me or strangle me with their meaty hands. Focus, Megan.

In an effort to distract myself and pass the time as pleasantly as possible until Jess returns, I explain about Jess's son having his first fender bender.

"Let's cut to the chase, Megan. Why are you really here? What do you want to ask me?"

CHAPTER 23

I TILT MY HEAD, feigning ignorance. "What do you mean?" I shake my head. "I'm not sure I understand."

"Charmaine visited you yesterday," Emory says. "You know Karen is my patient, and she was Dr. Armistead's girlfriend."

"Why didn't you stop seeing her as a patient? Or report him?" I ask.

"As Charmaine told you, I didn't make the connection until recently that Karen and Dr. Armistead were a couple. By the time I realized, she was struggling with his decision to end the relationship and was making veiled threats toward him. I tried to warn him." He nudges his glasses for what feels like the millionth time.

You know that torture technique where the torturers let one drop of water drip onto the victim's forehead at random intervals until the victim is driven to insanity waiting for the next drip? That's what it's like waiting for Emory Solomon's next eyeglass-nudge.

"Charmaine said you tried to warn him subtly. Why didn't you warn him directly?"

Emory sighs. "I didn't want Mac to think I was threatening him."

"I don't follow."

"If I told him I knew he was having an inappropriate relationship with a former patient, he could easily have interpreted it as me threatening to report him. Even if I never did report him, he'd always know I had this information about him and could use it against him. It would have made our personal and professional relationship awkward. Karen told me he ended the relationship. I believe her. If I didn't believe he had ended it, I would have reported him." He nudges the bridge of his glasses again.

"Did you make the realization yourself, or did Jamila Jagger tell you about Karen and Dr. Armistead's relationship?"

"How would Jamila know?" He nudges the bridge of his glasses and squints at me.

I tell him about Jamila's chance encounter with Karen and Dr. Armistead at the movies. "When she met Karen, she may have recognized her name from the patient files of either you or Dr. Armistead."

"Jamila? Interesting…" He rubs his chin with his fingers. "Why would she kill him if she caught him doing something wrong? Wouldn't it be the other way around? Wouldn't Dr. Armistead kill Jamila to stop her from exposing him?"

I give the highlights of my theory that Jamila hacked into Dr. Armistead's computer and he found out. Emory follows along, intrigued. You'd think after listening to other people's drama all day, every day, he'd be indifferent to the ins and outs of Dr. Armistead's life, but he's enthralled.

"That makes sense," Emory utters under his breath, his gaze fixed on the wall behind the sofa.

"What makes sense?" I ask.

"Hmmm?" He comes out of his trance, looks at me, and nudges his glasses.

"You said, 'that makes sense.' What did you mean?" I ask again.

"Jamila was anxious during our dinner on Friday. She had trouble sitting still. I assumed it was social anxiety. She insisted on helping in the kitchen. You know, plating the food, carrying it to the dining room, that type of thing. I *assumed* she was trying to keep busy and be helpful."

"So, you're saying Jamila had the opportunity to put caffeine in Dr. Armistead's food and drink," I state for clarification.

"Quite possibly," he says reaching for his phone. "I'm texting Charmaine to ask if she noticed the same thing." His thumbs move quickly across the keyboard on his phone. He sends the text then looks at me and nudges his glasses. *I'm* tempted to text Charmaine and ask her how she copes with Emory's incessant eyeglass-nudging. "But this would mean it wasn't Karen," he says, shaking his head. "I was sure it was Karen."

"Sorry about that," Jess says, re-entering the room. "Is everyone OK?" She looks at me, and I smile and wink.

"It's all good. I think our time is up," I say, standing up and hoisting my bag over my shoulder.

We thank each other and say our goodbyes, then Emory holds the door for Jess and me as we leave.

"Megan..." He touches my elbow as I step into the hall.

I tell Jess I'll catch up. She steps into Adam's office to wait for me, loitering near the open door.

I turn to Emory and smile. "Yes?"

He moves in uncomfortably close. "Is the computer still in Karen's trunk? It needs to be surrendered to the police," he whispers, nudging his glasses.

"It was," I assure him quietly as I shift my weight to put a bit more space between us. "Darby Morris took Karen and the computer to the Harmony Lake Police Station."

"You mean Harmony Hills," Emory corrects me. "Harmony Hills is handling the investigation."

"No, I mean Harmony Lake," I insist. "Darby said someone from HHPD would pick it up. He said taking it to HLPD was the most immediate way to secure it while he questioned Karen."

"That's a relief." Emory purses his lips into a tight

smile. "Thank goodness it found its way into the right hands."

IT SMELLS WEIRD IN HERE. What is that smell? It's making my stomach roil.

"Hi, everyone." I smile and put the tray of coffee cups on the counter, then bend down to greet Sophie.

I try not to drink coffee after lunch, but today requires extra caffeine.

I stand up and reach for my coffee. The charity knitters–who never visited Knitorious on a Thursday until Eric started working here–aren't knitting. They're frozen in place with their knitting on their laps, and their needles paused mid-stitch. The tableau reminds me of the statue game we played when we were kids and would freeze and see who could hold their pose the longest. They look at me intently, like they're waiting for me to do a trick or something.

"Do I have something on my face?" I ask, thankfully distracted from the mysterious stench. I run my hand across my mouth and chin, checking for food. "Is everything OK?" I pause. They look at me, then each other. "What's going on?" I demand.

"She doesn't know," Mrs. Roblin says.

Does she mean me? She must mean me.

"What don't I know?" I ask, bracing myself for whatever it is I don't know.

Eric strolls out of the back room. We all look at him.

"Did you get my text?" he asks when he sees me.

I shake my head. "My hands were full." I nudge his coffee toward him. "And my phone is buried in my purse."

"She hasn't heard." Mrs. Vogel brings Eric up to speed.

"Charmaine was arrested in connection with the break-in at Armistead's office," Eric says calmly.

But it was Jamila. I showed Darby the proof.

I can't help but give a small gasp. "Charmaine Solomon?" I'm so stymied that I have trouble formulating a response. "It wasn't…" I shake my head as though it will make me less confused. "Who told you?"

"I heard it from Darby," he replies. "I'm not sure how everyone else found out." He gestures vaguely at the charity knitters who have now resumed knitting. Their eyes might be firmly fixed on their needles, but their ears are focussed on what Eric and I are saying.

"It's all over town," a charity knitter pipes up over the out-of-sync clicking of knitting needles.

"The texts started about twenty minutes ago," adds another one.

I reach into my bag, pull out my phone and, ignoring the slew of missed messages, check the time. Twenty minutes ago, I was in line at Latte Da waiting to order. Before that, Jess and I talked at our cars for about ten minutes after we left Emory's office. And before that, we spent about ten minutes chatting with Adam in his office.

It must have happened after Jess and I left Dr. Solomon's office. Surely, if he'd received a call or message while we were there that his wife had been arrested, he would've been too shocked to continue our session.

I take a deep breath and raise my coffee to my lips when the unpleasant stink once again assaults my nose. "Is that...cabbage?" I ask, my nostrils twitching as I try to place the odour.

"Cabbage rolls," Eric replies, nodding. "Would you like some?"

I don't like cabbage rolls. The smell is making me nauseous. I shake my head. "No, thank you."

"Mrs. Willows made them," Mrs. Roblin informs me. "There's plenty." Ah, of course, cabbage rolls are today's food offering to Eric from his fan club.

"They smell wonderful," I lie. I'm sure to someone who appreciates a good cabbage roll, Mrs. Willows's rolls smell tempting, but no cabbage roll will ever smell pleasant to me. "I ate." Another lie. "But thank you." I smile. "I have a few emails I have to respond to. I'll be in the back if anyone needs me." I shove my purse under the counter, grab the laptop, my coffee and phone, then hightail it to the back room.

The emails are a ruse. There's nothing in my inbox that requires my immediate attention. The truth is, I'm eager to prop open the back door and air out the store. I hold the door open and kick the brick in front of it to keep it open. I'm worried the cabbage-roll smell might cling to the yarn. I'm sure I'm not the only knitter who would never buy yarn that smells like over-cooked cabbage.

"Darby says Charmaine confessed," Eric explains, closing the door that separates the back room and the store. "Apparently someone caught her in the evidence locker, looking for the laptop Karen gave to Darby."

Why would Charmaine suddenly confess? So far, she has cooperated minimally with the investigation into Dr. Armistead's murder. What would cause her to go from barely cooperative to making a confession?

"Did she get the laptop?" I ask, opening the door to the store, then leading Eric to the open back door. We step outside and stand in the parking lot, careful to stay within sight of the backroom in case any curious charity knitters suddenly appear. "I don't want to close the door to the store, because I'm trying to dissipate that smell."

"Sorry about that," Eric replies. "It would be rude not to eat one. I heated it up in the microwave."

"Do you like cabbage rolls?" I've never seen him eat one, and I don't think I could stomach going home to this smell in the house.

"Meh," he says, wrinkling his nose. "They're not my favourite." He shakes his head. "Anyway, no, Charmaine didn't get her hands on the laptop. Forensics already picked it up."

"That's a relief," I say. "But it couldn't have been Charmaine who broke into Dr. Armistead's office. Could it?" Briefly, I doubt myself. "I proved it was Jamila. You saw the proof. Darby saw the proof. Jamila doctored her store's security footage, so she'd have an alibi. And she's on the footage at the medical centre at the time the break-in occurred. It doesn't make sense."

"They could be working together," Eric suggests. "If they are, the race is on for one of them to turn against the other in exchange for a deal. The truth will come out. We have to wait and let Darby do his thing."

I nod. "Trying to get to the laptop was a desperate move and isn't Charmaine's style," I theorize. "Charmaine is strategic. Every move she makes is carefully planned. It's hard to believe she'd spontaneously confess to a crime."

Something isn't right about Charmaine's confession. She gave it up too easily. If she had gotten her hands on the laptop, it would have been obvious it was her. There are cameras, locks, and procedures to keep evidence safe from prying intruders. But if she managed to erase whatever she doesn't want the police to find on that laptop, she would have been charged with evidence tampering or some such thing instead of computer hacking, stalking, or even murder. Charmaine might have decided that getting caught tampering with evidence is the lesser of two evils.

"Charmaine was at the medical centre the day of the break-in. You saw her on the security footage. She had the opportunity to break into Armistead's office," Eric reminds me.

"You think she faked a cracked tooth? As an excuse for being at the medical centre at the same time as the break in?" I ask. "Jess told me herself that Charmaine had an emergency procedure to fix it."

Eric shrugs. "Maybe she had time to get her tooth fixed *and* turn over Armistead's office. The police will figure out the timing."

I make a mental note to text Jess and ask her exactly what time Charmaine showed up with her cracked tooth, and exactly what time she left with her fixed tooth.

"This is my fault," I confess. "I told Emory about Karen having Armistead's laptop at her house. He asked me if she gave it to the police, and I told him Darby took it to HLPD until HHPD could pick it up." I look at my feet, hanging my head in shame. "I shouldn't have told him that. Emory must've told Charmaine where it was."

"If that's the case," Eric takes my hand and tilts my chin up with his index finger, forcing me to look at him, "you helped solve it. If Charmaine didn't know the laptop was there, she wouldn't have been caught trying to get to it, and she wouldn't have confessed. She confessed to breaking into Armistead's office, she didn't confess to murdering him. His killer could still be out there." He tucks a stray curl behind my ear.

I disagree. I know the two crimes are related. The knot in my stomach insists they are.

"My gut tells me otherwise," I say.

"Are you sure it's instinct and not the smell of cabbage rolls you feel in your stomach?"

"I'm positive."

CHAPTER 24

I inhale deeply, sniffing for any trace of cabbage roll. I think it's gone. I hope it's gone. I came in early to check the odour situation at the store and air it out again if necessary.

"What do you think, Soph? Can you smell anything?" I ask as I detach her leash. "Let's leave this open just in case." I use my foot to slide the brick up against the back door, forcing it to stay open.

"Good morning, gorgeous," I say to April, answering my phone as I put Sophie's full water bowl on the floor.

"So, how's the smell?" she asks.

"It's either gone, or I'm immune to it. I propped open the back door to air out the store, just in case."

A chill from the breeze coming through the open door sends a small shiver up my spine. I gather my pumpkin-coloured, hand-knit cardigan around my neck as thunder rumbles in the distance. It's supposed to rain today, and there's a foreboding thickness in the air.

April is tending to her dad and packing while her mum runs errands. When her mum returns home, April will leave to pick up our girls. While April and I talk about the weather and how it might impact her drive to Toronto, then to Harmony Lake, I put in my AirPods and get busy processing the online orders that have come in since the last time I shipped online orders.

"I can't believe Charmaine would do something like that," April says after I tell her about Charmaine's arrest and her shocking confession.

"That's what I said," I agree. "But why confess to something she didn't do? And why else would she try to tamper with the evidence?"

"I don't know," April replies. "But her connection to Dr. Armistead must be deeper than we think."

"How do you mean?" I ask. "Aieeee!" I scream, pulling away from the hand gently touching my back. "You scared the life out of me." I put my hand on my chest.

"Megnificent! Are you OK, what's going on?"

"Sorry, April. I didn't mean to scream in your ear. Eric snuck up behind me and almost gave me a heart attack." I swat playfully at his arm with the skein of yarn I'm holding. "April, I'm going to put you on hold for a sec."

"Sorry, I didn't mean to scare you," Eric apologizes,

trying unsuccessfully not to laugh. He hands me a coffee and nods at the skein of yarn I just smacked him with. "Is that your weapon of choice? It's not very lethal."

"It would be if the intruder has a wool allergy," I reply, defending my pathetic choice of weaponry.

"If someone with a wool allergy is stupid enough to break into a yarn store, they deserve what they get," he chuckles.

"Why are you here?" I ask. "You said you weren't coming in until this afternoon."

"To get your keys. I'm taking your car for an oil change and tune up, remember? I wanted to get it done before you left for Toronto. Here, take my keys in case you need them." He hands me his keys.

"That's thoughtful of you," I say, digging my keys out from the bottom of my purse. "But I'm not going to Toronto, anymore," I remind him. "April is picking up the girls on her way home."

Eric shrugs. "I know, but it's booked. I may as well go."

"I'm back," I say to April, taking our call off hold after Eric leaves.

"He loves you," April informs me when I tell her Eric booked my car for service before my road trip today. "Some people say, I love you, and some people take your car for an oil change, vacuum your dryer vents, and cover your air conditioner."

"Eric does all of the above," I respond. "Mostly out

of love, but partly to keep his mind off this murder case that happened on his turf, but he's not allowed to investigate."

The first sip of coffee burns my tongue. I move the cup to the far corner of the counter and place it in time-out so it can think about what it's done and cool down enough not to scald me.

"What were we talking about?" she asks.

"Charmaine's surprise confession, I think?"

"Right!" April declares. "We were trying to figure out why Charmaine Solomon would want to hack into Dr. Armistead's computer."

"Whatever the reason," I respond, "could it be serious enough for her to want to kill him?"

I glance at the window just as Eric drives by in my car.

"Charmaine isn't a murderer!" April insists.

"And I didn't think she was a blackmailer, but she is," I counter.

We bounce ideas back and forth and come up with a few weak but possible reasons to explain why Charmaine might try to access Dr. Armistead's computer. None of them are supported by evidence, and none are a strong motive for murder.

"Maybe Darby is right," I admit, "and the spyware on both my computer and Dr. Armistead's have nothing to do with his murder."

"*Alleged* spyware," April reminds me. "Right now, all we have is Karen's word that Dr. Armistead found spyware on his laptop. The police haven't confirmed it yet."

"You're right," I admit. "We can't eliminate Karen as a suspect yet. If Emory is telling the truth about Dr. Armistead ending the relationship, she has the strongest motive of all."

"And she knew about Dr. Armistead's allergy and where he would be the night he died," April adds. "You know who else is a good suspect?"

"Who?" I ask.

"Emory Solomon," April replies. "He had access to whatever Dr. Armistead ate and drank that night, and he knew Dr. Armistead was having an illicit relationship. Maybe Emory killed him for making the profession look bad."

"You don't think that's far-fetched?" I ask.

"Not to a crazy person," she justifies.

"Emory is so soft-spoken and non-threatening, though," I remark. "Dr. Armistead told Karen they were having dinner to discuss Dr. Armistead possibly purchasing Emory's practice. Why would you kill someone who you hope to sell something to?"

Cautiously, I attempt another sip of coffee. Ouch! Still too hot! What the heck? Coffee from Latte Da is never this hot. Must be a new barista, or a new machine, or something.

"The dangerous ones are always non-threatening," April tells me. "It's a ruse. They use it to their advantage. Lulled into a false sense of safety, the victim lowers their defenses, and boom! The culprit strikes!"

"If we were placing bets, I'd put my money on Jamila," I say. "She knew about Karen and Dr. Armistead, she has a history of digitally stalking people, I've seen her pick a lock with my own eyes, and she deleted Adam and me from her store's security footage, then insisted we weren't there."

"I think you're right," April agrees. "Jamila makes the most sense, but Charmaine must be involved somehow, or she wouldn't have tried to compromise evidence and admitted to breaking into Dr. Armistead's office."

My phone dings and I pull it out of my pocket.

Jess: Good morning! I looked at our office security footage and the footage of the main entrance for the twenty-eighth. Charmaine came straight to our office upon entering the building and exited the building immediately after leaving our office. There's no way she had time to break into Dr. Armistead's office and destroy it.

"She's still typing," I tell April after I read her the text message from Jess.

"If Jess is right, Charmaine couldn't have broken into his office. We're back to Jamila," April points out.

Jess: But her husband left our office right after Charmaine got in the dental chair. He didn't come back until she was done. In fact, after her procedure, she sat in our waiting room for a few minutes until he came back to get her.

"Oh. My. God."

"What is it, Megastar? What did she say?"

I read the text to April.

"Emory?" I ask in disbelief. "Why? What motive would Emory Solomon have for murdering Dr. Armistead?"

April says something, but it doesn't register in my brain because I'm in shock. In shock over the realization that Emory Solomon is the break-and-enter bandit and possible murderer.

I watch anxiously as three dots bounce on the screen, indicating Jess is typing another text.

"DID YOU HEAR ME?" April shouts. "You need to contact Darby. *Now*. He needs to know *now*."

"I hear you," I respond blankly. "She's still typing. I'm waiting in case there's more?"

"More?"

"More evidence."

"Megabear, screenshot those texts and send them to me. Just in case."

"Good idea."

I do as I'm told and send the screenshots to April.

"Got them," she confirms.

Jess: I'm with the property manager. We're looking at the footage from the 14th. I only recognize one person. They enter the building after Dr. Armistead leaves, and they leave the building shortly before he comes back.

Me: Who is it?

Jess: Hang on.

"Who is it?" April asks when I read her Jess's texts.

Suddenly, or finally, because every second feels like an hour while we wait for Jess to reveal the name, a photo pops up in my text conversation with Jess. A grainy, still image from the security footage in the medical centre lobby. I click the photo and enlarge it.

"Emory!"

No way!

I'm overcome with a sudden urge to close and lock the back door.

"Are you sure?" April asks. "Send me those texts, just in case."

I send the texts and photo to April, then indulge in a brief moment of panic.

"I was in his office yesterday, April!"

"I know. Listen, you need to text Darby. Right now."

"I will. Just let me close the back door and lock it. I feel too vulnerable with it open." I slip my phone into the pocket of my cardigan and walk toward the back of the store. "What if Charmaine's arrest made him more unstable, and he's out there all…murdery…and looking for revenge?"

Halfway between the counter and the backroom, the back door closes with its distinct click. Eric! He must have forgotten something.

Briefly, a wave of relief washes over me.

Very briefly.

Sophie starts barking.

It's not Eric. She doesn't bark at Eric. She rarely makes a noise when he shows up, except for the occasional high-pitched yelp-whine.

This isn't the friendly, excited bark that she uses for other friendly visitors either.

Each bark is punctuated with a snarl. This is a warning bark. Low growls between each snarly bark warn the intruder that Sophie means business. Her upper lip is curled back, and she's baring her small but powerful teeth. I've only seen her do this once before; earlier this week when Charmaine was here.

"Eric?" I call out, hoping Sophie is wrong.

But Sophie is never wrong.

"Not Eric."

I stop abruptly in the doorway between the store and the back room.

"You," I say, taking a backwards step away from the back room.

Away from danger.

CHAPTER 25

"Are you expecting someone else, Megan?"

"Yes. Eric will be back any second." I summon my most convincing voice.

"I don't think so." Emory Solomon smirks and shakes his head. "Two old ladies knitting at Latte Da said Eric won't be here until this afternoon."

Each backwards step I take away from Emory, he takes an equal step toward me. I need to position myself with something between us. We already passed the harvest table, so the counter is my next best option.

"Megster! Is that Emory?" April asks through my AirPods.

"Yes," I say to April and Emory. "He's not working until this afternoon, but he'll be back any minute. He lives upstairs."

"I'll take my chances," Emory says, not sounding at all concerned about being interrupted by a muscle-bound, six-foot-plus cop who does hand-to-hand combat training as a hobby.

Evidently, Dr. Emory Solomon has lost his mind.

"Clear your throat if you're in danger," April says to me, before she yells to her father, demanding to know where his cell phone is.

"Ahem... hem... hmph." I bring my hand to my throat to make it look real for Emory. I also fuss with my hair and ensure my curls are covering my AirPods. If I'm going to die here and now, April will hear everything and can tell my story. I hope she heard me clearing my throat over Sophie's loud barking.

"Frog in your throat?" Emory asks, using his forefinger to nudge the bridge of his glasses closer to his face. "No worries. I have something that will clear that up."

He pulls a syringe from the pocket of his tweed sports jacket.

I hate needles and the sight of this one, in a psychotic murderer's hand, makes me shudder.

"Is that caffeine? Did you have some left over after you murdered Dr. Armistead?" I ask. "I hate to disappoint you, but I'm not allergic to caffeine. Between my coffee and chocolate habits, I probably have a much higher caffeine tolerance than most people."

Emory shakes his head. "It's not caffeine." He nudges the bridge of his glasses and smirks. "It's Benzylpenicillin."

OK, that would kill me.

Benzylpenicillin, also known as penicillin G, is the liquid form of penicillin. The form used in injections.

I knew I shouldn't have included my penicillin allergy on my New Patient Information form yesterday!

"Where did you get a vial of penicillin?" I don't care where he got it; it's a stall tactic. I need to keep him talking while I come up with a plan to get Sophie and me out of here alive.

"He has penicillin?" April whispers through the phone. "How does he know about your allergy?"

"I have my ways." He winks. It's the creepiest, most unsettling wink ever.

I glance behind me. Almost at the counter now.

"Why do you want to kill me? Wasn't killing Dr. Armistead enough?"

"Because this is all your fault," Emory hisses. "I won't allow Charmaine to take the fall for me, and if I have to go down, I'm taking you with me."

The cap is still on the syringe, a good sign. A sign that he isn't planning to kill me right away.

Can I make it to the front door, unlock it, and get out before Emory catches me? Risky. Especially in these peep-toe ankle boots. Stupid heels! What was I thinking, putting form before function?!

I could run through the display window. I'd be scratched up and bloody, but it would attract the attention of everyone around. Would I be able to burst through the window? Or does that only happen in movies and on TV? If it doesn't work, he'll jab me with the needle, and I'll probably be dead before anyone can get in here to save me. I don't want to die in the display window. I don't want to die period. Also, if I die, Emory gets what he wants. That can't happen. I won't let him win.

"It's my fault you killed Dr. Armistead?" I ask.

"No, it's your fault the case is still open, and it's your fault Charmaine was arrested and charged," Emory replies. "Armistead's murder should've been an open-and-shut case. I planned it so the evidence would point to Karen. And if by chance the police eliminated Karen, I made sure there was enough evidence to frame Jamila. But you inserted yourself into the investigation and wouldn't let it go. Now my wife's reputation is ruined, and her career is over. Because of you."

"To be fair," I say calmly with my hands in front of my chest, palms facing out, "I wouldn't have gotten involved if your wife didn't order Jamila to spy on me."

The counter is between us now.

Sophie is at my feet. When we stop walking, she stops barking. She sits at attention, intermittently curling her upper lip and emitting a low-key growl, just loud and frequent enough to remind us of her unwavering diligence. Her gaze is laser-focussed on Emory. He seems oblivious to her presence.

"I'm still here, Megapop. I'm listening and recording everything I hear. I'm calling Darby on my dad's phone. Help is coming. Whatever happens, don't hang up. I love you!"

I love you too, April.

"I understand why you're angry at me, but why did you kill Dr. Armistead? What did he do to you?" Please keep talking and leave the cap on that syringe.

"Because I'm tired of working hard, playing by the rules, and barely earning a living wage. Do you know how hard it is to watch someone—who's a bad therapist, by the way—have their patients handed to them while they break all the rules and sit back getting rich?"

"Not really," I admit quietly. "I get that Dr. Armistead broke rules when he dated a former patient. And I know he's done at least one other shady thing in the past."

Emory laughs and tosses his head back. "See?" he asks when he lowers his chin again. "That's exactly what I mean. He did whatever he wanted and got away with it. Where was karma to teach him a lesson?"

Not sure whether this is a rhetorical question, I shrug and shake my head trying to appear sympathetic. "What do you mean when you say his patients were handed to him? Did he inherit his practice or something?"

Emory puts the syringe of penicillin on the counter and places his hand on top of it. He's a little less agitated than he was a few moments ago. I need him to let his guard down a little more so I can make a run for it.

"Let me answer your question with a question,

Megan." He nudges his glasses with his finger again. He really should get them tightened.

Focus, Megan. "OK," I say.

"If Armistead weren't dead, would you and Jess have come to me or him for your appointment yesterday?"

"Um…" I don't know how to answer this. If Armistead were alive, Jess and I wouldn't have gone to either of them.

"Just tell him you hadn't thought about it," April whispers in my ear.

"To be honest, we hadn't thought about it," I reply. "I mean you were the only option so…"

"Exactly!" Emory slaps his hand on top of the syringe, keeping it securely under his palm. "I work in Harmony Lake. The residents of Harmony Lake should be *my patients*. They should come to *me* for their counselling and psychotherapy needs. Am I right??" His eyes are bulging, and he's nodding enthusiastically. "But they have this small-town paranoia that everyone is watching them and talking about them, so instead of coming to me, they go to Harmony Hills where they can see a therapist more discreetly."

"I see. That must be frustrating." By showing him some sympathy, I'm hoping he'll be less eager to kill me.

"He's completely lost it, Megan. Please be careful." This must be serious if April is calling me Megan instead of a punny nickname.

"He used to gloat about it. He'd tease me about my small-town practice and how much time I must have to pursue other interests," Emory explains. "Do you know how many referrals I've received from Dr. Armistead? Ever?"

"I have no idea."

"Guess."

"I don't know," I shrug, mentally grasping for a reasonable number.

"Just GUESS!" He slams his fist on the counter.

"TWENTY?" I shout while at the same time, April shouts, "Fifteen" in my ear.

"None. Zero. Zilch. Nada." Emory touches the tip of his thumb to the tip of his fingers, making a zero.

"Wow. That's…."

"Awful?" He finishes my sentence. "Unprofessional?" He finishes it again. "Sel-fish?" He prolongs each syllable.

"It certainly sounds unfair and frustrating," I sympathize. "So, were Dr. Armistead's patients supposed to transfer to you after he died? Was that the plan?"

"Partly," Emory admits, nudging the bridge of his glasses. "But mostly, I had to kill him because if I didn't, he would've gotten me in trouble, and he would've gotten away with it. There's no way I was going to allow him to ruin my life and walk away unscathed."

When Emory nudges the bridge of his glasses yet again, I notice how thick the lenses are. I bet he can't see a thing without them. He'd probably be defenseless and unable to chase me. Focus, Megan. Keep him talking.

"What did he threaten you with?" I ask. "I believe you, by the way. I know for a fact that a few years ago, Dr. Armistead tried to bribe a cop, and when the cop refused, he filed a complaint and got the cop in trouble. I know he was capable of doing bad things and hurting people." I want to convince Emory we're on the same side.

Emory takes a deep breath and lets it out. "When I found out he was dating Karen, I knew it could be his downfall. I became determined to prove it. This would be the thing he couldn't weasel out of. I recruited Jamila to help me. She owed my wife a favour, you see."

"Charmaine and Jamila both told me how Charmaine used her influence to prevent Jamila from being charged when she was caught hacking computers for the mayor."

"Because that's the kind of person my wife is. She's selfless and forgiving." Emory annunciates each word clearly and emphatically.

I would have said opportunistic and corrupt, but I'm not about to argue with someone who's clenching a vial of something that would kill me, so I nod and summon my most sympathetic and understanding smile.

"What did you recruit Jamila to do for you?"

Once again, he nudges the bridge of his glasses. If I had an eyeglass repair kit handy, I'd offer to tighten them for him just so I wouldn't have to watch him constantly nudge them anymore.

"She gave me the password to Mac's computer. She knows it because she's done tech support work for him."

"She didn't install spyware on his laptop?" I ask suspiciously.

"No," he replies. "That was me. But it was no use. He deleted Karen's patient file from his database. The only proof I found that she was ever his patient was an old patient list. Not enough to prove that he was breaking the rules. He would have slithered out of an accusation."

The patient list Emory just mentioned must be the same one that was posted online.

"But Dr. Armistead found the spyware and knew it was you," I say as though I already know it's true and not just a theory. "Did he threaten to expose you?"

Emory nods. "I didn't know he'd found the spyware. He didn't let on that he knew it was there or that he suspected I did it. I only intended to leave it on his computer long enough to get the evidence I needed to prove he deserved to lose his license. But the evidence wasn't there so…"

"You went back to his office on the twenty-eighth to delete the spyware, or steal the computer, or something, but it was too late. Dr. Armistead switched computers. The computer you tampered with was gone. Angry and frustrated, you destroyed his office," I say, finishing his thought. "Who taught you how to pick a lock?"

"Charmaine," he replies. "Years ago. It's a handy skill to have."

Apparently, it's also a common one. I'm starting to feel like the only person in Harmony Lake who doesn't know how to pick a lock.

"We have to learn how to pick locks," April whispers as if she's in my head.

"But Jamila was at the medical centre on the twenty-eighth. Why was she there if you were acting alone?"

"My wife was having a dental procedure. If the dental office called because Charmaine had some kind of emergency, I would have to go. Jamila was there to finish the job if I couldn't."

Very conscientious.

"Why was Dr. Armistead at your house for dinner last Friday?" I ask. "You obviously didn't like each other. Why did you invite him over?"

"That's when all of this went wrong," Emory explains, and yet again nudges his glasses. "I told him Charmaine and I might be moving away from Harmony Lake, and I invited him to dinner under the guise of discussing referring my patients to him. I planned to confront Armistead with my evidence about his relationship with Karen. In exchange for not reporting him to our regulating body, I wanted him to take his practice elsewhere and refer his clients to me when he left town."

"I take it he didn't agree," I probe.

He shakes his head. "On the contrary. He showed me his proof that I hacked into his computer and compromised his patient files. He wanted money—money we don't have—or he said he would report me. My career would be over, and I would face criminal charges. I had to stop him."

"And you just happened to have lots of caffeine lying around?"

"It's easily obtainable online. I didn't want to use it, but was prepared to use it. He left me with no choice."

There it is. His confession.

"You're doing great, Megalicious. I'm recording everything." April's reassuring voice in my ear gives me comfort and makes me less afraid.

"I put it in his pudding and his after-dinner scotch," Emory continues. "Immediately after dinner, I dispatched Jamila to save us a table at the pub, and Armistead and I had our little disagreement. I showed him my evidence, and he showed me his. He left quickly and…You know the rest." He waves toward me in a sweeping motion, then nudges the bridge of his glasses with his index finger.

Emory says he didn't want to use the caffeine but was prepared to if necessary. However, he fed it to Dr. Armistead *before* they had their after-dinner confrontation. He knew exactly what he was doing. This was premeditated murder, not a spontaneous crime of opportunity.

"Why did you post Dr. Armistead's patient list?" I ask.

"I had Jamila do that. It was intended to distract you." He nudges his glasses again. "It didn't work. When Charmaine and I ran into you at Tiffany's on Monday, she mentioned you seemed to be sleuthing and asking a lot of questions. I hoped the list would give you something else to focus on."

If I made a drinking game where I take a sip of wine every time Emory nudges his glasses, my liver would fail, and I would die.

"It almost worked," I tell him. "I was worried about more private information being posted if I kept asking questions, but I persevered. So, Charmaine doesn't know you killed Dr. Armistead?"

Emory shakes his head. "She's convinced it was Karen or possibly Jamila. I have her fooled. She'd never consider me a murderer. But she does know that I installed spyware on Armistead's computer."

"That's why she tried to find it in the evidence locker yesterday," I theorize. "And why she confessed. She was protecting you. She loves you."

"I love her too," he garbles almost intelligibly. Emory's eyes well up, and he lifts his hand off the syringe and pinches the bridge of his nose between his thumb and forefinger, lifting his glasses toward his forehead.

This is it. This is my opportunity to get away.

CHAPTER 26

WHILE MY RIGHT hand sweeps the syringe off the counter, my left hand reaches across the counter, tears the glasses from Emory's face, and tosses them toward the display window. The syringe slides along the floor and disappears under the shelves of discounted yarn.

Sophie jumps into action, adding to the chaos by barking and snapping at Emory's ankles.

Taking advantage of his semi-blind confusion, I try to run around the counter and past him. He reaches out and grabs the sleeve of my sweater. Before he can get a better grip, I wriggle my arm out of the sleeve, then rip the other sleeve from my other arm, and let the cardigan fall to the floor.

I grab the coffee from the time-out corner of the countertop and throw it at his head.

Instinctively, Emory raises both hands to his coffee-soaked face.

"Run, Soph!" I yell, running toward the back door.

Her snarling and growling get fainter as I get closer to the back door.

I stop and turn. With the hem of a pant leg in her mouth, Sophie tugs it repeatedly and growls. She's preventing Emory from getting up. She's stopping him from coming after me.

"Come on, Soph! Let's go! Sophie!"

"Run, Megan. Get out. Sophie will be fine," April shouts in my ear.

No. I can't do it. I can't leave Sophie behind.

I tune out April's voice encouraging me to run. I look around, searching desperately for inspiration.

The brick we use to prop open the back door is on the floor just inside the door.

I run into the back room and lunge toward the brick.

It's heavier than it looks, but brick in hand, I run back to the counter.

Sophie still has Emory's pant leg clenched between her teeth. Snarling, she tugs and shakes her head vigorously while dodging his attempts to kick her away with his other foot.

If he hurts Sophie, so help me, a life sentence will be the least of his problems.

Clawing at the floor with both hands, he tries to slide his body away from the determined corgi while also frantically groping the floor in front of him, presumably in search of his glasses or the syringe of penicillin.

I run around the counter to Sophie, being careful not to get within arm's reach of Emory.

"Sophie, come!" Focussed on keeping the intruder down, she ignores me. "Soph! Let's go!" I reach down, place my hand under her belly, and slide her backwards toward me. "It's OK! Let's go!" She yanks her head away from him, tearing off a swatch of pant leg. She lets me pick her up as she releases the swatch of fabric from between her teeth.

Holding Sophie under my left arm like a football—she's also heavier than she looks—I clutch the brick in my right hand and run to the other side of the counter.

Almost on his feet, Emory lurches toward us. I leap back and avoid his reach. Sophie snarls and snaps threateningly.

He's mostly on his feet, albeit unsteadily. He's disoriented. Probably because he can't see without his glasses, or because the corgi attack combined with the unfamiliar surroundings have made him discombobulated, or all of the above. Nevertheless, Emory perseveres. He reaches for the counter to steady himself and is able to stand up all the way.

"Overhand or underhand? What's the best way to throw a brick?"

"Overhand! I don't know. Just throw it!" April instructs.

I hurl the brick toward him.

Because the brick is heavy and I am weak, it barely hits him. But it hits him nonetheless, awkwardly on the shoulder, with just enough impact to knock him off balance. He slips on my discarded sweater and the coffee covered floor, allowing Sophie and I to get away from him while he recovers.

"Great! I just gave him a brick. He has a brick!"

"Just run, Megan!" April cheers.

At the back door, I fiddle with the locks. It takes me longer than usual with only one available hand, but I manage to turn the first lock, then the second.

Sophie's barking elevates in volume and urgency, causing me to turn around.

Dragging my coffee-soaked cardigan behind him with the foot that Sophie attacked, Emory is in the doorway between the store and the back room. His left arm hangs limply at his side, and he squints hard as he flails his good arm in front of him with the brick gripped tightly in his hand.

Still looking behind me in case Emory lobs the brick at us, I throw the back door open and run.

I make it two steps when I run into a wall of… person?

Without taking his eyes off Emory, Eric puts one hand on each of my arms, lifts Sophie and I off the ground, moves us out of his way, and runs inside.

When he places us on the ground, I lose my balance on the uneven asphalt in these impractical heels. I stumble backward, struggling to stay upright and not drop Sophie. I stagger backwards into the corner of the door frame and come to a stop when it digs into my upper back. At least I didn't fall and injure Sophie and I in the process.

"Ouch!" I blurt.

Distracted by my outcry, Eric turns and looks at me with his left fist clenching the lapel of Emory's tweed sport jacket. Emory raises the brick above him; he's about to smash it into Eric's head.

"Eric! Brick!" I shout, pointing behind him with my free hand.

"Eric, turn around!" Connie is beside me. Where did she come from?

Eric releases Emory's lapel, raises his hand, and grabs the brick, blocking Emory's attempt to smash Eric in the head.

Despite having only two fully functional limbs and impaired eyesight, Emory doesn't let go of the brick and struggles to regain control of it from Eric.

Eric makes a fist with his right hand and delivers an upper cut to Emory's jaw. The thud of fist against bone is followed by a grunt from Emory, who immediately drops to his knees and releases his grip on the brick. His head hangs low, with his chin almost resting on his chest.

Eric lowers the brick to his hip, then tosses it aside.

Connie wraps her arm protectively around me, digging her fingers into my shoulder and pulling me close to her. I wince slightly because my back hurts where it hit the door frame.

Still on his knees, Emory raises his head and looks

up at Eric. His jaw bulges where Eric punched him. His misaligned jaw, limp arm, and damaged leg are all on the same side, making him look more like a stroke victim than a freakishly determined, maniacal killer. He wriggles. I think he's trying to get up. Emory's determination is resolute. I wish I was as committed to anything as Emory is to not staying down.

When he sees the door, Emory lunges his upper body toward Connie, Sophie, and me. Instinctively, Connie and I cringe and lean away from him. Instinctively, Sophie barks and growls while making doggy paddle movements with her front paws as if she's trying to swim toward our attacker. Sophie and I have very different instincts when it comes to how we react to danger.

Eric once again grabs Emory by the lapel and restrains him. Eric makes a fist with his right hand while lifting Emory up slowly by his lapel. Eric pulls back his fist. Oh my god, he's going to punch Emory again!

"Eric, No! Enough!" I yell.

"Finish him off, Eric!" Connie shouts beside me, pumping a fist in solidarity with Eric.

Connie and I have very different instincts when it comes to how we react to violence.

Darby Morris sweeps past us so quickly the breeze he leaves in his wake moves my hair.

He grabs Eric's fist and positions himself between Eric and Emory.

Eric lets go of Emory's lapel and steps back. Emory collapses forward.

A flurry of blue police uniforms descends on the store and the parking lot. Too many voices speaking at the same time, the clomping of boots on pavement, and the idling engines of patrol cars drown out the thumping of my racing heart.

"Finish him off?" I ask, looking at Connie. "Really?"

"Yes. That horrible man deserves everything he got and more!" Connie insists.

With Darby on Emory-duty, Eric turns away from them. The white-hot anger emanating from him is palpable. He looks agitated. His brow is furrowed. His jaw is clenched. His fists are clenched. Everything is clenched.

I follow Eric's gaze as he takes in the scene around him. We make eye contact, and he narrows his eyes and moves aggressively toward us. Reflexively, Connie and I recoil in unison. Eric puts his hands up in front of him like he's surrendering.

"It's OK. It's over," Eric says.

Poof! His anger is gone.

Sophie makes that high-pitched yelp-whine she only makes for him. I can feel her tail wagging under my arm. I shift my weight and switch Sophie to my other arm because the one I've been holding her with is cramping. Eric holds his hands out to take her from me, and Sophie practically leaps into his arms. I shake out my arms and stretch my neck. Connie brushes my hair away from my face and tucks it behind my ear, her hand grazing my AirPod.

I forgot about April!

"April! April? I lost her." I pat my hips and butt area, searching for my phone, then remember where I put it. "My phone is in the pocket of my cardigan." I'm too far away and the AirPods lost the Bluetooth connection to my phone.

I'll miss my pumpkin-coloured cardigan. I've worn it every fall for the last five years.

"It's OK, my dear. We'll call her from my phone," Connie replies.

Since they're no use to me without my phone, I remove my AirPods and place them in Connie's waiting hand. She drops them in her purse and takes out her phone. "I'll call April and fill her in." Connie gives me a quick, tight shoulder-squeeze, and I try not to grimace when it hurts my back. She steps away from the commotion to talk to April.

"Is your back OK? I'm so sorry." Eric's eyes are full of worry and regret. "I can't believe I hurt you. I didn't mean to. I *would never*…"

I reach out and touch his forearm. "It's fine," I say, interrupting him before he can finish his sentence. "You didn't do it. I lost my balance and stumbled into the corner of the doorway." I point to my cute but non-functional ankle boots. "I wore the wrong footwear to outrun a killer."

"I'm so sorry," he starts to apologize again,

shaking his head. I wave away his comment. "We'll get the paramedics to check you over and look at your back."

"I think he needs the paramedics more than me." I point to Emory who is face down on the floor with his hands secured behind his back.

"Hi, Megan."

"Hi, Amy."

Amy is a police officer with the Harmony Lake Police Department. Seeing another friendly face, I'm suddenly overwhelmed. My throat is thick, and my eyes fill with tears. I take a minute to compose myself.

"Would you like to sit down?" Amy asks. "My patrol car is right here."

A few minutes alone to process what happened sounds like a good idea.

"Thank you, Amy, we'll wait upstairs. The apartment isn't part of the crime scene." Eric looks at me. "Is it?"

I shake my head.

"April is fine. I told her you'll call her as soon as you and your phone are reunited," Connie says, approaching us.

"Amy, do you think I'd be allowed to leave for a little while?" My question raises multiple objections from both Connie and Eric. "I want to take Sophie to the vet. She seems fine, but I'd like to have her examined, anyway. She put up quite a fight."

"Let me call the Animal Centre. I'm sure when they

find out it's for Sophie, they'll be more than happy to make a house call."

"Thank you, Amy. That would be great."

Amy winks and rubs Sophie's head before she walks to her patrol car.

The Animal Centre is Harmony Lake's all-in-one animal shelter, veterinary hospital, animal sanctuary, and wildlife education centre. Sophie's previous owner was the founder and executive director. Sophie has a special relationship with the staff and volunteers.

Eric cuts a path through the horde of police officers so we can make our way inside to the stairs. He positions himself between the stairs and Emory, so Emory and I can't see each other. Though I highly doubt Emory can see much of anything without his glasses.

Eric places Sophie on one of the steps, and she races up the stairs to the apartment. Connie follows her, and I follow Connie.

CHAPTER 27

AFTER CHECKING MY VITAL SIGNS, the paramedic examines my back. She says there's no visible mark or swelling. It's tender when she pokes around, but not as tender as it was earlier. Together, we decide it's a minor bruise or soft tissue damage, and I'll bounce back in a day or two.

A uniformed officer comes upstairs to tell us the vet is here. Eric offers to take Sophie downstairs instead of bringing the veterinarian upstairs to his crowded apartment. Connie insists she'll go in his place and calls for Sophie to follow her downstairs. The paramedics pack up their gear and leave shortly after.

"I need a coffee so bad," I say, pulling away from Eric's tight embrace. "Want one?"

He shakes his head. "I saw your first coffee all over the floor of the store. The store's a mess, Megan. It looks like ten people had a struggle, not two. Are you sure you weren't hurt?"

"I'm fine, honestly," I assure him as I put a pod in the coffee machine and close the lid.

"I'm sorry I wasn't here." His eyes and face are downcast. He's blaming himself.

"None of this is your fault," I remind him. "You couldn't have known a deranged psychotherapist would walk into my closed store determined to kill me. No one could've known. Trust me, if I thought it was even a tiny possibility, I would have worn different shoes and left my pumpkin-coloured cardigan at home."

"I think I might've killed him if he hurt you," he confesses, looking relieved to say it out loud.

I nod. "I was scared you were going to punch him again."

"I wasn't, I swear," he insists. "I wanted to scare him. To make him feel as scared as you felt when he trapped you."

"I think it worked," I confirm. "For all of us."

"I'm sorry." He sounds defeated. "I didn't mean to scare you or Connie. I would *never* hurt you. Or threaten you..."

"I know," I interrupt before he launches into a long list of all the things he'd never do. I retrieve the mug of coffee and hesitantly take a small sip. Once burnt, twice shy, as they say. The temperature is perfect, so I take a bigger sip and put the mug on the counter. "This is the first time I've ever seen you angry. It was a shock. I mean, I've seen you annoyed and frustrated, but not angry. Not like this."

It was also the first time I've ever witnessed a real-life punch. The only punches I've seen before today were in movies or TV shows. They're scarier in real life.

"I wasn't angry," Eric corrects me. "I was scared. He was a mess, and I was terrified you were in worse shape."

If that's what scared-Eric looks like, I don't think I want to see what angry-Eric looks like.

I take his hand, and he winces and sucks in his breath.

"The paramedics should've checked you over," I say, looking at his red, swollen knuckles. How could this hand that gently rubs Sophie and delicately tucks my hair behind my ear almost break a man's face? If I hadn't seen it with my own eyes, I wouldn't believe it.

"I'll be OK. Nothing is broken," he says. "Battle scars." He smiles and winks, then raises my hand and kisses it.

"Why did you come back, anyway?" I ask. "You weren't gone long enough for an oil change and tune up."

"Your car never made it into the service bay," Eric confirms. "One of the charity knitters phoned me just as I arrived at the dealership."

"Lucky they have your phone number," I respond.

"Yeah, how did they get it?"

"They have their ways," I reply.

"Anyway, she said two knitters saw Emory at Latte Da, and he was acting strangely. They mobilized their forces and kept eyes on him while he wandered around Water Street. They called me when they saw him loitering behind the store. I came back right away."

"Thank you for coming to my rescue," I say, standing on my tippy toes to give him a kiss. "Again."

"I didn't rescue you," Eric insists. "You saved yourself. I just restrained him until Darby arrived. I might have saved Emory, though. I'm not sure he would have survived another round with you and Sophie." He smirks, then adds sheepishly, "But if you insist on thanking me, I won't stop you."

"Do you hear that?" I ask, mid-kiss.

I hear it again and recognize Sophie's distinct scratch on the apartment door.

"She might be your fearless defender, but Sophie's timing sucks," Eric jokes on his way to let her in.

Darby follows Sophie into the apartment. They make themselves comfortable in an overstuffed leather chair.

After a few pleasantries and Darby declines our offer of a beverage, he leans forward and opens his leather folio on the coffee table.

"The vet said to assure you that Sophie is fine, and in light of her heroic actions, she should get extra treats today," he says, scratching under her chin. She loves it and raises her head to give him better access.

"That's a relief," I say with a sigh.

"I'm taking her to the butcher later so she can pick out her own steak," Eric adds.

Darby asks about my back and any other injuries I have, then uncaps his fountain pen, lays it on his folio, and looks at me.

"What the hell happened down there, Megan? The store looks like a war zone, and Dr. Solomon's injuries are severe enough that he had to go to the hospital for treatment."

I shake my head and shrug.

"Was anyone else there with you?" Darby asks.

"Nope," I reply. "Just me and Sophie."

She perks up and wags her tail when she hears her name.

Darby points from Sophie to me. "You two did that to him? By yourselves?"

"Though she be but little, she is fierce," Eric says, quoting Shakespeare.

Is he talking about me or Sophie?

"Let's start at the top and work our way down," Darby suggests.

The top of what? I nod.

"Dr. Solomon wears glasses. He can barely see without them. Where are his glasses?"

"Somewhere near the display window or cozy seating area," I reply.

"And they got there how?"

I explain about the glasses while Darby takes notes.

"Can you explain the burn marks on Dr. Solomon's face?"

"I think there's a new barista at Latte Da," I reply. "Or a new machine, or something."

"I don't follow, Megan."

I explain how my coffee burnt me not once, but twice and was relegated to the time-out corner.

"So, that's why there's coffee all over the floor," Darby says. "What happened to Dr. Solomon's jaw? It's dislocated and possibly broken."

Eric raises his hand. "That one is on me," he confesses. "Self-defense. Emory was about to brain me with a brick."

"The brick we found nearby?" Darby clarifies.

We nod.

"And how did Dr. Solomon's shoulder get dislocated?"

"His shoulder is dislocated?" I'm stunned. "I swear the brick didn't hit him that hard!"

Eric tries unsuccessfully to stifle a laugh.

"Maybe when he slipped on my sweater on the wet floor, he fell in such a way that his shoulder dislocated?" I theorize.

"Good," Darby responds, writing in his book. "That explains how Dr. Solomon got hold of the brick he threatened Eric with. Do you always keep a brick in your yarn store?"

"We use it to prop open the back door when we're bringing in deliveries or airing out the cabbage smell."

"Of course, you do," Darby remarks.

"Now, what can you tell me about Dr. Solomon's shredded pant leg?"

I point to Sophie. I was hoping to leave her out of this. Our jurisdiction has tough dog biting laws. I'm afraid the authorities will quarantine her, or even put her down for biting Emory.

"She won't be in trouble for biting, will she, Darby? She was defending herself and me. If it weren't for her, we wouldn't have escaped, and at least one of us—me—would be dead. You know she's a good dog, Darby. She's gentle. She's never hurt anyone before. Ever. If anyone gets in trouble, Emory should be charged for trying to kick her..."

Darby raises his hand in a stop motion, and I cease my rambling defense of Sophie's actions. "Sophie's not in trouble, and she's not going anywhere. Did she sprain his ankle too?"

"He has a sprained ankle? I have no idea how that happened unless he did it when he slipped on the wet floor." I shrug.

Darby reaches into his suit pocket and pulls out a small evidence bag containing a pill bottle.

"Did Dr. Solomon force you to take any of these? They were in the pocket of his sports jacket."

I shake my head.

"Did he force you to take anything else? Or did you witness him taking anything?"

I shake my head. "I've never seen those. What are they?"

"Sleeping pills. A lot of them."

"Maybe they were for another victim?" I suggest. "He planned to kill me with the syringe of penicillin."

"We didn't find a syringe of penicillin with Dr. Solomon," Darby interrupts loudly.

"Because it's under the shelves of discounted yarn," I tell him, then explain how it ended up there.

I wonder who the sleeping pills were for? Who else was on Emory Solomon's kill list?

CHAPTER 28

Button-up sweater, eight letters. Simple. C-A-R-D-I-G-A-N.

Speaking of cardigans, I finished my new sweater in time to wear it to Thanksgiving dinner, after all.

Last Friday, I wasn't allowed back in the store until the police finished gathering evidence, so instead of waiting upstairs, Sophie and I went home, and I finished the sleeves. Then I washed it and blocked it. By Sunday it was dry and ready to wear.

When Darby finally released the store on Friday, Connie asked him to wait an hour before notifying me so she, Phillip, and Marla could clean it. I have the most amazing friends. Connie even opened for a couple of hours when they were done. She was able to deal with the initial rush of nosy neighbours so when I came in the next morning, I didn't have to dodge as many questions as I was expecting.

The situation is public knowledge now. Everyone in town knows Emory killed Dr. Armistead.

They know Charmaine tried to tamper with evidence that implicated her husband, and they know Charmaine and the mayor were secretly hacking computers, spying on people, and using the information to blackmail people.

Unfortunately, the part that hasn't become public knowledge is the role Jamila played in the scandal.

Jamila was able to negotiate immunity from any charges in exchange for her cooperation. Somehow, the residents of Harmony Lake interpret this to mean that Jamila is some sort of cyber superhero who used her tech skills to expose the mayor, Charmaine, and Emory and bring down the corrupt pillars of our small community.

Rumour has it, Jamila was a police informant, and the intelligence she gathered was so sensitive, that not even the chief of police, Charmaine, knew what Jamila was up to. It's not my place to correct the rumours, and I would never say anything that could jeopardize Jamila's cooperation with the police.

Despite being viewed as a local hero, Jamila is gone. She left town to visit her family for Thanksgiving weekend and didn't come back. Her brother came back in her place. He's staying in her house and taking care of the store. According to him, Jamila wanted to spend some time with their parents, and he offered to take care of Bits'n'Bytes until she comes back. I have a feeling she won't be back.

It sounds like the mayor won't be back either. By the time everything hit the fan last Friday, the mayor and her husband were in Boca Raton, Florida where they apparently have a second home that no one in Harmony Lake knew about.

Citing health reasons, the mayor sent an open email to the town, tendering her resignation effective immediately. It turns out she's a dual Canadian-US citizen, and she and her husband won't be back. Good riddance.

They say things happen in threes, and the third person to disappear when the scandal broke was Charmaine Solomon. Within minutes of being relieved of her duties, she packed a bag and hit the road. As far as I know, no one has heard from her, and yesterday a FOR SALE sign appeared on her and Emory's lawn.

"So, if no one else comes forward, this candidate runs unchallenged? Or do they win by default, and we skip the campaign and election?" April asks Connie.

"I have no idea." Connie shrugs. "In the history of Harmony Lake, this has never happened. We're in uncharted territory."

Because of the vacancy left by the mayor's sudden resignation, Harmony Lake is having its first ever mayoral by-election! The window for potential mayoral candidates to hand in their nomination packages and get their name on the ballot opened at noon yesterday.

So far, the only candidate is a big-boxer. We don't know if this is part of the big-box plot the mayor was trying to uncover with Jamila's help, or if the big-boxers are opportunists who are using the corruption scandal to make a power play.

I put down the crossword puzzle and pick up my phone. "According to the internet, if a candidate is unopposed, they'll be acclaimed on the day the election was scheduled to happen," I say, putting my phone on the counter.

"That won't happen," Connie says confidently, with a chuckle. "We're working on a plan." Nodding, she winks and lays her finger aside her nose.

"We?" April and I ask in unison.

Connie checks her watch. "We've called an emergency joint meeting of the charity knitters and the book club. There will be no corporate interference in my cozy little town. Not on my watch. Unless it's over my dead body."

I'm not usually a superstitious person, but I wish Connie hadn't made that last comment. No need to tempt fate.

April and I gasp. A meeting between the readers and the knitters is huge.

The campaign period only officially started at noon yesterday, but I already can't wait for this election to be over. Once we have a new mayor and a permanent chief of police, the people of Harmony Lake can lay this scandal to rest, and our tight-knit community can go back to being the hotbed of rest I know and love.

Adam: Lunch?

Me: Sure.

Adam: Pub at 1 p.m.?

Me: Sounds good.

"Anything important, my dear?" What Connie really means is, who are you texting and about what.

"No," I reply, smiling. "Just making lunch plans with Adam."

"Today?" April asks, giving Sophie a dog treat.

"Yup. Today," I confirm.

"Won't that be…awkward?" Connie asks.

I shrug. "I don't expect it will be more awkward than usual. It feels right somehow to see him today. Is that why you're both here? Are you checking on me?"

"Kind of," April admits. "How are you feeling?"

I shrug. "Bittersweet," I reply. "Sad it had to end, but happy we came through it in one piece."

"Are you sure you're all right, my dear?"

"I'm fine," I reply. "I truly believe we'll all be happier this way. It helps that we're both moving on. I'm with Eric now, and Adam is with Jess."

"Jess is lovely!" Connie interjects. "They're a beautiful couple."

Jess's Thanksgiving debut was a success. I think Jess was nervous at first, but she fit in immediately. Who wouldn't be nervous about Thanksgiving dinner with twelve new people? Jess and Hannah got along great. So well, in fact, that Jess and Adam drove the girls back to school the next day. It gave Hannah and Jess a chance to get to know each other and gave me the chance to avoid another day-long road trip. Everyone was a winner.

The thud of the back-door closing makes me jump. I check the time on my phone. A week ago today, almost to the minute, Emory Solomon closed the back door, locked it, and tried to kill me.

"Good morning, ladies," Eric says, entering the store and seeing Connie and April on the sofa. "A lady in the parking lot asked me to give this to you." He hands me a squishy plastic envelope.

"Yarn," I say, squeezing the package. I find a pair of scissors and open the envelope. Three skeins of yarn tumble on to the coffee table.

"These are lovely." Connie compliments the yarn while automatically petting and squeezing it.

"Custom, limited edition colours," I tell her. "This one is inspired by the colour of the lake." I point to the blue-green variegated skein. "This one is inspired by the mountains in the winter." I point to the brown yarn with cream speckles. "And this one is inspired by the Knitorious logo." I point to the purple-green self-striping yarn.

"What a wonderful idea! How did this come about?"

"Well, I kind of told the charity knitters I was working on getting some limited-edition yarn. It was a lie of convenience, but I want to be true to my word, so I commissioned these from a local dyer. My plan is to donate the proceeds from the sales of these skeins to the charity knitters to help fund their projects. I have to decide which colours and how many to order."

"Well, it's nice to see you, Eric, but we were just leaving," Connie announces, nudging April's elbow and standing up.

"We were?" April asks, then she looks at me and shrugs. "I guess we were." She smiles.

Connie kisses my cheek. "I'll pop by later, my dear."

"Text me if you need me." April winks and gives me a hug.

Eric hands me a maple pecan latte with extra whipped cream and a drizzle of chocolate and locks the door behind them.

"Thank you," I say, cracking the lid. "Where's yours?"

"I had one at the office already."

He's already been to the office and back? It's barely 8:00 a.m.

"You didn't have to leave work just to bring me a coffee," I tell him. "You could've sent someone else. Now that you're Chief of Police, don't you have people who run these types of errands for you?" I tease.

"*Interim* chief of police," Eric corrects me. "I want to be here when Darby comes by with your laptop. And visiting you isn't an errand." He smiles.

Harmony Lake's octogenarian deputy mayor is now

mayor until the election in the new year. Her first order of business was to contact Eric on Saturday and invite him to her house for tea on Tuesday. She asked him to step in as interim chief until the new mayor can recruit a permanent chief of police. Eric was hesitant to accept, but the deputy mayor is very grandmotherly and very persuasive. She plied him with tea and guilt until he gave in.

"Are there turkey sandwiches in the fridge for me for lunch?" Eric asks, jerking his thumb toward the back room.

As usual, there was more food than people at Thanksgiving dinner. Everyone left with leftovers. Since Sunday, I've made turkey pot pie, open-faced turkey sandwiches with gravy, turkey casserole, and too many turkey sandwiches to count.

"We're out of turkey," I reply.

"Yes!" he mumbles and pumps his fist triumphantly. "I almost answered the phone yesterday with 'Gobble Gobble' instead of 'Hello'."

I gather the plastic envelope from the custom yarn and toss it in the garbage pail under the counter.

"How are you feeling?" Eric asks.

"Fine," I reply.

"I know what day it is. I know what happens today."

"You mean the enrollment window for mayoral candidates to submit their nomination packages?" I ask, knowing this isn't what he means.

"Yes, that's exactly what I mean," he replies sarcastically. "That and your divorce will be finalized today."

"Oh, that," I respond. "I'm fine. I'm happy and sad, but I'm fine."

"Well, I'm here for whatever you need. And I just restocked your chocolate stash. We can go out for dinner, we can stay in. We can do whatever you want. If you want to be alone, I understand. Just let me know how to show up for you today."

"Thank you." I give him a hug.

Sophie runs to the back door as though she recognizes Darby's knock. Maybe she does, what do I know?

Darby puts his messenger bag on the counter and opens it. He slides my laptop out of the bag and places it on the counter. "Our tech people said it's completely spyware-free and safe to use."

"Thanks," I say, not sure I'm emotionally ready to trust this computer.

"Also, we solved the mystery of who the sleeping pills in Dr. Solomon's pocket were intended for."

"Oh?" My interest is piqued. "Who?"

"Himself," Darby replies. "Dr. Solomon emailed a long, rambling suicide note and confession to Charmaine. He used a delay feature, so it wouldn't send until the next day, when he thought he'd be dead."

"Wow," I say, then drop into a chair while I process what Darby just said.

I guess I should've realized this was a possibility when Emory said, "If I have to go down, I'm taking you with me." I assumed he meant if he had to go to prison, he would make it worth his while, not that he was planning a murder-suicide.

Darby reaches into his bag, pulls out an envelope, and hands it to me. "From Karen Porter," he explains.

In neat penmanship, the envelope is addressed to Megan and Eric.

While Darby congratulates Eric on his appointment to Interim Chief of Police, and they talk about cop stuff, I open the envelope and read the notecard inside.

It's a thank you note. In lovely handwriting, Karen thanks me for believing her when she came to me with the truth and for helping find Dr. Armistead's killer. She goes on to say that she hopes Eric and I will be happy together and to look her up if I ever need a chiropractic adjustment.

Karen is leaving for Europe. She's taking the trip she and Dr. Armistead were planning to take next year. Apparently, he left her his house in his will. She'll be away for six months, then decide what she wants to do with the house when she gets back. She ends the note by asking me to give Sophie some rubs for her.

I'll show Eric later.

As soon as I turn the sign from CLOSED to OPEN and unlock the door, my phone is abuzz with news of the two most powerful groups in Harmony Lake combining forces. Apparently, the charity knitters and book club are meeting right now, upstairs at the pub.

As the entire town waits in awe to find out how the powers that be will keep our town safe from corporate invaders, people wander up and down Water Street, in and out of stores, collecting and sharing information.

There is no shortage of speculation and rumours. While no one knows anything for sure, we all agree on one thing: this is historic. There are events in a town's history that are so monumental, future generations refer to time as before-the-thing-happened and after-the-thing-happened. This is one of those events.

Marla races through the door.

"Marla! Why are you here? Shouldn't you be at the meeting?"

"I've been dispatched to relieve you, Megan. You've been summoned."

"Summoned? Me? Why?"

What did I do? What could they want with me?

"There's no time to explain." Marla shoves my bag and cell phone into my arms and turns me toward the back room. "They're at the pub. Upstairs. Drive. It'll be faster than walking. They saved a parking spot for you by the door." She prods me to the back room and out the back door.

As I PULL up to the pub, a book club member zooms out of a parking space and a charity knitter standing nearby gestures for me to pull in. I guess this is what Marla meant when she said they reserved a spot for me by the door.

The charity knitter who gestured for me to pull into the parking spot holds the outer door for me. A book club member opens the inner door, allowing me to stride through without stopping. At the bottom of the stairs, a charity knitter moves the velvet rope aside so I can climb the stairs.

The upstairs area of the pub is available by reservation only. There are two function rooms, an office, and extra washrooms. The velvet rope at the bottom of the stairs keeps regular patrons from going upstairs looking for extra seating.

"Thank you," I mumble to each of them as I pass by.

At the top of the stairs is an open reception area with an ornate wooden railing overlooking the pub below.

I'm quickly able to determine which function room they're in when I see a charity knitter on one side of the closed door working on a baby bootie, and a book club member on the other side engrossed in, *The President Is Missing* by James Patterson.

"Good morning, ladies," I say with a smile.

"Good morning, Megan," the charity knitter says as the book club member knocks on the door.

"Someone will be right with you," the book club member says without looking up from her book.

The door handle turns from the other side. I take a deep breath and brace myself. I'm excited and nervous, like when I was seven years old and Katie Humphries was about to let me into her clubhouse for the very first time, but only if I did the secret knock perfectly.

"There you are, my dear! I knew you'd get here quickly." Connie puts a hand on my shoulder, kisses my cheek, and guides me into the room.

There's a mahogany board table surrounded by mahogany chairs with dark-green leather trim. Connie resumes her seat at the table. She is flanked by the former-deputy-now-current mayor on one side and another book club member on her other side. Across from them, Mrs. Roblin and Mrs. Vogel look up at me and smile without breaking the rhythm of their knitting. Eric sits between them. He looks up at me and smiles with a small wave. Why is he here? Adam is at the head of the table. Why is he here?

Am I being ambushed?

"Is this an intervention?" I ask meekly, slightly afraid I've found one dead body too many, and now the unofficial leaders of the town have taken it upon themselves to intercede.

"Of course not, Megan. Don't be silly. We only do those at the library," Mrs. Roblin assures me after everyone stops laughing at my question.

I think she's serious.

"Have a seat, my dear." Connie gestures for me to sit at the other end of the table. "And don't look so worried."

I sit and a charity knitter appears from nowhere offering me a glass of water. "Thank you," I say when she finishes pouring.

She disappears into the corner where she waits with a book club member.

"Time is of the essence, so I'll get right to the point," Connie says. "Adam has agreed to run for mayor on the condition that Eric agrees to accept the chief of police job on a permanent basis. We think they're our best chance at defeating the big-boxers."

"Adam would be a great mayor," I respond. "He's politically inclined, he's local, and his values are in line with most of the town's residents."

The knitters and readers sound like a leaky air mattress when they breathe a collective sigh of relief.

"We were hoping you'd say that," Connie says, smiling widely.

Adam pulls himself up to his full-seated height and clears his throat. "I have zero interest in recruiting a new chief of police," he begins, "especially when the best person for the job is already doing the job on a temporary basis."

I look at Eric.

"I want to talk to you first," Eric says.

Eric and I step across the hall to the other, unoccupied function room and close the door.

"You said you don't want to be 'chief of paper-work'," I start.

"I don't. But I don't want to risk working for another corrupt boss, either. You know what this town is like, Megan. After what happened with Charmaine, they'll never trust an outsider. If I say no, an outsider will be the only option. If I support Adam and make it clear to the town that I won't work for a pro-big-box mayor, it could help Adam's campaign and keep the big-box stores out of Harmony Lake."

He's right.

I tell Eric he has my support whatever he decides, and with that sorted, we re-join the meeting across the hall.

Adam signs a few pieces of paper, and the rest of us sign forms as his nominators. Connie and Mrs. Roblin think it will strengthen Adam's position if they, Eric, and I show our support by being nominators.

The meeting is adjourned, and Connie and Mrs. Roblin leave to hand deliver Adam's documents to the town hall.

With the knitters and readers gone, I close the door and turn to Adam and Eric.

"Are you sure about this?" I ask Adam.

"No." He shakes his head. "But look at the alternative, Meg. Harmony Lake would be full of drive-thrus and MegaMarts in a year."

"Real estate prices would skyrocket because of corporations buying land, and the next generation of residents would never be able to afford to settle down here and raise families," Eric adds.

"And you have to admit, we're a great team." Adam smiles.

I assume he's talking about him and Eric.

"I know you're right," I agree. "But I have a feeling this election could get messy. With the mayor gone, and the scandal that just happened, this is a big opportunity for the big-boxers. There's no telling what they might do to win."

"C'mon, Meg!" Adam says, chuckling. "This is small-town politics that we're talking about. Really small. How nasty can it get? It's not like anyone would kill to fix the election," he says confidently, then laughs.

Wouldn't they?

I don't laugh with him because I'm not so sure.

CONTINUE READING for a sneak peek of Crime Skein: A Knitorious Murder Mystery book 6.

CLICK HERE to to read an exclusive bonus scene from Son of a Stitch that wasn't included in the book.

CRIME SKEIN

CHAPTER 1

THURSDAY, January 14th

Tomorrow morning Harmony Lake will either stay the cozy, sweet town I know and love, or become a soon-to-be tacky resort town on the cusp of a corporate coup.

I'm hoping for the former, not the latter.

Harmony Lake isn't like other towns. We have a big-box policy to protect us from corporate invasion. I support the big box policy. I don't want big business to commercialize our lovely little lakeside sanctuary. Residents who *oppose* the big-box policy, and want to see our town overrun with drive-thrus and giant warehouse stores are known as big-boxers. They are a loud minority, made up of residents who would benefit from selling land to the corporate invaders.

Our quaint, family-owned businesses and restaurants make Harmony Lake the intimate and cozy refuge we call home. There are no drive-thrus, no neon signs advertising corporate logos, and no multi-level parking structures. Our town is a blissful oasis, free from the corporate landscape found in most cities and suburbs. The reason tourists flock here is to escape the hustle and bustle of their day-to-day lives and immerse themselves in our small-town charm.

"Is that a cat toy for the animal centre?" Sheamus asks, pointing to my knitting.

"Yes," I reply, nodding. "Nothing like knitting for a worthy cause."

Sheamus isn't a knitter, so I'm surprised he knows about the cat toy initiative for the animal centre.

Our local charity knitting guild is collecting knitted cat toys to benefit The Vanity Fur Centre For Animal Health & Wellness — known to locals as the animal centre. The animal centre is our local all-in-one animal shelter, veterinary hospital, animal sanctuary, and animal education centre. The donated cat toys will be sold in their gift shop and online store.

"No need to ask who you voted for, I take it?" Sheamus shouts over the buzz of the crowd, as he stands next to our booth at the Irish Embassy Pub.

"What gave it away?" I reply teasingly.

I brush aside my brown curls and point to the MARTEL FOR MAYOR button affixed to the front of my hand-knit sweater.

Today is election day in Harmony Lake's first ever mayoral by-election, a historic event in our tiny town.

Harmony Lake was a reliable hotbed of political rest until our town's predictable political balance was thrown into upheaval by a scandal so shocking that the former mayor and police chief were forced to leave town in a cloud of corruption and disgrace.

Today, the residents of Harmony Lake will choose between two potential leaders, and the future of our cozy town hangs in the balance. Everything is on the line.

"What did Sheamus say?" April leans over and asks in my ear.

April is my best friend. We thought a quiet post-ballot dinner at the Irish Embassy Pub would be a nice way to commemorate the end of the mayoral campaign. Apparently, the rest of the town had the same idea, and the pub is packed. Standing room only.

"He asked me who I voted for," I reply directly into her ear.

April smiles and nods. Her blue eyes sparkle and she tucks a few long, blonde strands of hair behind the ear I'm speaking into. Her year-round sun-kissed glows gives her the appearance of someone who just returned from a sunny getaway down south. All winter long, people assume she's fresh off a plane from some sun-filled destination or other, and are shocked when she tells them she has been nowhere. No one makes that mistake with me. My hazel eyes and fair, alabaster skin are more likely to elicit questions about what type of anemia I have. I don't have anemia; this is just how I look.

April leans forward and turns her head so her wife, Tamara, can yell into her ear next.

"He asked who Megan voted for," April shouts in response to her wife's question, while nudging her head toward me. Tamara nods and smiles, leans back in her seat, and gives us a thumbs up.

Sheamus is leaning away from me now and speaking into Eric's ear. I don't know what he's saying, but his full head of shocking red hair bobs up and down as he speaks. Whatever he's saying, Eric isn't very enthusiastic about it. He replies with the occasional shrug and a few uncertain smiles.

Eric Sloane is my boyfriend. We met over a year ago when the Harmony Lake Police Department borrowed him from another police force to investigate the first murder in our town's history. He solved the case — and a few more since — and moved here after accepting a detective sergeant position with the Harmony Lake Police Department. Eric is also my tenant; he lives in the apartment above my yarn store, Knitorious. We've been dating for almost a year. In fact, the anniversary of our first date is next week. Eric is planning something special to celebrate it, but whenever I ask him for details, he tells me it's a surprise.

Shamus leans toward me and jerks his thumb toward Eric. "Megan, convince yer man, here, to come by my place later for a bit of poker, will ya?" he yells, with a hint of Irish brogue, flashing me a wide grin.

"I'll see what I can do," I shout back with a wink.

Sheamus is wearing a lovely hand-knit scarf. It looks like two strands of bulky weight yarn held together. One yarn looks to be a variegated combination of greens and rusts, and the other is a complimentary solid cream. I want to reach out and touch it, but over the years I've learned that non-knitters think it's weird when knitters randomly reach out and pet their clothing. Or get within an inch to inspect the stitches. Or sniff it. When knitters spot hand knits in the wild, personal space protocols go out the window. I speak from experience.

I file away a mental image of the scarf and make a mental note to ask Sheamus about it when we find ourselves in circumstances more conducive to conversation.

Sheamus finishes speaking to Eric and moves along to spread his unique brand of blarney to a group of tourists at the next booth.

Sheamus O'Brien is the second-generation owner of The Irish Embassy — known as the pub, or the embassy to us locals. The embassy is as close to a genuine Irish pub experience as you can get without hopping on a plane and flying to Ireland.

"Ready to go?" Eric mouths to me from across the table.

His phone buzzes and vibrates. When he picks it up

to look at it, I notice how tired he looks. His eyes are heavy and his posture is more limp than normal, like he's wilting. Even the honey coloured flecks in his brown eyes seem duller than normal.

"Sure" I say nodding.

He puts down his phone, winks and gives me a warm smile that makes the butterflies in my stomach wake up and start fluttering.

I lean over and tell April that Eric and I are heading out. She informs me that she and Tamara won't be far behind us.

We pay the bill and wrap ourselves in our winter woollies because it's freezing outside. The temperature is at least minus ten with the windchill, and we're supposed to have a snowstorm tonight. Environment Canada issued a snowfall warning saying we should expect up to fifteen centimetres before morning.

We're about to get up from the booth when Adam waves to me from the door. I gesture for him to come over. Adam Martel is my ex-husband and the mayor presumptive of Harmony Lake. By the time the residents of Harmony Lake wake up tomorrow morning to shovel their driveways, Adam will hopefully be our new mayor and our big-box policy will remain securely in place for the duration of his term in office.

Adam and I were married for almost twenty years. We finalized our divorce in October. Our daughter, Hannah, is nineteen and goes to university in Toronto.

We have a virtual brunch with her every Sunday. I'm proud of how Adam and I handled our divorce. We were careful to make sure the implosion of our marriage had a minimal effect on the people we love, and we redefined our relationship and learned how to be friends. We're not married anymore but we're still family.

Adam is Harmony Lake's local lawyer. He's politically inclined and passionate about the small town where we live and raised our daughter; he'll be an amazing mayor.

"Good evening, Your Worship," I greet him playfully.

Your Worship is the appropriate Way to address a mayor. He better not get used to it, I don't intend to call him Your Worship ever again.

"It might be premature for that," he chuckles then bends down and we exchange a double cheek kiss.

Adam turns to Eric and asks him If he's going to Sheamus's place later to play cards. When Eric says he doubts he'll go, Adam tries to persuade him.

Yes, my ex-husband and boyfriend are friends. Good friends. Eric was new in town and had no friends in Harmony Lake, and despite living here most of his adult life, Adam didn't have many friends in Harmony Lake either. Before opening his own practice Adam was a workaholic senior partner at a law firm in the city. They bonded over a mutual love of golf and the rest is history. Sometimes it's weird that they're friends, but no weirder than the friendship I have with Adam's new partner, Jess.

Jess and I kiss cheeks, and April and I shove over in the booth so she can slide in with us.

"I'm surprised you're here tonight," I say to Jess. "With the snowstorm coming I didn't think you'd risk the drive."

Jess lives and works forty-five minutes away in Harmony Hills. She takes off her toque and shakes out her long strawberry blond hair.

"I wanted to be here tonight for Adam," she explains. "I won't stay long, I plan to get on the road before the worst of the snow starts."

"Full house tonight." Adam scans the pub, searching for an available table or booth.

"We're just leaving," Eric says. "Why don't you sit here?"

With that decided, Eric and I vacate the booth, giving Adam and Jess our seats.

Stepping into the cool night air is a relief. It took us at least ten minutes to get from the booth to the door because we stopped at almost every table and booth to say hi to friends and neighbours — one hazard of living in a small town where everyone knows everyone else. Stopping to chat while wearing two layers of clothes, a down-filled winter coat, a thick hand-knit ear warmer, cowl, and mittens is a recipe for overheating.

"Are you going to play cards with the guys?" I ask Eric as we walk up Water Street toward Knitorious.

"I don't think so," he replies. "I'm tired, and they always play on a weeknight when I have to work the next day."

"Maybe you're tired because you're working two jobs," I suggest. "It's pretty much a done deal that Adam will win this election. Tomorrow, he'll appoint you as the permanent chief of police. You can't be police chief, and Harmony Lake PD's only detective. It's too much. Have you given any more thought to hiring a detective to replace you?"

After the scandal that shook our town to its core, the deputy mayor asked Eric to step in as interim chief of police until the newly elected mayor could choose a permanent replacement. He's been doing two jobs for three months and it's taking a toll.

When Adam was approached to run for mayor, he made it a condition that he would only enter the race if, upon his election, Eric agreed to become the chief of police permanently. Eric accepted because he knows the locals — who are skeptical of outsiders on a good day — will hesitate to accept a police chief recruited from elsewhere.

"I haven't had much time to think about it because I'm so busy." Eric gathers his scarf around his neck and takes my hand. From inside his coat pocket, his phone makes the notification sounds that have become the soundtrack to our lives lately. "I hope to promote someone from within because I don't think the town is ready to accept any new people, especially someone in a position of authority."

I keep my face down and look at my feet to avoid the sharp sting of the frigid January air on my face.

"Ms. Martel, Police Chief Sloane, so lovely to see you both."

I look up when I hear my name.

Saxon Renaud. Ugh! What an unpleasant way to end the day.

Eric looks up at the same time as me and utters a curse word under his breath, then plasters a fake smile on his handsome face.

"Mr. Renaud." I nod, intending to continue walking.

"Saxon," Eric nods, also still walking.

Saxon steps in front of us, forcing us to stop.

"Hi Rick," I say with a smile to Saxon's hired hench-man, Rick Ransan.

"H-hi Megan," Rick smiles.

Rick is such a pleasant person. Why does he hang around with someone as insufferable as Saxon Renaud?

"Rick." Eric nods.

"H-h-i Chief S-Sloane." Rick returns the nod.

In what qualifies as the weirdest thing I've seen today, Saxon uses the long metal tip of his whangee handle umbrella to draw a line in the snow that's beginning to accumulate on the sidewalk. A line between where Eric and I stand and where Saxon and Rick stand. Is it some kind of metaphorical or literal battle line?

Watching Saxon scrape the tip of his umbrella along the sidewalk, I notice that instead of wearing boots, which would be a practical footwear choice for a night like tonight, he's wearing his signature penny loafers — complete with pennies, even though we haven't made pennies in this country for years — and rubber overshoes with no insulation value.

Saxon Renaud carrying an umbrella during a blizzard isn't strange to me. He carries his umbrella with him everywhere he goes, all the time, no matter the weather situation. It's like an extension of his right arm; the umbrella is Saxon's quirk.

Using it to draw a line in the snow, however, is new. At least it's new to me. I've never seen him do it before. He's also fond of using his umbrella as a cattle prod to protect his personal space, and make people — women — jump out of his way. I've been on the receiving end of his prodding, and it's infuriating. Saxon Renaud is a hard person to like.

I sigh. "What's up, Saxon?" I ask, since he has made no attempt to tell us why he stopped us, or to explain the weird line he drew in the snow.

I'm tempted to use the toe of my boot to erase his stupid line, but I resist the urge. The snow is falling faster now, and the line is already disappearing anyway.

"Chief Sloane, I was hoping to run into you," Saxon says, ignoring me and my question, and looking up at Eric. "I'm willing to give you one more chance to change your mind and accept the permanent chief of police position when I'm confirmed as mayor tomorrow."

Eric shakes his head, rolls his eyes, and chuckles breathily. "No thank you, Saxon," he replies, still shaking his head. "I told you, I would *never* be police chief in a town that would have you as mayor."

"Are you sure?" Saxon asks again. "I suspect you might regret it tomorrow morning."

"A risk I'm willing to take." Eric grins. "Now if you'll excuse us, gentlemen, it's chilly out here." Eric tightens his grip on my hand and walks straight at them, forcing them to part and let us through.

I glance behind us to make sure Saxon and Rick are out of earshot, then quicken my pace to keep up with Eric. He's almost a foot taller than me, and his strides are longer than mine. "The only way Saxon Renaud might win this mayoral election is by cheating," I assert with confidence.

"He won't win," Eric agrees. "There's no way. I'd bet my life on it."

I know he wouldn't *literally* bet his life on it, but I wish he wouldn't tempt fate by saying that.

We both turn to check one more time and make sure the two men haven't doubled back and are walking behind us, listening to our conversation. We glimpse them disappearing into the pub.

"It looks like we left just in time," I remark.

"Yep," Eric concurs. "It might get pretty heated in the pub tonight with both candidates there."

CHAPTER 2

"REMIND me again why we vote today but don't get the results until tomorrow?" Eric asks as I unleash Sophie and take off her sweater after our walk.

Sophie is my corgi. She comes to work with me every day. If Eric and I go out after work, she hangs out in his apartment until we get home. Sophie has a full suite of toys, food, dishes, sweaters, and even a bed here. Knitorious and Eric's apartment are her homes away from home.

"Well," I start, "this year it's due to the weather. Because of the snowfall warning, voting hours were extended until 10 p.m. to give residents who commute enough time to get home to Harmony Lake and cast their votes."

"And in previous years?" he asks.

I shrug. "I don't know. Tradition, I guess? You know how much this town likes tradition."

It's snowing heavily now, and visibility is bad. A fresh layer of snow covers everything like a blanket and makes our already-picturesque town look even more postcard worthy. The glow from the slivered fraction of the waxing moon, and the streetlights reflecting off the new-fallen snow makes the light coming in the windows brighter than usual for a January night.

I hem and haw about whether to go home or stay at Eric's apartment for the night. He convinces me to stay by warming my favourite flannel pyjamas in the dryer and showing me his PVR full of mindless TV shows we like to watch.

There are advantages to dating my tenant; I sleep above the store when the weather is bad, and my morning commute is only thirty seconds.

"MEGAN." Eric gently nudges my shoulder. "Babe, wake up. We fell asleep watching TV. It's late, go to bed."

Disoriented and groggy, I take a deep breath and force open my heavy eyes. Overwhelmed by the harsh glare of artificial light, I shut them again. The last thing I remember is knitting a mouse ear and trying to stay awake for the big reveal on the home renovation reality show we were watching. Eric fell asleep checking his email on his phone within ten minutes of the opening credits, and was snoring softly on the sofa next to me. I felt myself being lulled to sleep by his rhythmic breathing and fought to stay awake. I guess I failed.

"Why are you dressed?" I ask, squinting while my eyes adjust to being awake. "Is everything OK?"

"I was called into work," he replies. "They called me to a hit and run out on Lake Access Road."

"In a snowstorm?" I asked, still confused, but better able to focus and take in my surroundings.

"Not everything shuts down because of terrible weather." Eric smiles and holds out his hands. "I'll be back as soon as I can."

I take his hands and let him pull me to my feet. I walk him to the door and wrap him in hand knits until I'm satisfied he's protected from the cold and wind, remind him to drive safely, and kiss him good night. After locking the door behind him, Sophie and I trudge off to bed.

SOPHIE'S SHRILL bark startles me awake and I jolt upright to a sitting position.

"What the matter, Soph? Do you need to go outside?"

Without looking at me, the corgi barks again and launches herself off the bed. Her paws don't touch the floor until she lands in the hallway outside the bedroom door. She scampers off toward the apartment door.

Turning on lights as I go, I follow Sophie and find her whining and scratching at the apartment door. Then I hear it. Someone is pounding on the outside door, downstairs. It's the middle of the night. I squint at the clock on the stove. 1:12 a.m. Eric hasn't been gone very long. I can't believe I fell asleep so fast. Who's knocking at this hour?

Sophie and I descend the stairs while the pounding continues. Sophie, having twice as many legs as me and being built for speed, gets to the bottom first and yelps, then scratches the back of the door. This is her friendly yelp, the one she uses for friends. She knows and likes whoever is on the other side of the door.

I'm about to pick up the brick we use to prop open the back door — just in case — when I hear a familiar voice.

"Sophie? Is that you? Meg? Are you there? It's me!"

Adam? What the heck is he doing here?

"Adam?" I ask through the closed door.

"Yes, it's me. Can you open the door, please?"

I open the door, and there stands Adam, his hands shoved in his pockets, the collar of his navy-blue pea coat turned up against the wind, and his hair and shoulders covered in a dusting of big, fluffy snowflakes. He blinks a few snowflakes from his eyelashes, and I step aside so he can come in.

"What's wrong?" I ask.

Adam kicks the brick wall next to the door to knock the excess snow off his boots, then steps inside.

"I'm stranded," Adam replies, using his bare hand to shake the snow from his salt and pepper hair.

"How are you stranded?" I ask, "You live ten minutes away." Dramatic much?

I use my bare hand to dust snow from the shoulders of his coat. He's not wearing a hat, a scarf, or mittens.

He's inadequately dressed for regular January weather, never mind a blizzard.

"I can't find my keys," Adam explains. "I think they fell out of my coat pocket at Sheamus's house. I can't start my car, and my phone is dead. Even if I walk home, I can't unlock the door."

"Did you go back to Sheamus's house to see if your keys are there?"

He nods. "I searched around outside the house, and the path from the front door to my car, but nothing. For all I know, they fell in the snow. Sheamus isn't there. No one's there. The poker game ended abruptly, and we cleared out in a hurry. I lost my keys in the commotion. I was hoping Eric could drive me to your place so I can get the spare set of keys, pick up my car, and go home."

"Eric's not here," I explain. "He went to work because of a car accident, or something."

"Can you drive me to get the spare set of keys?" Adam asks.

I shake my head. "My car isn't here. I walked to work this morning — yesterday morning — whenever."

Adam huffs in frustration, rubs his hands together vigorously, and uses them to cup his red ears.

"Crash in the spare room." I jerk my head toward the stairs. "It's too late and snowy to do anything tonight. We'll find your keys in the morning."

Adam agrees and after lending him one of Eric's t-shirts and a pair of sweatpants, I set him up in the small spare room. When Sophie and I check the door to make sure it's locked, I notice Adam's dead phone on the breakfast bar. I plug it into the phone charger in the kitchen, then Sophie and I shuffle off to bed. Again.

Drifting off to sleep for the third time tonight, I replay my conversation with Adam in my head. Why did the poker game end abruptly? And why did they leave Sheamus's house in a hurry? What did he mean when he said he lost his keys in the commotion? What commotion? Between being dazed from waking up prematurely, and shocked at finding Adam on the doorstep in the middle of the night, it didn't occur to me to ask questions. As sleep takes over my brain, I make a mental list of questions I want to ask him in the morning.

Friday, January 15th

I'm a morning person. This time of year, I'm awake before the sun is up. I know everyone isn't an early riser and try to be considerate.

That's why, after I shower and dress, I tiptoe around the small apartment trying to make as little noise as possible. The door to the spare bedroom is still closed and I don't want to wake Adam.

Eric isn't home yet from wherever he went in the middle of the night. He must be exhausted. Intending to text him and see how he's doing, I grab my phone, quietly close the apartment door, and sneak downstairs with Sophie to get ready for our morning walk.

"Which sweater do you want to wear today, Soph?" I ask, holding up a sweater in each hand.

If Sophie prefers one sweater over the other, she doesn't share it with me, so I choose for her. I bundle myself up, then help Sophie into her purple, cabled, turtleneck sweater and unlock the back door.

Walking through the park, I'm grateful the windchill has eased and it's less frigid this morning. The world is still and silent, except for the occasional echo of a branch in the distance cracking under the weight of last night's snowfall, and the snow crunching beneath our feet and paws as we walk. The snow is smooth and untouched, shimmering in the pre-dawn light. Tree branches curve toward the ground, reaching lower than usual, yielding to the weight of the snow on top of them. My heart is bursting with gratitude because I live in the prettiest town on earth!

"I was just about to text you," I say when I see Eric getting out of his car in the parking lot behind Knitorious.

"How'd you sleep?" he asks, then kisses me hello.

"Interrupted, and not long enough," I reply, walking through the back door he's holding for Sophie and me.

I unleash Sophie and take off her sweater, then take off my winter gear and put everything away.

"I'm going upstairs to grab a quick shower, then I have to go back to work," Eric says, heading toward the stairs. "After my shower, I'll tell you about the hit and run I attended last night. It was a doozy."

"Adam slept in the spare room last night. Be quiet because I think he's still asleep," I warn him.

Eric stops and turns to me, his eyes narrow and focussed. Hot intensity emanates from him. "Adam's here?" He steps toward me and narrows his eyes even more. "Why? What time did he show up? Where's his car? It's not in the parking lot."

He's using his cop voice and I feel like I'm being interrogated.

"Am I a witness, or something?" I ask, confused.

"We've been looking for Adam for hours. He's not at home, he's not at his office, he's not with Jess, and his phone is off."

"'We'? Are the police looking for Adam? Why?" I demand.

An anxious knot forms in my stomach. My heart pounds against my ribs. I feel panicky, and I'm not sure why.

Heavy shoulders, long arms, I remind myself and take a deep breath. Heavy shoulders, long arms is a mantra I learned in a yoga class once upon a time. It reminds me to let go of the tension in my neck and shoulders.

"Someone saw his car driving away from the hit and run," Eric replies. "His car isn't in his parking spot at the condo, it's not at his office, it's not anywhere."

"It's at Sheamus's house," I inform him. "But the

witness must be mistaken," I insist, wondering who the witness is.

Eric mumbles something about already checking Sheamus's house while he unlocks his phone and starts typing with his thumbs.

"Adam showed up here after you left," I say. "He lost his keys. He couldn't have been driving on Lake Access Road."

Eric pauses his thumbs mid-type, looks up at me and says, "LAWYRUP," then looks down at his phone again and resumes typing, presumably to dispatch a patrol car to Sheamus's house.

LAWYRUP is the lawyer-themed vanity license plate Adam bought himself years ago when he got the job at the firm in the city. Everyone in town knows his plate.

"The witness was close enough to read Adam's license plate in a blizzard?" I ask, dubious.

Adam drives the only late model maroon Jaguar sedan in town. But, I'm sure lots of cars would resemble his car, right? Most sedans look the same to me, anyway, and at night, in a blizzard, one sedan must look like another.

Eric fights back a yawn, musses his short, dark hair with one hand, and turns to climb the stairs. I follow him and Sophie follows me, but she zooms past both of us and reaches the apartment door first.

"Adam's not here," Eric booms from the spare room. "What time did he leave?"

I shrug. "I'm not sure, I haven't seen him since he

closed the bedroom door." I rack my brain trying to remember if Adam's coat and boots were downstairs when Sophie and I got ready for our morning walk. I can't remember. I turn toward the charger on the breakfast bar where I plugged in Adam's dead phone last night. Just a charging cable, no phone. Was his phone plugged in this morning after my shower? I didn't notice.

"He took his phone," I mutter. I look at Eric. "I'm sorry, I don't know when he left. I'm usually more observant than this, I don't know why I'm off my game today. He took his phone and it's charged. Try texting him."

"It's not your job to be observant, babe, it's OK," he reassures me. "You had a long night and you're tired."

Eric texts, then calls Adam's cell phone while he paces the living room.

He drops the hand with the phone in it to his side and exhales loudly. I assume Adam didn't answer.

I feed Sophie breakfast and drop a pod in the coffee maker.

Our phones ding in unison.

"He's acclaimed," Eric says, reading the text. "Adam is officially the mayor of Harmony Lake."

I got the same text. It's from Connie, my mother-friend. She sent it to the Modern Family group chat, a group text chat with me, Eric, Adam and his girlfriend, Jess, April and her wife, Tamara, Connie and her boyfriend, Archie, and Ryan and Lin who are Archie's son and his partner.

"I'm sure Saxon Renaud is already on his way to the town hall to contest the results and demand a recount," I remark.

"I doubt it," Eric says. "Saxon Renaud is dead."

CLICK HERE to continue reading Crime Skein

ALSO BY REAGAN DAVIS

Knit One Murder Two

Killer Cables

Murder & Merino

Twisted Stitches

Son of a Stitch

Crime Skein

Sins & Needles

Rest In Fleece

Life Crafter Death

In Stitchness and in Health

Bait & Stitch

Murder, It Seams

Neigbourhood Swatch: A Knitorious Cozy Mystery Short Story

Sign up for Reagan Davis' email list to be notified of new releases and special offers: www.ReaganDavis.com/email
Follow Reagan Davis on Amazon

Follow Reagan Davis on Facebook, Bookbub, Goodreads, and Instagram

ABOUT THE AUTHOR

Reagan Davis is a pen name for the real author who lives in the suburbs of Toronto with her husband, two kids, and a menagerie of pets.

When she's not planning the perfect murder, she enjoys knitting, reading, eating too much chocolate, and drinking too much Diet Coke.

The author is an established knitwear designer who has contributed to many knitting books and magazines. I'd tell you her real name, but then I'd have to kill you. (Just kidding! _{Sort of.})

http://www.ReaganDavis.com/

ACKNOWLEDGMENTS

I owe the biggest thanks you, dear reader. Your love and enthusiasm for the first three books in the series gives me the determination and inspiration to the series.

Thank you to Kim of Kim's Covers for another perfect cover.

Thank you to Chris and Sherry at The Editing Hall for correcting all my misplace punctuation and making the story readable.

Eternal love and gratitude to the Husbeast and Kidlets for everything.

Made in the USA
Columbia, SC
10 April 2023